**'Are you indeed a wanton, Eleanor?'
he demanded in a rough voice.**

'I did not mean—' she protested, but her words were cut short.

'I can see it in your eyes, as they follow me about the hall. Is this what you want?' Troye grasped her chin between his fingers and tipped her face up.

He lowered his head and his mouth came down on hers. His rough jaw scratched her tender skin, and she could smell and taste musky maleness laced with wine. Suddenly his hold loosened and his arms slid around her waist.

'I had forgotten,' he murmured, as he pressed his lips to her neck and for a moment breathed in the soft, sweet smell of her skin.

'What had you forgotten?'

'The feel of a woman.' His fingers smoothed down the curve of her back and she gave a little cry, her fingers clutching at his tunic. Troye realised her shock, that she had no experience of men, that no doubt this was her first real kiss, and cursed softly.

Catherine March was born in Zimbabwe. Her love of the written word began when she was ten years old and her English teacher gave her *Lorna Doone* to read. Encouraged by her mother, Catherine began writing stories while a teenager. Over the years her employment has varied from barmaid to bank clerk to legal secretary. Her favourite hobbies are watching rugby, walking by the sea, exploring castles and reading.

THE KING'S CHAMPION
features characters you will have
already met in THE KNIGHT'S VOW.

Novels by the same author:

MY LADY ENGLISH
THE KNIGHT'S VOW

THE KING'S CHAMPION

Catherine March

MILLS & BOON

Pure reading pleasure

First published in Great Britain 2007
Large Print edition 2007
Harlequin Mills & Boon Limited,
Eton House, 18-24 Paradise Road, Richmond, Surrey TW9 1SR

© Catherine March 2007

ISBN: 978 0 263 19408 1

Set in Times Roman 15 on 17 pt.
42-1007-88255

Printed and bound in Great Britain
by Antony Rowe Ltd, Chippenham, Wiltshire

THE KING'S CHAMPION

For the Quartermaster
With love

Prologue

Arundel Castle—20 April 1289

To celebrate spring the King had called a royal tourney. The scent of grass and apple trees bursting into blossom sweetened the air, welcome after the harsh and long winter. Yet their pastel hues of pink and cream paled in comparison to the bright colours of the hundreds of pavilions mushrooming across the meadows surrounding the castle. Some were of plain canvas, belonging to knights of lesser standing who hoped to win rich prizes and prestige with their skill at the joust, but most were striped in a varied combination of expensive colours, and on the lusty breeze heraldic banners waved from the topmost point of each pavilion.

The grounds were bustling with knights and squires, horses and heralds, strolling ladies and their lords, the noise of blacksmiths hammering at dented armour and cast shoes adding to the hubbub floating on the air. The sky spanned a cloudless blue above them and children romped in the sunshine, bursting with energy after many days confined indoors during the winter months.

Two knights sauntered, one very fair and the other dark, looking about with interest. They conversed earnestly upon the merits of their opponents, and occasionally commented on the several attractive *filles de joie* today present; they smiled politely at the former, with a small bow, and grinned broadly at the latter, with a brazen wink.

Their progress was hampered as two children suddenly burst from between a row of pavilions, striped in red and yellow and flying the banner of Lord Henry Raven of Ashton. The fair knight exclaimed and jumped back, clutching at his friend's elbow in a warning gesture as two wooden swords chopped through the air.

'*Allez!*' shouted the one child, attacking the other with fierce swipes from side to side that greatly impressed the knights as they watched.

The children were dressed identically in linen tunics and chausses, cross-gartered, and the fiercest of the child-combatants had a blue scarf tied about his head. Although smaller than his opponent, he charged down boldly with lithe, graceful strides, swinging his sword with an accurate and controlled measure that soon had his opponent stumbling and crying, 'Pax!' as he fell to the ground. His opponent gave a war-like whoop of triumph and promptly sat upon his fallen victim, waving his sword in a circle and announcing his victory in a gleeful tone.

The two knights clapped and called out their admiration for such a fine display of young swordsmanship, and then the child turned and pointed a delicate chin over one shoulder, staring at them, with solemn cornflower-blue eyes.

'Why, 'tis a girl!' exclaimed the flaxen-haired knight.

'Saints!' His companion was equally amazed, 'Have you ever seen the like, Austin?'

Dropping to one knee, Austin Stratford cupped her chin with gentle fingers. 'Does your mother know what you are about, little maid?'

Without a blink of her very blue eyes she smacked his hand away with a sharp blow of her wooden sword. Austin exclaimed and leapt to his feet. He sucked his smarting knuckles whilst his friend looked on and made little attempt to smother a chuckle.

'I pity the man who weds that little vixen,' Troye de Valois stated with a taut smile.

'I shall not wed!' declared the little girl, swift and stout in her retort. 'I shall fight in the tourneys and be champion of England, like my uncle.'

'Indeed?' Austin smiled, his eyes skimming over the perfect oval face, certain that one day she would grow into a great beauty and her fate would be otherwise. 'And who is your uncle, if I might beg my lady's pardon to ask?'

'Ellie!' groaned her defeated playmate, 'let me up!'

The girl rose lithely to her feet and offered her hand to the boy, who huffed and moaned and dusted the back of his tunic with a great show. She turned sideways and eyed the two knights, who seemed very tall to her as she craned her little neck. The one was fair and had a laughing mouth, the other was very dark, his eyes more black than brown and his silence intimidating. There was a controlled tension about him that held a hint of menace. Quickly she looked away from him and addressed herself to his more amiable friend.

With great pride she puffed out her narrow chest and announced, 'He is Remy St Leger, champion of England, and there is none who can best him.'

'And you say he is your uncle?' The two knights exchanged a glance.

'Aye.' She stood, leaning on one hip, her sword pointed down between her feet, clutching the hilt with her small hands, her very pose that of a young knight.

'How old are you, little maid?' asked Austin.

'I shall be ten on St George's Day.'

He asked gravely, a wary eye on the small hands clutching her wooden sword, 'And why would a lady want to fight, rather than wed? 'Tis no easy task being a knight.'

She snorted derisively, her slim nose pointing to the sky as she scoffed, ''Tis boring being a lady! All they do is sew and eat sweetmeats and waste time on idle chatter. Why should I not participate in the joust? The German Hildegaarde something-or-other does, and there is a Turkish lady, I can't 'member her name, she does too. And sometimes they beat the men, puny creatures that they are! Look how easily I beat Rupert. He's my brother, you know, and two years older than me. And bigger.'

'Shut up!' Rupert cuffed her on the shoulder, his face flaring red.

Austin hid his amusement, and turned to his friend with a smile in his eyes.

Troye de Valois envied him his easy charm that enabled him to converse with everyone, whether they be kings or knights or ladies, or even little children. Making an effort, he stated in the boy's defence, in his low, solemn voice that by nature held more a thread of steel than laughter, 'Your brother is still a boy, but one day he will grow into a man. Men have much greater strength in their arms and shoulders than ladies do.' He eyed her delicate bone structure and guessed that she would never develop the brawn of the German and the Turk. 'Your female frame would never stand up to a man's.'

She misheard him and declared indignantly, 'I am not feeble!'

Troye backed away with hands upraised, as though in surrender to this fierce verbal assault, and Austin would have ruffled her hair had it not been bound up within the confines of her blue scarf, auburn tendrils escaping here and there. Instead he smiled and bowed to her, 'I wish you good luck, my lady—'

'Eleanor!' a strident voice called. 'Eleanor, where are you?'

'Nurse!' Eleanor and Rupert exclaimed in unison with round-eyed guilt, and together they ran off, scarce giving the two knights a backward glance.

The knights watched them go and then fell into step again, the feisty little girl-warrior soon forgotten as other matters claimed their attention. Troye intended to make his mark in the tourney, and he had both talent and courage enough to do so.

On the final day of the tournament he was drawn to ride against the famed Remy St Leger. As he waited for the signal to charge, and his horse pranced and champed against the firm rein checking him, he remembered the little girl and looked down the long length of the list. After a week of jousting it was dusty and the ground rough from the trampling of many hooves. At the far end sat St Leger on a big black Hanoverian stallion. His visor was down and he gleamed in silver-plate armour, big and solid as he sat firmly in the saddle. St Leger was thirty-four years old and Troye scarce five and twenty. By Troye's reckoning he had been champion too long and now it was time to make way.

'*Laissez-aller!*' cried the Marshal, waving his banner that signalled they should charge.

Troye touched his spurs to his horse's flanks and gripped the lance beneath his right arm tightly. The ground trembled as the two horses galloped at each other full tilt, and the crowd on either side of the lists held their breath. The two knights were well matched, each rock-steady in the saddle, their glance unwavering through the narrow slit of their visors as they thundered towards each other. A crash of wood on steel, the rendering split of a lance, and then the dull thud as a rider was sent crashing to the ground.

For a moment there was a stunned hush, and then a gasp of horror, as all eyes turned from the fallen champion, and stared at Troye de Valois. His few supporters cheered, but most were shocked. For the two knights, however, there was no regret on either side, only male acceptance of youth and that some things must come to an end if others were to have a beginning.

Troye was triumphant and gave a yell, shaking his clenched fist in the air, the adrenalin pumping fast through his veins and bunching his muscles with heady excitement. Yet later, at the end of the day, when he went to the King's dais to collect his prize, Troye saw a little girl with long auburn hair clutching at the rails as she stood in the gallery above watching the proceedings. He recognised her and smiled, but she only stared solemnly back at him. She turned and ran to a blonde woman who could only be her mother, judging by the similarities in fine features and blue eyes, despite the startling difference in hair colouring that gave him a moment's pause for doubt. Yet the child flung herself down in the vacant seat beside the woman and folded her arms across her little chest. Troye collected his gold ingot, his handsome features giving cause for many an admiring glance from the ladies in the stand. His own true love was many miles from London, and his vows to her he did not take lightly. Yet there was one female he cast his glance to—the maiden who would a knight be, and he bowed to her, smiling at her grudging little nod in salute of his victory, a gesture remarkably mature for one so young.

Ellie was devastated to see her uncle fall in the lists. She had felt the sting of tears at the back of her eyes, and yet they were staunched by her traitorous admiration for the knight who had this day proven himself the victor. He was very handsome indeed, very strong and bold and skilled at all forms of the art of combat. Ellie could not help but lose her heart

to him. Soon they left Arundel and set off for home.
Her uncle recovered quickly enough from his broken
arm and bruised head, and her Aunt Beatrice announced her heartfelt relief that at long last her
husband was ready to concede that his body was not
as strong as his ego, and the time had come to retire.

Her father, Lord Henry Raven of Ashton, did not
take them to tournaments again for a very long time,
and when at the age of twelve Ellie experienced the
changes that shaped her for womanhood, she put
away her tunic and her wooden sword, at her
mother's insistence. She resigned herself to being a
lady. She found other pursuits to enjoy, and as the
years passed she found that it was not such a burden
to be a lady. Indeed, she took great pleasure in
dressing in becoming gowns of silk, of learning how
to manage a household efficiently, and from her Aunt
Beatrice she learned simple herbal remedies for
everyday ills. Ellie greatly enjoyed listening to the
tales told by travelling troubadours, tales of heroic
deeds performed by handsome knights of exceptional
courage and valour. None of them could compare to
her Uncle Remy, of course. In her eyes he was the
most handsome, and the most brave, of all knights in
the kingdom, yet he was, after all, her uncle and he
could not fill the space in her heart that yearned for
love. A space that she had already assigned.

Her mother groomed her for her future life, which would be as wife to a knight of good standing and mother to his children, gently schooling her in the arts of being a lady and a woman. Ellie became aware that her face was considered to be beautiful and her slender form desirable. As she grew older she noticed that both had an effect upon the opposite sex, yet she felt that much was lacking in all the males of her domain. What Ellie wanted was a hero. A real man, a man of strength and honour and courage and valour, a man who had fought in battles and overcome all adversity, and who was not afraid to stand up and be counted, as in the troubadour's tales. She knew of such a man, and over the years had heard his name mentioned many times. She was fourteen when she realised that all men must measure against the standard that was Troye de Valois.

Such a man did not exist in Ellie's very small world, for most of the eligible knights had gone to Wales over the years to fight the King's good fight, or now to Scotland as Edward sought to bring to heel the passionate and rebellious Scots. There remained at Castle Ashton, and in their neighbourhood, only young boys training as pages and priests; officials of the king's new judicial system, sheriffs and reeves and judges; ancient men too worn and weary to climb into the saddle and resigned to a life as Lord Raven's hearth knights. Perhaps if it had not been so, and she had met young knights in the usual way, she would not have clung to the image of Troye de Valois. She harboured him ardently within her heart, where neither logic nor absence could persuade her love to fail. She waited impatiently, anxious for Mother Nature to complete the nurturing process and for her body and her mind to emerge as a full-grown woman.

On his eighteenth birthday Rupert was selected to join the King's Own Guard, serving as a cadet in the elite company of men guarding the king's life with their own. Eleanor pointed out to her father that it was unfair that Rupert should have this advantage while she, a marriageable heiress, rusticated in the countryside. Her mother fully agreed that only at the court of King Edward would a suitable husband be found for their Eleanor and, at last, they made the journey to London that Ellie had dreamed of for many years. She was sixteen, and her greatest asset was not in the shine of her long auburn hair or the beauty of her face, nor the graceful shape of her figure, but the inner glow of love that shone from within. Her love for Troye de Valois had never ceased nor faltered over the years and, while her parents pondered on suitable bridegrooms, Ellie had no doubts about the man whom she wished to marry.

Chapter One

Cheapside, London—August 1295

Crowds of people had been waiting all morning for the procession that was now approaching, and a wave of cheering billowed on the warm morning air. The blast of trumpets vibrated on an elusive breeze, stirring dozens of colourful banners that adorned the stands on either side of the lists, and echoed in miniature by the pennons fastened on the end of the lances carried by the knights who would be competing in the tourney.

Resplendent in full armour, the knights gleamed silver-bright in the sunshine, helm-less that they might be seen by the adoring crowds, who had their well-loved favourites, and their loathlings. Above the noise of cheering, the jingle of harness and clop of many hooves upon the dusty road as they entered the stadium, there was also the sibilant hiss of jeering. It was well known that some knights won by ruthless methods other than skill, and whilst all knights must possess a brutal aggressiveness or lie slaughtered upon the field of battle, the manner in which it was applied was a matter hotly debated.

At the head of the procession rode the marshals and the constables, dressed in their frogged livery and full of smug satisfaction at their own importance, for it was they who would keep order, it was hoped, when male tempers raged hot and uncontrollable. Yet they were not held in adoration as the knights were, who each followed behind his own herald. At the forefront of the twenty knights invited to compete this week rode the champion of England, and the people's darling—Troye de Valois.

His chestnut stallion danced, swinging his noble head as Troye held the reins with skilful yet casual ease. His dark hair had recently been cut short to the nape of his neck, so that in the hot summer sun he did not sweat unduly within his great helm. The crowd cheered even louder at his passing. Harlots hung from balconies and windows, eager to catch his attention. From their fingertips fluttered flower petals and ribbons cut from their chemises, for there was nothing more erotically alluring than a handsome man graced with a pair of broad shoulders and clothed in a masculine aura of strength, courage and danger.

Troye narrowed his eyes against the sun and the adulation, in equal measure. He had no doubts that once his rear end landed too often upon the dusty ground, he would be darling no more. At thirty-one he harboured no illusions about the younger men eager to bring about his downfall, and he smiled with rueful acknowledgement, waved his hand in salute, thanking the people of London for their praise, and yet prepared for their inevitable rejection.

Turning his horse into the stadium, he lined up with the other knights before the gallery of spectators, dominated by the King's dais, bedecked and swagged with colourful bunting and garlands of ivy and ribbon rosettes. The sun slanted sideways, burnishing his deep tan and accentuating the hollow cheeks of his lean, handsome face.

In the stands, a fair-haired beautiful woman, Lady Joanna, called to her daughter, a smaller version of herself, with dark auburn hair tied back with silk ribbons.

'Eleanor,' her mother complained in a weary voice, 'do stop jumping up and down and craning your neck like a swineherd. It is most unladylike.'

'But I cannot see Rupert,' Ellie responded, sitting down upon the bench and trying to peer through the dust and the glinting armour and the crowd of horses, with blushes and youthful awkwardness disguising her interest in one knight who was not her kin. And was he not the most handsome, the most strong, of all knights? Her heart glowed and fluttered as she gazed upon the face that been naught but a memory for so long.

'He'll be well to the back,' said her father, reclining in his chair and leaning over to pick up her mother's hand and kiss her knuckles.

Ellie rolled her eyes skywards, exasperated. Why couldn't her parents be like normal people? They were for ever kissing and cosseting, much to her embarrassment.

'What is that look for, demoiselle?' demanded her father, with a small smile touching the corners of his mouth, 'Your mother is worried. Might I not comfort her with a kiss?'

Ellie folded her arms over her waist and hunched her shoulders, looking away as she muttered, 'In private, aye, but not here, where everyone can see.'

'There is naught wrong with a little affection,' rebuffed her father, and then added quickly, all too aware that his daughter was no longer a child, 'between married couples, that is.'

Lady Joanna smiled at her husband, and murmured in her low, serene voice, 'Leave her be, Hal. She chafes that it is her brother who rides in the joust and not herself.'

'Hah!' snorted Lord Henry, 'that will be the day! 'Tis sport for men, not maidens, and you would do well to remember that, young Ellie.'

Ellie sighed. 'Yes, Father.' Her reply was dutiful

and full of respect, for she had much love and admiration for her father, yet she burned and fretted against the restrictions of her sex, for more reasons than were apparently obvious. How she longed to run to Troye de Valois and throw her arms around his neck and tell him how much she loved him! Suddenly, unable to contain herself any longer, she leapt to her feet and pointed, with an excited shriek, 'There he is!' She ran to the rails and waved. 'Rupert! Rupert!'

Her brother steadfastly ignored her, his eyes averted as the cavalcade rode by, exiting from the stadium, yet he felt a blush creep up his cheeks as the other knights made ribald comments about the pretty red-haired wench clamouring from the stands.

''Tis my sister,' barked Rupert with a scowl, 'so shut your mouths!'

This only brought forth more raucous crows and teasing quips, and some serious speculation that resulted in sudden overtures of friendship, in the hope of making an introduction to a wealthy young heiress who was not only of noble English blood, but beautiful too. Rupert, though only eighteen years old, had a sensible head on his young shoulders and was wise to their stratagems. What he knew of these knights, having fought and caroused alongside them all this summer past, in Scotland and Gascony, left him in no doubt that they fought hard, and played harder. The thought of such men making close acquaintance with his little sister somehow made him bristle and leap to protect her. Besides, it was not his say-so regarding Ellie—any honourable intentions must go through his father first.

While the knights retired to their arming tents in the field beyond, the crowd was entertained by the heralds, who gave eloquent, and often extravagant, introductions, relaying to all and sundry not only their master's name and country of origin, but his ancestry, heraldic banner, victories and character. Only knighted nobles were allowed to participate in the joust and this was part of the glamour that attracted the commonfolk: for them the knights were men not of their ilk, but demigods—stronger, faster, braver than any mere mortal man—or so they wished to believe.

Ellie sat bored and fidgeting, fanning herself in the sultry afternoon heat while the speeches droned on, sucking on a lemon sherbet that too quickly melted and left her with sticky hands. She was desperately eager to see Rupert and speak with him, remind him to keep his guard steady and not to look away too soon, naïvely convinced that without her advice he would fail. Conveniently she forgot that so far he had survived quite well without her. This was his first summer on the tournament circuit, and it had taken some persuading to convince her mother to make the journey to London to watch him compete. Lady Joanna had not wanted Rupert to participate in the joust in the first place, and sought to avoid the spectacle of her son being attacked at all cost. Yet she had been worn down by the pleadings of her husband and her daughter and had seen the necessity and opportunity of making a suitable match for Eleanor amongst the great gathering of nobility.

On Ellie's other side sat her Aunt Beatrice, her dark hair streaked with silver and yet her brown eyes and soft skin still beautiful despite her middling years. 'Shall I go and find Uncle Remy for you?' asked Eleanor artfully, seeing how her aunt darted frequent and worried looks to the entrance.

'Nay…' Lady Beatrice patted her hand '…he will be in the arming tent giving Rupert some last-minute advice, no doubt, and 'tis no fit place for a lady. He will be here anon.'

Ellie pursed her lips in frustration, and slumped inelegantly on the bench, disgruntled with her lot in life and earning a reprimand from her mother, who was ever mindful of the fact that beautiful, unmarried and privileged girls like Eleanor were constantly watched and appraised.

Ellie was roused from her maudlin mood when a blast of trumpets heralded the first joust of the day. At this stage of the tournament it was the young, inexperienced knights who rode first, and Rupert was amongst them. Eleanor looked up as a pair of boots pounded on the wooden steps and along the narrow gangway of the gallery. Her Uncle Remy ran lithely to where they sat, casting a smile on his wife as he sat down, and leaning forwards to reassure Lady Joanna that all would be well for Rupert.

'Did you tell him to keep his guard up?' asked Eleanor urgently. 'He tends to look away too soon.'

'Aye,' laughed her uncle, his blue eyes bright with a teasing glint. 'Don't fret, little one, he is a man full grown and this is not his first joust.'

'Though 'tis the first I have watched,' complained Lady Joanna, her lips pinched white in a worried grimace.

When at last Rupert brought his caparisoned charger on to the field and faced his opponent, it was his sister who leapt to her feet, shouting encouragement along with the commonfolk who cheered from the far side of the lists. Until, that is, her mother gripped her wrist and jerked her down, with a swift admonishment to sit still and be quiet. Her father and her uncle laughed, and then they too were leaping to their feet and shouting as the ground thundered to the pounding of galloping hooves and the air vibrated with rowdy cheering.

Rupert was drawn three times in the list, and three

times he vanquished. As the sun dipped in the afternoon sky and the joust came to an end at seven in the evening, there was much rejoicing in the Ashton camp. Ellie and her family retired to their pavilions, pitched in the meadows beyond Cheapside. It was inexpensive and convenient accommodation, compared to the taverns of London that were infested with disease and thieves, but still it lacked in homely comforts. Lady Joanna and Lady Beatrice supervised the boiling of hot water and the cooking of supper upon vast cast-iron cauldrons set on open fires. Rupert had his own tent amongst the competing knights, on the far side of the same crowded meadow. Ellie endeavoured to slip away and to rush to her brother, eager to hear from his own lips how it had felt to be victor three times today, and eager to have news of Troye de Valois.

It was no easy task and was full dark by the time she managed to make the feeble excuse of visiting the privy, and then change her course for the knights' encampment. The cool evening air and the darkness threw a cloak over the field that in daylight she had few qualms about traversing. Now she trod warily, leaving behind her the comforting domestic noise of clattering spoons and gossiping serfs, to encounter the coarse laughter and strident music of the revelling knights. This was a foreign world, and Ellie feared her father's wrath should he find out where she had been. She picked up her pace and jogged her way between the striped pavilions, but in the dark and the dancing shadows thrown by the flames of open fires she felt disorientated and struggled to locate Rupert's tent.

A hot sense of panic began to prickle over Ellie, as leery glances from several groups were cast her way, and she pulled up the hood of her dark blue fustian cloak. It must be here! she thought, gazing about in bewilderment. As she paused to look around her, seeking the red-and-yellow stripes of Rupert's tent and the banner of the house of Raven, three knights seated on tripod stools about their campfire called out to her.

'How much?' they shouted, waggling a purse of coins.

She stared at them, bemused, and then turned and hastened onwards, deciding to call out to locate her brother.

'Rupert!' Her voice sounded thin and reedy, and was swallowed up by the noise all around her. 'Rupert!'

'Ho, little lady!'

Two fellows lurched around the guy ropes and pegs of the nearest tent, bumping into her as they stumbled with drunken awkwardness. Her hood fell back and Ellie gave a small cry of alarm as an arm snaked around her waist.

'Mind your step, my beauty!'

Rough fingers jerked her chin up and she cringed against such violation, for no man, except her relatives, had ever touched her. The stink of wine fumes wafted from their mouths and Ellie pushed at the arm holding her.

'Well, now, you're a pretty little wench if ever I did see one! How much? For both of us.'

There was that question again, and Ellie gasped, as now it dawned upon her their meaning—they thought she was a harlot! With an angry exclamation she shoved again at the man nearest, and was surprised to find that he did not yield. An entirely new experience, to have her command thwarted.

'Let me go! My brother will kill you—'

This was met with uproarious laughter and suddenly the two men exchanged a glance, nodded in agreement and dragged her off into the dark shadows of an alley way behind a row of tents. Her scream was cut off by a sweaty hand clamped to her mouth and the wind was knocked from her ribs as she was flung down upon her back, hitting the hard ground with a thump. Quickly she recovered and fumbled at her waist for the dirk she had concealed there, whipping it out and pointing its gleaming silver tip at the man who had straddled her.

'Let me go! Now!'

To her dismay her demand was met with only more

laughter. Cruel fingers crushed her wrist, so that she yelped and was forced to drop the dirk.

'Shut up!' hissed the man, all merriness gone as he now panted with excitement and struggled to unlace his breeches, 'This won't take long and we will reward you well enough.' He turned to his companion, 'Hold her hands, Will, while I get this poxy knot—'

His friend seemed uneasy, 'She don't speak much like a whore, maybe she is a lady—'

'A lady!' snorted the other. 'What would a lady be doing down here? Nay, it's just a game, isn't it, lovely?' With a grunt of triumph he wrenched open his breeches and reached for the hem of Ellie's gown.

She gave another scream and struggled wildly as she felt his knee jerk her legs apart and his fingers sought the linen loincloth that she wore. Her silky white hose dislodged in the process, sliding down in undignified folds about her ankles, and her heart hammered at the dreadful prospect of what was about to be done to her. She felt dizzy and with sick despair she turned her head away and closed her eyes, raging with impotent fury at her fate.

Then suddenly a black shape hurtled through the darkness and the man crouched on top of her went flying backwards. She glimpsed the blur of a fist as it smashed once, twice, three times into her abuser's face, with swift and brutal efficiency. Blood spurted from his nose and he spat broken teeth upon a gurgle of shock and pain, before he was grabbed by the scruff of his tunic and thrown a goodly distance away from Ellie. Her rescuer then turned to deal with the other man, but he had already seen who it was meting out justice and fled with all speed into the darkness.

Panting slightly at his exertions, the knight knelt at her side. Ellie stared at him, too shocked to utter a word of thanks. She felt nauseous and the world spun in a whirling circle before her glazed eyes. She shuddered as again she felt male hands move beneath her skirts—but his were impersonal, quickly investigating hands that touched her loincloth briefly and then pulled up her hose and refastened her garters. He murmured soothingly, reassuring her in a deep male voice that he meant her no harm.

'You are still intact.' He breathed a sigh of relief. Then she felt his fingers cup her face and turn it to the distant glimmer of firelight, 'What are you doing here, a little maid with no escort?'

She sat up and stared at him, niggled by a faint sense of recognition, but it was too dark and she could not see his face in the shifting firelight and the faint moonglow. She felt so alone and lost and very foolish. Suddenly, without warning, she burst into tears.

'Shh,' the male voice commanded, 'you are safe. I will protect you from all harm.'

His arms went around her slender back and she leaned against him, sobbing upon his hard, warm chest. He let her cry for a few moments, and then wiped her tears with his thumb and persuaded her to rise.

'Come, let me escort you to your family.'

With angry impatience at her own female weakness, she dashed away the tears from her eyes and muttered, 'Thank you, sir, for your help, but I will find my own way.'

He gave a short laugh. 'I doubt that! And you have not answered my question. Why are you here amongst these rough knights? 'Tis no place for a maiden.'

'I am looking for my brother. Rupert Raven.'

'Ah, I see. So you are indeed Ellie.' He led her between the pavilions and the light from a nearby fire illuminated them. 'You have grown since I last saw you, little knight.'

Troye de Valois! Ellie gasped. She felt the hot tide of a blush sear her neck and cheeks, at once both elated and mortified. How perfect, how fine indeed that Troye should be the one to rescue her, and yet how terrible to meet again in such shameful circumstances! Ellie could not think of a word to say to him and they walked in silence as he led her between the tents. She realised that she had been completely off course, until at last he lifted the striped yellow-and-red flap of Rupert's tent and they entered the golden glow within.

The tent was not solely occupied by Rupert, who sat lounging on a cushion with a young woman sprawled upon his lap, her frothy petticoats hitched well above her ankles and her bodice immodestly low cut. Eleanor stared, taking in her brother's two companions as they reclined in various postures of debilitated drunkenness, a stench of wine fumes emanating from the empty bottles cast upon the ground.

Rupert looked up from a ribald conversation with his friends, and then suddenly leapt to his feet as he spied his sister, spilling the doxy to the floor.

'Ellie! In God's name, what are you doing here?' With a guilty start he tugged together the open neck of his tunic, where the harlot had been exploring his chest hairs with her accomplished fingers.

Her rescuer spoke for her, giving Rupert a stiff bow and a disapproving glance. 'She was looking for you and—'

'I became lost!' interrupted Ellie swiftly, her eyes, as she lifted them to the tall man at her side, suddenly pleading. She quelled a sigh as in the glow of lamplight she looked upon Troye's face that featured in so many of her dreams, both waking and asleep. Yet now, in the cold hard light of reality, his eyes looked at her in an impersonal way that she had not anticipated.

'You should take better care of your sister, Raven, for she was wandering about the camp alone. 'Tis no surprise she was attacked.'

Ellie cast her eyes to the ground at this revelation, embarrassed beyond measure by his words.

'I am sorry,' he said to her, noticing her expression and pursed lips, 'but such an incident as I have just witnessed cannot be hushed up. I must report it to the constable and the men who nearly raped you shall be caught and punished.'

'What!' exclaimed Rupert.

'Aye,' confirmed her rescuer, 'two men attacked her. I have no doubt one shall be easily identified, by his broken nose and two missing teeth.' Then he turned to Rupert and made a deeper bow. 'I trust you will escort your sister safely homewards.'

Rupert replied with a bow of his own, 'My thanks, sir.'

Troye paused as he turned on his heel to leave, and smiled gently down at her, 'Did I not warn you once that your female strength would be no match for a man's?'

Ellie was forced by good etiquette to reply, 'Indeed. I thank you, sir, for your assistance.' But the words did not come easily, forced in a barely audible whisper from the constriction of her throat.

Troye threw a stern glance to her brother. 'I would suggest that you keep a closer eye on your sister. This is no place for maidens.'

A vivid blush stained Ellie's cheeks and then he turned and silently left, a dark, lithe shape that moved with all the ease and swiftness of a shadow.

Rupert apologised to his friends and the doxy, for whose services he had paid for the next two hours. It irked him sorely to be deprived of them, but he latched on his sword. With gruff impatience he took his sister by the elbow and dragged her in his wake as he left the tent.

'What the hell did you think you were playing at?' he demanded harshly, striding fast and unerring through the rowdy campsite towards the quieter domain of the family pavilions.

Rupert was easily head and shoulders taller than herself, and she struggled to match his long stride. As they hurried a drunken reveller stumbled into their path, but with a growled oath of unusual viciousness Rupert easily threw him off with one sweep of his forearm.

Ellie stared at him from the corner of her eye. All their lives they had always been close, and had spent much of their childhood playing and getting up to mischief in each other's company, yet she had the uneasy conviction that this Rupert, the man, she did not know.

'I wanted to speak with you,' she said in a small voice. 'I wanted to hear from you how it was riding in the lists.' Sudden tears crowded in her throat and pricked the back of her eyes, her heart confused and hurting by both her brother's anger and her meeting with Troye. The tears threatened to fall at any moment.

With a sigh, glancing at her woebegone face,

Rupert halted, his hands gently gripping her arms and turning her towards him. He bent his head and stooped to peer at her downcast eyes. 'Listen, de Valois is right about one thing. We are no longer children. We are not free to run about as we did then. You are a young woman now, Ellie, a very pretty young woman, and there are men that, given half the chance, would eat you whole for breakfast.'

She sniffed, and wiped the heel of her hand over her damp cheeks. 'I meant no harm. I just wanted to talk with you.'

'I know.' Relenting in his anger, he hugged her and patted her shoulder as he felt her slender frame shudder with racking sobs.

'Oh, Rupert…' she pressed her cheek to his tunic, her fists clenched to her bosom as she folded herself into his comforting embrace '…I was so frightened! I thought I could fight them off. I've never feared anyone in my life, but I was so helpless!'

'Thank God for de Valois.' She was silent and he looked down at her, adding, 'You were less than gracious in your thanks to him.'

She shrugged, uncertain of the tumult of emotions that Troye de Valois had awoken in her, and for a moment wondered if she could confide her secret yearnings to her brother. But the moment passed, as Rupert gave her a little hug and then briskly walked on. She had no choice but to follow in his wake.

'Come, let us hurry,' declared Rupert. 'No doubt Mother is beside herself with worry, and God knows what havoc Father is wreaking in his search for you.'

They exchanged a glance and in silence continued on. When they reached their cluster of pavilions, Lady Joanna spied them and with a heartfelt cry of relief picked up her skirts and ran to meet them. Ellie stumbled to her mother and gratefully surrendered herself to her fierce embrace.

'Oh, wretched, wretched child!' exclaimed Lady Joanna, holding Eleanor away from her and smoothing her auburn hair back from her brow. 'Where have you been? Your father has gone to call out the guard in search of you.'

Rupert groaned and quickly despatched a serf with a message that Eleanor had been found, and then quailed as their uncle approached, striding towards them with a thunderous frown upon his brows.

'Where in God's name have you been, girl?'

Ellie faced her uncle, throwing a conspiratorial glance to her brother and hoping he would not betray her as de Valois had. 'I only went to see Rupert, but then I got lost. But we found each other in the end.'

'Stupid girl! Don't you realise that a tourney campsite is no place for a lone female? Why, 'tis teeming with mercenaries and harlots and thieves and all manner of lowlife that you would have no wish to encounter!'

She hung her head in guilty silence, casting a surreptitious glance to Rupert from beneath her lashes.

'Calm yourself, uncle,' soothed Rupert, 'she has come to no harm and I am sure…' he glanced down at the bowed head of his sister '…*very sure* that she will not make the same mistake again.'

'Is that so?' said another voice, the deep, angry voice of her father as he strode into their midst. 'What have you to say for yourself, Eleanor?' Lord Henry grasped his daughter by the chin and jerked her head up. 'And do not lie to me, girl, for I am in no mood for deceit!'

Ellie gasped, for she had never seen her father so angry, and she glanced with wide, frightened eyes to her mother, who intervened on her behalf, touching a soothing hand to her husband's arm. 'Easy, Hal, all is well. She was merely lost, but Rupert found her and brought her straight home.'

'Indeed?' Her father pierced her with his dark brown gaze, 'That's not what I hear.' The others looked at him in questioning consternation. 'I have heard an entirely different tale from Troye de Valois.'

Her uncle and father exchanged glances. 'What has he to do with this?'

With reluctance Lord Henry admitted, 'It seems we owe him a debt of gratitude, for he came to report an attempted rape and gave good evidence of the suspects, and the victim.'

'Good God!'

'Eleanor—' her mother turned to her, with flutter-ing alarm '—is this true?'

Eleanor and Rupert exchanged a glance. Then her brother turned on his heel and called back over his shoulder that he would find Troye de Valois and bring him back to explain the truth.

'Nay, Rupert!' protested Eleanor as her father snatched at her upper arm. 'Father, it's not—'

'Don't try to deny it, girl,' he snapped with great fury, turning to address her mother. 'What did I tell you? Blood will out!'

'Nay, Hal! Please, leave her be.'

But her father turned a deaf ear to her pleading mother, who stumbled in their wake as he grabbed hold of a wooden spoon from the cook's table and dragged Eleanor to his pavilion. Once within he pushed Eleanor against the table and forced her face down with his hand between her shoulder blades. He flung up her skirts and began to strike her across the buttocks with the wooden spoon.

'Hal, please,' shrieked her mother, desperately trying to catch hold of her husband's arm as it rose and fell in a fury. 'Stop, for the love of God! She is my daughter, through and through, mine! All mine, never his!'

'Blood will out, Joanna, but I will teach her a lesson and beat the wanton from her first.'

Chapter Two

Eleanor was beyond crying out after the first initial shocked cry, and leaned across the table in taut silence as her father smacked her. He did not apply much force; whilst each blow stung, it was her pride that suffered the most.

'Remy, stop him, please, please stop him!' sobbed Lady Joanna.

Her uncle stepped forwards then, the only man big enough to tackle her father, and grasped hold of Lord Henry's arm, forcing it down and grinding out between clenched teeth, 'Enough, Hal. There is no need for this.'

Her father snorted. 'Is there not? Then what was my so-called daughter doing amongst a campful of tourney knights, unescorted? Lies and dissipation I will not tolerate!'

'You have not even given Eleanor a chance to explain.'

'Hah! What would we hear but lies, just like her—'

'Don't!' screamed Lady Joanna, with such force that their ears rang, 'You promised, Hal,' she wept, 'you promised me that you would love them. She's a good girl, high spirited and strong-willed, but none the less a good girl.'

Seeing his wife with tears streaming down her cheeks and her beautiful, fair face twisted and reddened with fear and horror, he suddenly dropped the wooden spoon and released Eleanor, jerking down her skirts. 'Go!' he commanded her. 'Get from my sight.'

Slowly, her back aching and her buttocks smarting, Ellie raised herself up from her punishing stance and turned slowly to face her father, and when she spoke her voice was a trembling whisper that wrenched at his heart. 'Please forgive me, Father, if I have done wrong.'

And then she turned and staggered to her mother, who folded her tightly into her embrace and, together with her Aunt Beatrice, took her away.

Alone now, Remy turned to his brother-in-law and said quietly, 'Your fears are unfounded, Hal. I have to agree with Joanna, there is naught of her father in Ellie.'

Lord Henry turned away, sickened with himself, enraged at the cruel twist of fate that was now rearing its ugly head to torment them. 'What to do?' he asked in bitter despair. 'What to do? She will hate me now. Ellie has always been slow in her forgiveness of a wrong. But how greatly I fear the vice of the father shall be born in the children.'

Remy clasped his shoulder, offering his support. 'By nature there is a measure of vice in all of us. But I believe you have nurtured her so well—indeed, both of them—that it is no more than the usual. I know you mean well, Hal, but let things be for a day or two. You will see, Ellie will love you still, as the good father you have always been to her.'

'Good!' Hal snorted in self-disgust. 'I have never in her life, nor mine, beaten a wench before.'

'Nay, but in a fit of hot temper we all do rash things we later regret. She will forgive you.'

In the adjoining pavilion Ellie lay face down upon her cot covered in soft furs, too numb with shock and misery to cry, to even speak, and lay staring at the canvas walls, while her mother and her aunt whispered conspiratorially behind her. Rupert returned and knelt beside her, stroking her hair and whispering that he had been unable to locate de Valois, but on the morrow he would find him and let him speak his truth. Eleanor roused herself, sniffing as she reached out and clutched at her brother's sleeve, her voice muffled and strained as she begged him not to.

'Please don't, I have no wish for him to know of my disgrace.'

'But you have done nothing wrong!' protested Rupert, 'Mayhap you have been foolish, but 'tis nothing like what Father thinks. Troye de Valois will set him straight.'

'Nay!' sobbed Eleanor. 'Say nothing.'

Reluctantly Rupert departed, and after a word with his mother and restraining himself from tangling with his father, he returned to his own tent on the knights' side of the field.

All night, and the following day, she would talk to no one, and lay still and silent upon her bed, refusing all food and even water. Worried, Lady Joanna sent for her son, and paced restlessly until at last he came, but as she rushed to him she contained her outburst as she saw that he was accompanied. Questioningly, she frowned at Troye de Valois as he bowed to her with quiet respect.

'What is he doing here?' she asked, somewhat ungraciously, too concerned for her children to bother with niceties.

'I thought that he could speak to Father, and reassure him that what happened was not Ellie's fault.' He turned to de Valois, and with a lift of his eyebrows encouraged him to speak.

'It is so, lady. Your daughter did nothing wanton

and her only error was to be naïve enough to think she could wander through an encampment full of drunken men unmolested.'

Lady Joanna smiled at him then, and sent a serf to fetch her husband, before turning to Rupert with a worried frown, 'She has not spoken, nor eaten, nor even swallowed a drop of water since...since last night.'

''Tis shock,' supplied Troye, thinking to be helpful and unaware of the full events, 'but she's young and strong and will soon recover.'

'Nay...' Lady Joanna shook her head '...my husband was very angry and—and he...beat her. I think that has upset her more than anything else.'

Troye politely stood aside while mother and son conversed in whispers; when Lord Henry entered the tent and cast upon him an enquiring, speculative eye, he bowed with respect, although as the King's champion he had no need to bow to any man. Troye wasted no time, and carefully explained that he had no doubt that Eleanor had not behaved in any way to encourage an interest in her. 'She tried to fight them off and save her honour, but if I had not chanced to hear her scream and come to her aid, she would not have had strength enough to succeed. Rest assured, my lord, your daughter is not a wanton and her honour is intact.'

This was a thought that had not occurred to Lord Henry as of yet, and he spoke sharply to his wife. 'You have examined Eleanor? She is virgin still?'

'Of course,' murmured Lady Joanna through stiff lips, a guilty blush flaring upon her cheeks as she had not considered such an examination necessary and her blush deepened as her son and his companion stared uncomfortably at their boots.

'And you,' Lord Henry spoke with equal abruptness to Troye, 'what state was my daughter in when you found her?'

'Well, naturally, she was very distressed—'

'That was not what I meant! In what state was her clothing?' Lord Henry leaned very close, his eyes full of glittering danger. 'Was she…undressed?'

'Nay, my lord!' Troye protested hotly. 'It was as I have told you. Her clothing, and her honour, were all intact.' He thought it best not to mention that he had, in fact, refastened her hose and garters, sensing that even this brief assistance to a distraught and dishevelled damsel would send her father into a paroxysm of rage.

Lord Henry released a pensive sigh, and then ionked a brief, grudging bow to Troye, 'My thanks for your assistance. We are grateful. I trust,' he said with grave warning, 'that this will not be a topic for campfire conversation. My daughter's reputation relies upon your discretion.'

'You have my word.' Troye bowed and then turned to leave with Rupert, who hurried to where his sister lay in her pavilion. Troye halted outside and laid a hand upon Rupert's arm. 'I would like a word with her first, in private. With your permission.'

Rupert eyed him for a long moment, taking his measure, and then nodded and scanned the neighbourhood. 'Be quick. I will stand guard.'

Both acknowledged in silence the suspicion that Lord Henry would not take kindly to a knight such as Troye de Valois being alone with Ellie, even if it was just to speak to her.

It was dim within the pavilion, after the bright glare of the late afternoon without. Troye stood still for a moment and let his eyes accustom themselves, and then he looked about at the comfortable but far-from lavish furnishings that signified her family were well off, but certainly not extravagant. There were several brass-bound coffers spilling linens and furs, some small tables holding silver goblets and a tray of untouched food, two X-shaped chairs and numerous furs and carpets strewn about on the canvas ground sheet. Four cots were placed against the edges of the tent and in one of them he discerned a slim female shape, only recognisable to him by the long swathe of dark auburn hair that hung down and swept to the ground, obscuring her face.

Troye crept softly across the space and then squatted down upon his heels, whispering gently, 'Ellie?'

She started, with a small gasp, and turned her head

towards him, her eyes narrowed with fearful alarm. 'What are you doing here?'

'Rupert told me that your father was upset, and I came to explain to him what occurred.'

Silent tears began to streak from her eyes and track down her cheeks. 'My father thinks I am a wanton, so please go, lest his fears be true.'

Troye smiled, a slight, puzzled frown creasing his brows. 'But you have done nothing, and I have told him so.' He reached out then, and brushed aside her hair so that he might better see her face, and her expression. 'Come, where is the brave little knight who would fight the world? A knight cannot collapse in defeat at the first obstacle, and life is full of obstacles.'

She smiled then, weakly, raising her eyes to his as she lay upon her stomach, twisting her neck a little the better to see him, 'Do not mock me, or tease, for I have not the heart to laugh.'

''Tis better to laugh than to cry.'

'Go away!' She shifted then and rolled to her side, wincing as pain shot through the back of her thighs and buttocks.

Troye frowned. 'I heard that your father beat you.'

'Aye, and how I wish I was a man, like Rupert, for I would strike him back! But I am only a weak female and have no choice but to allow men to overwhelm me.'

''Tis not weakness,' he admonished in a whisper,

glancing quickly over his shoulder to the shadow of Rupert as he kept lookout, 'but respect for your father. He was afraid, and that is why he lashed out.'

'Afraid of what?'

Troye shrugged. 'That I am not sure of, but I implore you, little maid, to get up and stand firm, as any knight would.'

Ellie sighed with heavy exasperation, goaded by a niggling dislike for the way he spoke to her, as though she were just a child. 'Very well.' She rolled awkwardly and rose with stiff and aching difficulty to her feet. She swayed a little, light-headed from weeping and lack of nourishment, and then gasped as his arm went about her waist and steadied her. She laid a hand on his chest, at first to hold him back and then out of curiosity as her fingers splayed and she felt beneath their tingling tips his warmth and hard muscles.

She tipped back her head and looked up at him, for though she was not as small as her Aunt Beatrice, who was tiny and dainty, neither was she as tall as her mother. The top of her head reached to his chin, and with her eyes wide and wary she noted that he was certainly the most handsome man she had ever seen. His dark hair was fine and cut close to the neck and his level brows neither too coarse nor too thin. Her eyes roved over his face, noting his nose that would have been elegant if it had not been broken at some stage in his life, mayhap more than once. The slightly flared nostrils, and his square forehead and lean, hollowed cheeks were all very masculine. Her gaze lingered for a moment on his mouth, with its curved lower lip and narrow, well-disciplined upper. His eyes were a very dark brown, and now they narrowed.

She felt his hands let go of her waist, yet they stared at each other for long moments, and then abruptly he took a step backwards, as though he had suddenly found himself teetering upon a cliff edge and sought to evade the danger.

For a moment Ellie could not resist lifting her glance to look at his mouth, and the faint shadow of stubble upon his firm jaw. She wondered how it would feel to be kissed by him, to feel his lips on her lips, to feel the rough scrape of his chin, so very male, against her tender skin.

Her emotions were obvious to him and he sighed, looking away from her lovely face and curious eyes. 'I am of no use to you, child, so waste not your time looking at me in such a way.'

Ellie felt a blush burn along her cheeks and she dropped her gaze, yet her pride goaded her to ask, 'Am I so ugly that you would turn away from me, sir?'

'Nay, you are not ugly. The fault is mine, not yours.' He was not one to divulge his private affairs, but he took pity upon the doubts that shadowed her eyes and her tender, innocent ego, 'You are a very beautiful young girl. One day you will make someone a fine wife.' Then he bowed in farewell and his footsteps were a soft sound upon the ground as he left her.

Ellie sighed, and watched as Troye de Valois departed, not at all sure what her reaction should be. Her confusion was mounting. She jumped with nervous guilt as another figure entered the tent, but it was only Rupert and she ran to him, glad for his company.

'Oh, Rupert! Tell me, is Father still angry?' She clutched at his arms in her anxiety.

'Nay, he is full of remorse and is convinced that you must hate him.'

She shook her head in denial, and then looked up at him with a puzzled frown, 'They…' She hesitated and then ploughed onwards. 'They said such strange things last night, Rupert. Did you hear?'

'Nay—' his frown matched hers '—what do you mean?'

Ellie shrugged. 'Nothing. No doubt I misheard or misunderstood.'

Rupert did not press the point, accepting that last night she had indeed been confused and upset. 'How are you this morn, Ellie? Still sore?'

She nodded. 'It will pass. At least he did not strike me in the face.'

'Father would never do that.'

'Nay. I suppose not.' But suddenly her childhood had evaporated and she was no longer certain of anything. 'How was your day? Did you fare well in the joust?'

He smiled. 'Aye. But tomorrow I must face de Valois.'

She shuddered, at once fearful and yet not wishing to break her brother's confidence by admitting that she did not think he could best de Valois.

'Don't worry, little sis, even I do not expect to beat the King's champion in my first season. 'Tis only a learning experience. Come now,' he chivvied her in a cheerful tone, 'the king has invited almost everyone that is anyone to the palace for a night of feasting and merrymaking. We will dance and I will find you some of your favourite marchpane sweetmeats and we will forget all about this unpleasantness. How about that?'

Ellie smiled, and nodded, yet sadly aware that she could not easily forget the burning flicker that had been ignited in her heart and threatened to burst into a sweet flame that would consume her.

Chapter Three

They went by barge to the Palace of Westminster, and Ellie welcomed the cooling breeze that whispered off the River Thames, the waters dark and smooth and lapping gently as the sun waned on this late summer's evening. The sky was burnished a vibrant coral-pink, a colour that matched the silk of her close-fitting gown, the sleeves and bodice edged with gold embroidery and seed pearls. She had dressed carefully, hoping to see Troye and that he would notice her appearance. The clinging folds of the gown draped her slender yet feminine hips and full bosom, the colour a perfect background for her auburn hair that hung loose and rippling to her hips, her head covered with a filmy organza veil held in place with a gold circlet.

She sat a little apart from the others as the barge rowed down the river, gliding with little more than a splash of water as the oars dipped into the river and

the prow pushed its gradual way towards their destination. Her father had come to her earlier and made
his peace, and she had accepted, yet in her heart she
knew that all matters between them would never be
the same. She watched him now, sitting with his
casual grace beside her mother, his arm loosely about
her waist and laughing at some jest Uncle Remy
made. Aunt Beatrice leaned back in the circle of his
arms, and she looked radiant in a gown of dark green
velvet. Ellie envied them, these four, these two
couples, and she felt the bitter pang of loneliness for
the first time in her life. She felt that she no longer
belonged within the family circle, and that knowledge disturbed her.

The embankment at Westminster was lit with pitch
torches, flaring small pools of golden light as the
passengers from many river barges and gondolas
drew up and alighted.

'Stay close,' whispered Lady Joanna urgently as
they climbed the stairs and traversed the deeply
shadowed lawns edging the palace.

The great hall was brightly lit and already noisy
with music and laughter and the hum of cheerful
chatter. Ellie looked about, seeking her brother, who
had promised to meet up with them later when his
duties were done. Jousting in tournaments was for his
amusement and training, as it was for many other
knights, but not his living. He had just recently been

placed in the cadet corp of the King's personal body-guard and his duties were to serve the knights who guarded the King from all harm. The King's Own were men harvested from the most loyal families in the kingdom, fighting men who had proven their valour and skill upon the battlefield, amongst them Austin Stratford, Sylvester de Lacy and the King's champion, Troye de Valois. She kept a look out for her brother, for where he was Troye would be too, both of them in service to the King.

Ellie was fascinated by the colourful gathering of people, brightly clothed in rich fabrics of velvet and silk, and the snippets of conversations that she over-heard, laced with rumour and gossip and bawdy jokes, before her mother or aunt hastily moved her away. The crowd laughed and drank, dancing and feasting, with all the merriment and intensity of those who knew the King was footing the bill for this jollity.

Rupert sent a message with a pageboy to say that he would be off-duty at the tenth hour. Ellie danced with her father and her uncle, and once with a group of girls similar in age, but mostly her family kept her within the close confines of their protection at all times. Ellie chafed at the restriction, for she knew that Troye must be here somewhere and she longed to see him, to speak with him.

She could scarce concentrate on anything at all, as her gaze winged its way about the hall, to the King's dais, hoping to catch a glimpse of Troye de Valois, yet it was so crowded and such a distance away she could not see him.

Rupert appeared then, holding one hand over her eyes and with the other depositing an object in her hands.

'Guess,' he commanded with a laugh.

Long familiar with his teasing games, Ellie exclaimed, 'A white kitten with a black tail!'

'Nay, goose.'

'Um…' Ellie pretended to be flummoxed and agonised over her choices '…a dove? A silk scarf? A handful of London air?'

Rupert released her with a heavy sigh, and Ellie opened the wooden box, prettily decorated with mother of pearl, and murmured her thanks at the sight of plump marchpane sweetmeats nestling within a bed of satin. Standing on tiptoe, she reached up and kissed her brother's cheek, 'Thank you, but you should not have wasted your coin.'

'I didn't.' He grinned. 'I, er, charmed them off a lady-in-waiting.'

She punched his arm in mock-admonishment, and then quickly set aside the box as he whirled her off into a prancing set. The evening picked up its pace and seemed to fly by, as her parents could little object to her dancing in a group when her own brother was part of it and looked on with a careful and watchful eye.

During the dances they swept past the King's dais and there, at last, she found Troye. He stood behind the King, to his right, alongside four other trusted and experienced knights who would guard the King from all harm and lay down their lives for him if necessary. Troye watched the gathering but, hard as she tried, she could not seem to catch his eye.

The music for a particularly lively rotundellus had just come to a halt, the drums ceasing in their banging and the reedy notes of several recorders and a twanging rebec had stilled when a sudden shout from the yeoman guards ranged about the hall went up.

''Ware! Arms!'

Into the hall whirled five black-cloaked and hooded figures. A collective gasp bounced to the rafters from the gathering of guests and they jostled themselves out of the way, tripping and bumping one another, skirts rustling and heels tapping in their haste. Then the black apparitions flung off their cloaks and five acrobats were revealed, dressed all in white, with black ruff collars and their faces painted to match the black-and-white theme. Laughter and a sigh of relief echoed from the crowd, and the rasp of steel as swords half-drawn from their scabbards were now slotted home, the King's bodyguard retreating from its protective phalanx about their liege.

'It's only a disguising!' cried Aunt Beatrice,

peeping out from behind her husband's broad back, where he had thrust her at the first hint of trouble.

It was a common enough form of entertainment, to run into a hall disguised in dark cloaks, and then throw them off, make their performance of either singing or dancing, charades or acrobatics, and then run off again. Ellie emerged from behind her brother and watched with interest the tumbling, white-faced acrobats, and clapped along with everyone else before the disguisers picked up their cloaks and ran out of the hall.

The moment of tension had not blighted anyone's enjoyment of the revelry. Indeed, to face the uncertain prospect of violence, and possibly death, had only served to whet their appetites for more pleasure. The noise levels rose to a roar, strong Gascon wine flowed freely from casket to goblet, and sumptuous offerings of food crammed on side tables were soon consumed.

'Oh, look, it is a line dance! Do let's join in, Rupert.'

On either side of the hall the guests formed a line, each couple on opposites sides. When it was their turn they skipped the dancing steps into the middle and then down the length of the hall, until halfway, where they were met by a couple from the other end of the line. In the middle the two couples danced together, and then swapped partners. It was one of Ellie's favourite dances, being very lively, and gave her a chance to dance with new partners. And to pass in front of the dais. And perhaps to make Troye a little jealous as she danced with other men?

Her cheeks were flushed and her eyes glowed brightly as her feet tapped out the intricate steps, with a smile on her berry-red lips. She danced with a very dark man, who had a hook nose and shaggy brows and whose name she did not know, but he held her hand lightly and smiled at her, a gold earring glinting in one ear. She thought he looked like a pirate, and then they separated and she skipped away to join the end of the line.

The dance required stamina, and it was some long moments before she reached the head of the line again, in front of the King's dais, where he sat back, looking on with a bored expression upon his face. She tried to see if Troye de Valois watched her, but his face was just a distant blur. She smiled across at Rupert and it was just about to be their turn to go down the middle when again came that warning cry.

''Ware! Arms!'

There was a brief titter this time, and the dancers scarce halted in their bobbing as five cloaked intruders ran into their midst. Ellie stayed where she was, their entrance blocking her path, and she looked on with a faint hint of expectation on her face, which quickly evaporated as the disguisers threw off their cloaks and drew swords from their scabbards, the scraping sound echoing a warning about the hall.

The royal bodyguard reacted immediately, the hiss of steel as they drew their own swords and surrounded King Edward spurring the guests into a collective scream. The floorboards suddenly shook as heels drummed in their haste to run from the impending conflict. There was no doubt this time that the King was under attack, yet Ellie stood rooted to the spot, aghast and mesmerised by the skirmish that erupted before her very eyes.

She had lived her entire life sheltered behind castle walls, protected and cosseted. She had heard tales of battle and only envisaged it as a playground for the exploits of valour and chivalry. Now she was stunned as silver blades arced through the air and cut through flesh and bone, blood spurting in a crimson fountain and spraying across the floors, the walls, and her gown. The masked attackers were no match for the knights, who had honed their skills for years in battles and tournaments for just such a moment.

Steel clanged on steel. There were guttural shouts and coarse oaths shouted as the King's bodyguards fought off the five masked assassins. The hall had erupted into pandemonium. Hundreds of people shoved and grappled to squeeze their way through the already crowded doorways to flee from the danger. Ellie was knocked to the floor. She looked up to see

Troye de Valois standing over her as he parried the less-than-skilful swordplay of one attacker. As she cowered she watched him bludgeon his opponent with swift strokes, knocking him to the ground and then forcing him to relinquish his weapon. With one quick thrust Troye stabbed the man in the heart and he gurgled an instant death.

The dead man lay only a few feet away from her and now Ellie began to scream, as blood spattered her and she recoiled. Rough hands seized her arm and dragged her off the floor.

'Get out!' shouted Troye harshly.

She scrambled to her knees, and then to her feet, crashing against the solid rockface that was Troye's chest as he jerked her backwards with one hand and fought off an assailant with the other. Her heart pounded as sword blades flashed so close to her head that her veil lifted and shivered in the breeze of their wake. Following the urgent insistence of Troye's hand gripping her arm, she tried to flee, but her heel slipped in a greasy pool of blood and she fell to her knees, her screams of horror rising to piercing intensity. Troye tugged her up again and pulled her along, throwing her with some force towards the crowd of people scrabbling for the exit.

'For God's sake, get out!' he shouted at her, and then he turned away, leaping once more into the fray as he and his men quickly dealt with the remaining intruders.

'Eleanor!'

She started at the sound of that familiar voice, and with a sob flung herself into the open arms of her Uncle Remy, burrowing into the massive, protective width of his broad chest. Being head and shoulders taller than most people, he managed to force his way through the crush, and soon had her out into the cool dark of the evening air. He hurried to where the rest of the family waited, half-carrying Eleanor as her knees suddenly buckled and refused to hold her upright. Her mother gave a desperate cry at the sight of her.

'It's all right,' Remy hastened to reassure them, 'it's not her blood. No harm has come to her.'

Ellie sank into the warm embrace of her mother's bosom, while her Aunt Beatrice used her veil to wipe the blood from her face, both women making soothing sounds as Ellie stared blankly with shock.

'Let us depart,' suggested Lord Henry.

There were swift murmurs of agreement, yet Rupert hung back, knowing full well where his duty lay. 'I must return to the hall.'

Lord Henry stretched out a hand and clapped his son on the shoulder, 'Fare thee well, Rupert. We will see you on the morrow.' With a rueful glance thrown at his womenfolk, he concluded drily, 'Our duty lies elsewhere. The fight is yours.'

Rupert nodded, and melted away into the dark

shadows of Westminster without a backward glance as his family hurried across the lawns to the stairs leading down to the embankment and their waiting barge.

It was a silent journey, punctuated only by the clunk and splash of the oars as they rose and plunged through the oily black waters of the river, and by Eleanor's hiccups as she sniffed, a violent shivering now taking hold of her as shock set in. She could scarce believe what had happened, and through it all she could only see the crimson of blood and the face of Troye de Valois. Never in her life had she seen such an expression upon a man's face. Such grim determination, such brutal ruthlessness. Again she shuddered, as goosebumps flared across her skin. And yet her heart had been thrilled, for he was her hero. Her heart had spoken, saying aye, this is the one, the other half that would make the emptiness within her complete, and no counsel from her head would alter her heart's desire.

With relief she alighted at Cheapside and with her family made haste to seek the comfort and safety of their own camp. Ensconced within the shadowy tent bearing the banner of Raven, Lady Joanna prepared hot spiced wine to ease their shock.

Uncle Remy lifted his goblet and said, 'Here's to

Troye de Valois. Once again he has saved our Eleanor.'

The others murmured in agreement, even Lord Henry reluctantly, and, with a small frown, added his own toast of gratitude. Ellie took a few sips and felt the warmth spread through her body, and then with a whisper she excused herself and hurried to her own tent. Quickly she stripped off her bloodstained gown and flung it away. She washed in water that was cold but ready to hand; it was not until she was clean and dressed in her nightshift that she sank down upon the furs of her cot and covered her face with both hands.

It thrilled her to think that Troye de Valois had indeed saved her life. She could so easily have been cut down in the fray, her slender body sliced like a ribbon by the threshing swords. And yet gratitude was not the emotion that came foremost to her mind. Aye, her heart might well be smitten by the heroics, but in her mind she could see only the horror. Valour and chivalry were clean and bright and beautiful attributes, but there could be no honour in bloodlust. She ached to know whether Troye was all right, if he had survived the attack unharmed. It irked her bitterly to think that she could not go to him, tend his wounds if he had any, hold him and comfort him. But soon, one day, she would be able to do all of that. For it was obvious to her that they were destined to be together.

So thinking, she lay down, hugged her pillow and smiled as she fell asleep.

In the morning Lord Henry wasted no time in taking his family to Cheapside, impatiently chivvying his wife and daughter as they dressed and broke their fast on bread and cheese. As they took out combs and ribbons impatiently he muttered that they were lovely enough to have no need to waste their time, and his, upon needless 'titivating'. Mother and daughter exchanged a glance, Lady Joanna making comment upon the use of such a word, and yet taking pity on her husband as she realised his anxiety to meet up with Rupert and hear all the details of last night's fray.

Remy, still a warrior at heart despite the comforts of marriage, was also eager to hear more news of the night before. Remy and Lord Henry discussed the whys and wherefores and whatnots of the attack upon the King as they rode to the tourney field, and Ellie listened with curious ears, eager to hear the name Troye de Valois. She felt a glow of pride that he received nothing but praise this morn, for a man who failed to earn the admiration and respect of her kin was, in her eyes, no man at all.

At the tournament they seated themselves in the canopied stands, as the crowds came drifting in while the sun rose higher in the blue sky. Chatter ebbed and flowed on the breeze, the smell of dust and horses, roasted pork and smoke from the cooking fires, drifting and swirling around the arena. It would be another very bright and hot day, and already ladies were seeking the shade of awnings and fanning themselves with parchment and sipping lemonade kept cool in barrels of Thames water.

Seated in their stand, Ellie watched as a pageboy came tripping up the steps and handed her father a rolled letter, tied with a red ribbon. Lord Henry nodded his thanks and turned away, to one side, while he opened it.

Eleanor looked about, eager to catch a glimpse of the jousting knights, seeking out a particular profile, dark eyes and broad shoulders, but Troye de Valois was not yet out on the field. Her curiosity about him was too powerful to resist and she asked her father questions that were vaguely disguised, in the hope of finding out more about him.

'Do you think life is very hard for Rupert?' she asked, as they sat close together on the benches, her mother chatting to her Aunt Beatrice as they appraised the fashions of the other ladies.

Her father looked up from the parchment letter he was perusing, with a frown, and glanced at Eleanor, 'What do you mean?'

She shrugged. 'Well, I wondered what life must

be like for Rupert, now that he is serving in the King's Own.'

Lord Henry carefully rolled up the letter and retied the scarlet ribbon. 'Aye, life will be harder than the easy comforts of living at home. But that is what a knight expects, little comfort and no thanks. A bedroll upon the floor, or a muddy field, food not fit for hounds, and the soldier's curse of long separations from his loved ones.'

'Then why do it?' asked Eleanor.

Her father smiled, and looked away into the distance. 'That is a question that could have many answers, my little dove. For some men, being a warrior is all they know, for others they are escaping pain of some kind, and for a few, a very few, they seek the glory of valour.'

'Once I would have been a knight,' said Eleanor, 'but now I am heartily glad that I am a lady.'

'So am I.' He chuckled and kissed the top of her head, 'Now, fear not for Rupert, he can well take care of himself.'

She had the grace to blush, aware that she could not confess her concerns were not all for her brother. Roundly she chided herself for allowing her thoughts to dwell upon Troye de Valois, and briskly reminded herself that thoughts of Rupert should come first. After all, who was Troye de Valois? They had scarce spoken more than a few words to each other and, though he lived in her heart and her dreams, the truth was that he had not yet become a reality, a part of her life that she so longed him to be. But these facts neither daunted nor diminished her feelings. She felt a happy glow and smiled as she envisioned a rosy future, for she was young and beautiful; surely, by now, Troye must know that her hand was on offer for marriage? It was only a matter of time before he approached her father with a proposal.

Eagerly she watched as the jousting began. How great was her impatience as the lesser knights took their turns, their horses thundering down the length of the list and the crowds cheering as one or the other was knocked from the saddle by a thrusting lance. Towards mid-day, at last, Troye de Valois rode out, much to the delight of his adoring onlookers, for Eleanor was not the only one smitten.

She watched avidly as Troye dispatched his opponents in quick and ruthless succession, yet she was relieved that Rupert was not riding. He had lost his footing carrying the body of a would-be assassin down a stairwell the night before, and was now sitting on the sidelines, nursing a twisted ankle and feeling like a chump as his comrades teased him. The day's competition ended all too soon and the crowds began to drift away, discussing the merits and faults of their favourite combatants and eagerly anticipating the crowning glory.

* * *

The jousting knights had the following day off to rest and prepare, in readiness for the final contest on Saturday. In the afternoon the King again opened his court at Westminster and as Eleanor entered the hall she felt the sting of goosebumps prickle on her skin. But the floorboards had been scrubbed clean, the guard had been doubled and there was a defiantly festive air to the gathering as the court gathered to eat and drink and make merry. The King was overheard to say that no paltry assassination attempt would have him cowering away in his chamber.

''Tis not our way, my lords, for the English to cower in fear!'

'Nay, indeed, your Majesty!'

'A toast…' the King raised his goblet '…to the fighting spirit of Englishmen!'

His salute was echoed, but one of his closest chancellors murmured that it would not be wise to make too much of the matter, for the Scots might yet try again and it would do the King no good to become lax.

'Bollocks to them!' cried Edward, rising from his elaborate chair upon its royal dais. He waved at the musicians to play, shouted for more wine, exhorted his subjects to partake of the mountains of delicious food laid out on tables in an adjoining chamber, and called for the five guardsmen who had fought like lions to defend his life the night before.

From out of the crowd they came, five young men standing together, looking sheepish at all the attention, amongst them Austin Stratford and Troye de Valois. They were tall, broad-shouldered young men, with that lean and confident look in their eyes that proclaimed their profession as fighting men.

'See ye these fine lads, such knights as no kingdom on God's earth has the good fortune as I to have their allegiance. Tonight I reward them, for with their own lives they did mine protect and save. I have not a scratch upon me. Anything they want, they shall have. Come, Sir Austin, tell me what it is you most desire and it is yours.'

Sir Austin looked about with a bemused glance, and he half-turned to Troye de Valois with a silent plea for assistance. Troye merely shrugged, as much at a loss as Austin, for what, indeed, would any Englishman dare ask of his King? Taking pity on the floundering and blushing Austin, he turned to the King with a small bow and murmured, 'We seek no reward, your Majesty, for we have merely done our duty.'

Someone called out a cheer of approval for Troye's reply, and others still clapped their hands, until the entire hall applauded and cheered. And then, as the King exhorted the ladies present to dance with these fine fellows, Troye stepped forward and begged permission for a private word. The King eyed him shrewdly, reluctant to single out one amongst the five for any favouritism, however true it might be that Troye de Valois was indeed his favourite knight. He valued the noble attributes of honour and courage and strength, all of these clearly abundant in Troye. So it was that he refused Troye permission for a word in private, and yet granted him leave to speak, here and now.

Troye looked about as the guests jostled closer, eager to fuel their lust for gossip, and a flush stained his face beneath its summer tan. To one side he saw the beautiful face of young Ellie, her eyes wide and just as curious as all the others. How he wished he could have prevented her from hearing in public his news, for it had not escaped his notice that she had feelings for him, a childish crush, no doubt, but he had no desire to hurt one so young and innocent. His jaw clenched as he bowed deeply to his King and murmured in a tense voice, ''Tis a matter I would prefer to discuss in private, your Majesty.'

'Indeed?' The King stroked his beard and looked about. 'Come now, Sir Troye. We must have no secrets here amongst brothers at arms, for secrets are weapons that our enemies could, and would, use against us.' He turned and climbed the dais steps, seating himself upon his ornate chair and eyed Troye with a frown. 'Could this matter you wish to discuss have anything to do with your absence from court last autumn and winter?'

For a wild moment Troye wondered if the King already knew, and his heart hammered painfully in his chest. With downcast eyes he replied, 'Your Majesty is indeed wise.'

'I am only guessing, Sir Troye, for every rumour in the kingdom reaches my ears eventually. But rumours remain just that, until the truth is admitted.' Edward's eyes were very hard, any warmth rapidly fading as his worst fears seemed about to be realised. 'Spit it out, lad, for I am not a patient man.'

'Your Majesty—' Troye took a deep breath and seized both his fate and his courage as valiantly as he could '—Sire…I have married.'

A gasp escaped from the guests crowding closer, eager to hear the goings-on. From the corner of his eye he saw Ellie press one hand to her mouth and one to her heart. Her face paled visibly.

The King fiddled with the great signet ring on his right hand, his eyes never leaving Troye for a moment. 'And marriage is a crime you feel a need to confess? I had thought it was more of a blessing, to be celebrated.'

'Your Majesty, I beg your indulgence and your great mercy, for I have married the one woman I truly love and will always love, as you have loved your Eleanor. But, sire, forgive me, I beg you, my wife is a Jewess.'

'What!' roared the King, his shout echoing the collective cries of astonishment about the hall. 'So you have married a woman of the Jewish faith? When I have expelled from our kingdom these—these heathens, these leeches and troublemakers!'

'It is not so, sire,' Troye protested. 'They are good people, my wife is a kind and gentle soul—'

But the King would not listen. In his anger he signalled for the yeoman guards to come forwards and ordered them to take Troye to the Tower, where he was to be imprisoned while he gave further thought to the matter. They hustled Troye away, the crowd parting like the Red Sea as he passed between them, his jaw set and his gaze defiant.

Ellie could only stare, as the blood seemed to drain from her face, from her very heart, and disappear. The hall seemed to whirl and tip in a crazy slant, as the dizzy impact of shock hit her.

Troye was married.

He loved another.

These two sudden facts were hard for her to understand, and there was only confusion and astonishment for the moment; the pain and the tears would come later. She watched, like everyone else, as the guards marched him away, wondering what would happen to him, how long would he spend imprisoned in the grim confines of the fortress known as the Tower. Who was the woman that had claimed her Troye?

Whatever the answers to these questions, one fact remained—her dreams were shattered.

Chapter Four

News of Troye de Valois's disgrace swept through London like fire leaping across dry summer fields. It crossed all boundaries and both commonfolk and nobles of the Court knew of his downfall. The final contest of the tournament had to be cancelled. Tents were uprooted, the lists dismantled, and disgruntled traders relying on the rich pickings of the tournament day muttered darkly. Lord Henry Raven supervised the packing of his own pavilion and bid his son farewell.

'Send word to us,' he said to Rupert, 'should you need anything.'

'And let us know when there is any news on de Valois,' added Remy St Leger, his fondness for the younger knight growing as his foolishness, all for the love of a woman, became apparent. 'I would know how the idiot fares.'

Rupert nodded his agreement, and stooped to kiss

his mother and hug his sister farewell. He noted the pale silence of the latter, and clasped Ellie's shoulder with one hand as he asked her, 'Is there aught amiss?'

Ellie shook her head, and reached for the reins of her horse as she prepared to mount. 'Give me a boost up, please.'

Her brother ably lifted her into the side-saddle and watched as she fussed with her skirts, avoiding his eye. She gripped the reins firmly and then forced a smile as he patted her horse and wished her goodbye.

'Fare thee well, Rupert.'

'And you, little sister.'

She turned her horse about, ready to fall in beside her mother and aunt as they rode behind their menfolk, and then she paused and called out to Rupert, 'He will be all right, won't he? Troye de Valois.'

Rupert realised then where her sorrow lay, and he smiled gently. 'Aye, he will be all right.' He came up closer and beckoned for her to lean down, so that he might whisper close to her ear a private confidence. 'The King's anger was only for show, to save face. I hear from an aide close to him that he already knew of the marriage but he waited for Troye to confess. At worst he will spend thirty days in the Tower and be fined for his misdemeanour, but for his honesty and his courage the King holds him in high esteem and no doubt it will all soon blow over. Have no fear for him.'

Ellie nodded, relieved for Troye's sake, but this news did nothing to ease the pain in her heart. Then she said goodbye and touched her heel to her horse's flank, cantering off as her father called out for her to hurry along.

The journey home to Castle Ashton in Somerset took four days, and while they seemed the longest days of her life, as she struggled to come to terms with the empty space within her heart, she valued the time spent in the saddle that kept her busy. When they reached home there would be time enough to be alone with her thoughts. The prospect filled her with a dull gloom, for always she'd had hope for the future, a future that she would spend with Troye, but now all hope had been taken from her and she was left with…nothing.

Tired as she was by the long hours of riding on country roads, the summer heat and dust almost unbearable, she lay awake at night. She slept in a tent with her parents, and listened to her father snore, her mother occasionally moaning at him to turn over. She wondered where Troye was sleeping tonight, if he was still in the Tower, if he had a comfortable bed and had been given a meal…and then tears slipped silently from the corners of her eyes as she realised that she must banish all thoughts of Troye, for he belonged to another.

* * *

Yet as the days and the weeks passed, and still she continued to think of Troye, her heart would not easily accept the firm advice of her mind. The stubborn creature insisted that all its love was reserved for only one man—Troye. No matter what she was doing, whether it was working on a tapestry with her mother, distilling herbs with her Aunt Beatrice, hunting with hawks in the fields with her father, always thoughts of Troye came to her unbidden. At night he was still the last image on her mind, and the first when she awoke.

To make matters even harder to bear, she could tell no one of her feelings. How could she confess to even one as understanding as her own mother that she loved a man she barely knew? A man that had never so much as kissed her and one that was married to another. It hurt beyond measure, to think of him with this unknown woman, that all this time he had loved her and there had never been any hope that she, Ellie, would be the one he would love. She wondered what his wife was like, this Jewess, and concluded that she must be very beautiful and very clever indeed to have captured the heart of the King's champion.

Summer faded into autumn and the leaves dried upon the trees to gold and bronze, fluttering down to the ground all around Castle Ashton. The wind rose and the dark grey clouds of winter came down from the north and brought with them flurries of early snow. Ellie retreated into silence and, though it was noted that she seemed to be pining, her appetite greatly diminished and her eyes having lost their bold sparkle, it was assumed by her family that she missed her brother and she merely passed through the moods and vagaries that afflicted youths as they evolved from child to adult, from girl to woman.

Ellie indeed wrestled with her emotions, swinging from one day to the next with a determination to forget all about Troye and then desperately longing for a miracle that would somehow bring them together. Quite how this would happen she had no idea. On days when she was determined to break the hold Troye had upon her heart, she flirted outrageously with any young man that came to Castle Ashton, arousing her mother's alarm and her father's ire. And yet when these young men departed, having gained not so much as a kiss from the saucy little Ashton girl, Ellie would retire to her chamber. There she would fling herself down upon her bed, racked with such great sobs of tears that she feared her ribs would crack. However hard she tried, her heart compared all men to Troye and found them sorely lacking. They did not look like Troye, or smile like him, or have the timbre of his voice, or his manly smell.

Her attempts to find new love failed and she lapsed

into solitude, seeking balm for her soul, convinced that she would never love again. Convinced that for some unknown reason she must wait. She could not fathom why she felt this stubborn need to wait. Wait for what? For Troye? How could that be? she demanded of the stars in the sky, as she stood at the open window of her chamber and gazed up at the heavens, with an aching heart.

When spring came, her father insisted on a grand feast with music and dancing to celebrate her seventeenth birthday on St George's Day. He invited all the local gentry, especially those with eligible sons. But by now Ellie had resigned herself to loneliness and unrequited love and would have nothing to do with any of them. Lord Henry was incensed at the waste of time and coin, as she refused to even hear of any offers made for her hand in the days following.

It was Lady Beatrice who noticed how eagerly her little niece ran to any messenger with a letter from Rupert in far-off London. It did not escape her attention that it was news of Troye de Valois that Ellie so eagerly sought. They had heard, of course, that Troye was released from prison, having spent a mere ten days within its confines. The King fined him five hundred marks for his insolence and then banished him from Court for a year. In effect, he sent him home to spend time with the wife he so dearly loved and for whom he had been prepared to risk all. When Ellie had heard this she was at once relieved that Troye was out of prison and safely home, and yet a twinge of jealousy warred with admiration for a man who could so dearly love a woman, even if that woman was not herself.

Lady Beatrice tried to talk to her niece and explain that time was a healer and that her feelings of pain and rejection would pass; that one day Ellie would meet another and all would be well. Ellie simply nodded, and smiled, and turned away. There came little news after that, except that Rupert, and therefore Troye, went away on campaign to Scotland. She shuddered to think of the experiences they would have fighting against the Scots, who, from all accounts, were barbaric savages. After some months Rupert sent a note to say that Troye had been grievously injured, had been relieved of his duties and sent home to his family in York to recover.

Eleanor was surprised at the pang she felt, after all this time, her concern for him, for his pain and suffering, and to think of him with the wife who nursed and cared for him. She could not endure any such thoughts. She tried to banish them by devoting herself to occupations of one kind or another: tending plants in the herb garden that she and her aunt had created at Castle Ashton, and on rainy days she stayed in her chamber writing out a transcript of the

Bible, each page beautifully and painstakingly decorated with intricate illustrations. Under the guidance
of their priest, Friar Thomas, she worked diligently
and he announced how pleased he was with her
devotion and even began to drop hints to Lord Henry
that he had fine hopes of Ellie finding her vocation
as a nun, much to his lord's displeasure.

Yet another winter and another spring passed and
then came a surprising change to her solitary existence. Remy St Leger rode over from Hepple Hill
with glorious and most unexpected news—Beatrice
was with child. There was great celebration, for they
had kept the news quiet until they were certain that
this time Beatrice would carry the child and already
she was well into her second trimester. They were all
overjoyed, for a child of their own had been the one
perfect blessing to crown the love that Remy and
Beatrice had shared these many years. Bearing a child
so late in years for a woman of Beatrice's age was a
risky matter, but all was being done to safeguard the
health of both mother and child and she would remain
at Hepple Hill until after the birth.

Ellie decided that she would be of more use to her
aunt if she went to stay with her at Hepple Hill, and
with the blessings of both her parents she set off a few
weeks before the baby was due to be born. While
Beatrice was forced to lie abed, bored and frustrated

and yet desperate to sustain the life of her unborn child, Ellie assumed the day-to-day tasks of running the keep. She made sure that her aunt received fresh, nutritious meals every day and supervised all the preparations and accoutrements needed for the birth, and for the baby. It kept her busy, and helped to pass the time, time being the essential element needed to help heal the heartache she suffered.

When the birthing day came, despite Beatrice's fears and Ellie's inexperience as midwife, the baby was born with little trouble, a beautiful lusty boy, healthy and fair like his father. The ecstatic parents named him Tristan.

Ellie could scarce bring herself to leave Hepple Hill and her soft, sweet-smelling, cuddly baby cousin until, on St George's Day, Lord Henry realised with a shock that his daughter would be twenty and she was still unwed. He summoned her home at once.

Almost at the same time a messenger arrived from London, with a short and yet commanding missive from the King. It seemed he had the need to take another wife and all unwed, eligible maidens were ordered to pay their respects at Court. Herewith, and forthwith, Lord Henry was ordered to bring his daughter Eleanor.

Eleanor noticed that her father was plagued by the delivery of several more letters, and he seemed most thoughtful, a slight frown between his brows as he gazed in silence upon the letters before him. Something was afoot, she was sure, and her suspicions were only deepened when that afternoon her father rode off to Hepple Hill, clearly to consult with her uncle.

Lord Henry engaged in idle chit-chat with Beatrice, praised her honey cakes and sipped the mulled wine she offered, admired his new nephew, but eventually she sensed her brother's distraction and withdrew, leaving the two men seated with their wine, in warm and trusting companionship.

Remy leaned one ankle on the other, legs outstretched, and gave Henry a shrewd look. 'Come now,' he said with a smile, nodding his head at the four scrolls of parchment that Henry clutched in one hand, 'what is it that troubles you, my brother?'

Henry sighed, rose from his seat and paced about for several yards, tapping the letters against his thigh before turning and waving them aloft. 'I have received no less than four marriage offers for Eleanor.'

Remy sat up. 'Indeed? Well, that is good news for 'tis surely time for Eleanor to wed. And no surprise to me, considering that Eleanor is a pretty and wealthy young woman. Why, then, are you so troubled, friend? Whatever it is that grieves Ellie, surely this nonsense has gone on for long enough?'

'Aye, I could not agree with you more. I know my

duty to Eleanor, and that she needs to make a good marriage, before it is too late and she has past the age when offers will still be made.' Henry sighed, 'Today I have no less than four, five if you include the King, yet…I find none of them suitable.'

Eyebrows raised in question, Remy waited patiently for an explanation.

'The first offer,' continued Henry, raising the first letter, 'came from Taddeo Visconti, the Italian count from Florence. A wealthy and titled man, a handsome fellow and neither too young nor too old.'

'But?'

'But…but there is something I greatly mislike about him…something brutal. And I would not have my…daughter live so far away from me.'

'Then we strike him off. He is refused.'

Henry sighed, and then nodded. 'Aye. He is refused. The second offer came from Austin Stratford, a very likeable and amiable chap, but without a title and no means other than what he earns upon the tournament field and the King's pay. I fear he is looking for a rich heiress, and though that alone holds no blame, I doubt he would make my Eleanor happy. He has no means with which to protect her and his personality is such that no doubt she would lead him a merry dance.'

'Then he too is refused. Who's next?'

'Casper von Eckhart, the Hun.'

Remy sat up and snorted. 'The devil take him! He will break her within days and I have no liking for his sort in our family line.'

'Quite,' agreed Henry. He sat down then, a pensive frown upon his brow. 'And then there is Neville Talbot, who to all intents and purposes would make an excellent match. He has a fine estate and his own fortune. He seems of fine character and yet…'

His finely sculptured nostrils flared and Remy murmured, 'And yet I have heard that his liking is for boys.'

Henry met his brother-in-law's eyes and looked away. It was a subject difficult to prove and to cast such aspersions upon a knight would be a grave offence if proven false. But still there were rumours, and Henry could not be deaf to them, for Eleanor's sake.

'You are between a rock and a hard place.' Remy leaned forwards earnestly, elbows on his knees, 'I would be most careful of Casper von Eckhart. He is a dangerous fellow and takes insult far too easily. Your refusal should be made in the sweetest of terms.'

Henry spread his hands in a helpless gesture. 'I heartily agree with you. Let us not forget the fate of his last bride.'

For long moments they sat in silence, staring at the crackling fire flames, pondering, both of them remembering the tale of a young woman from Kent that von Eckhart had taken a fancy to, yet he had been refused by her wealthy landowner father. Von Eckhart had then kidnapped his intended bride, had used her so badly that the maid had thrown herself from a cliff and into the sea before he could drag her to the altar. The Hun was reputed to have in his pay a formidable force of free lancers, soldiers no longer in the employ of the King and thus free to be engaged as paid soldiers by anyone who had enough gold coin to buy the use of their lances. Henry worried that his own garrison, depleted by recent wars in Wales and Scotland, was not sufficient to withstand an outright attack upon Ashton, or even an ambush. He needed Eleanor to be united in marriage with a knight powerful enough to hold both her and Ashton safely. Rupert would inherit the title and estates, but it would be to their advantage if his sister was married to someone others would brook no argument with, and who would come to Ashton's aid if ever such a need arose.

Henry frowned over the four letters he held, offering marriage to Eleanor. None of them were what he hoped for, and Remy could offer little advice. All he could say to Henry was, 'A husband must be found for Eleanor, soon, but be on your guard.'

'Aye, I agree wholeheartedly with you there. And you are quite right in saying this nonsense has gone on for long enough. I cannot for the life of me fathom what ails the girl, but I will see her wed before the summer is out!'

They were each silent for a few moments, and then Remy stated the obvious, 'Then it is to Court you go.'

Lord Henry groaned, little eager for the expense and inconvenience of removing his household to London. But Remy was right. Eleanor would attract no suitable offers tucked away in the country. By God, the girl was twenty years of age and still an unwed maiden! He would be failing in his duty of care if he did not with all haste see her settled into a suitable marriage. He rode home to Castle Ashton in deep thought, and on his arrival surprised his wife by announcing that she should prepare and pack the necessaries for a visit to the capital by the end of the week.

There was a great flurry of activity. Lady Joanna was as determined as her husband that this time a match would be found for Eleanor. She set all her seamstresses to work night and day sewing several new and very elegant velvet gowns for her daughter, in beguiling shades of sapphire and emerald that would, surely, attract some notice. From a locked chest under her bed Lady Joanna took out several pieces of jewellery, fine necklaces and delicate bracelets of gold that would proclaim Eleanor's standing as a young woman of noble and wealthy family, as well as enhancing her natural beauty.

* * *

They arrived in London late on a damp, dismal afternoon early in May. As guests of the King they had been allocated a suite of rooms in the Palace of Westminster, and as the parents of one who served in the King's Own Guard these rooms had been finely furnished and servants allocated to see to their every need. Eleanor's maid unpacked for her in the bedchamber she would use, while her parents retired to their more sumptuous room on the far side of the antechamber where they would gather during the day, when not in the great hall. She stood by the mullion-paned window of her bedchamber and looked out beyond the sweep of green lawn of the embankment to the grey shimmer of the Thames. Beyond she could see the rooftops of the city of London, but it all seemed remote to her. She would much rather have been at home, working in her herb garden or on her calligraphy. But to please her father she had succumbed to his will, or, at least, allowed him to think that she had succumbed.

Eleanor was well aware that her father intended to find her a bridegroom; though she would put no obstacles in his way, and she would be obedient to his wishes and willingly marry the fellow chosen, she would find neither joy nor purpose in so doing. With a sigh, Eleanor turned away from the window, and washed her hands in the bowl of warm water the little maid held out to her. Then she sat down as her hair was brushed and tidied, a veil placed over the long, shining auburn tresses and fastened in place with a gold circlet.

A knock roused her from her reverie and she looked up as the door swung inwards.

'Rupert!'

Eleanor leapt from her chair and hurried towards him. Brother and sister embraced and then she leaned back and looked up at him. It had been over a year since they had last seen each other. He seemed much older, to her eyes, than his mere two-and-twenty. She asked him how he fared and he nodded, murmured briefly that he was well, but she knew her brother and could sense the soul-sick weariness that plagued him. She gave him a final embrace and then stepped to one side as they walked arm-in-arm to the antechamber adjoining. Here her parents rose with cries of joy as their son approached, and a manservant set about pouring wine and offering cakes while the reunion ensued. They sat together, Eleanor perched on the arm of Rupert's chair, her hand affectionate and re-assuring on his shoulder, once again a family. They laughed and talked and then Lord Henry suddenly realised that the evening meal would soon be served in the hall. As their parents made ready and fussed over a loose ribbon here and a tardy lace there, Rupert stopped Eleanor with a hand on her arm, whispering urgently by her ear, 'There is something I must tell you.'

But time was not on his side and Lord Henry chivvied them along, anxious not to offend the King by appearing late at his table. The moment was lost and they made their way along the wide, stone-flagged corridors that led to the main banqueting hall. They passed many other guests and residents of the court—not only privileged lords and ladies, courtiers and those in waiting, but members of the King's Counsel and men of military bearing who served in the King's army. There were many guards in their smart uniforms and gleaming swords, who thronged the hall in ever-ready watchfulness. Eleanor eyed them, but they were all young and unfamiliar, there were none that she knew or remembered. Rupert had advanced to the rank of lieutenant and his duties were many and varied. Eleanor resolved to ask him about these, to encourage him to confide in her whatever it was that so burdened him. She had some inkling of the stresses and strains of a soldier's life from his letters, but still she sensed there was something more.

At the end of the meal Lord Henry and Lady Joanna enjoyed making re-acquaintance with friends they had not seen in some while, and Eleanor excused herself, feigning a headache and asking Rupert to escort her back to her chamber. He readily agreed and they left the hot, noisy clamour of the brightly lit hall and walked together down a long corridor, cool and dim, intermittently lit by flaring wall sconces that threw vast shadows upon the walls and whose flames danced at every passing movement of air.

'Are you truly well?' Eleanor asked her brother gently as their footsteps tapped in unison and they had a moment of quiet to themselves. 'I sense that…'

She paused, as they approached three people, deep in conversation, their voices hushed, standing to one side of the corridor and just below the flickering light of a wall sconce. As they passed, Eleanor noted that one of the group was a knight in the uniform of the King's Own, and she looked at his face. Their eyes met, a swift stab of recognition passing between them. He was familiar and yet much changed. The black eyes were still the same, and the handsome face, yet there were subtle differences. His dark hair was liberally peppered with silver. His face seemed worn, but she knew not if by time, the weather, or some other force, yet certainly he seemed much aged. Even though it felt as though her body moved with infinite slowness, she did not stop. In her mind's eye she could see herself cry out, lift her skirts in both hands as they billowed about her ankles while she turned and ran to him, but in reality all she did was look back over her shoulder as she kept on walking. He too looked, turning his head slightly, his dark eyes following her as she passed, but Troye de Valois made no move, nor sign, towards her.

As though from afar she felt Rupert's hand beneath her elbow, guiding her, supporting, and he must have heard her swift intake of breath, seen the expression on her face as she turned to him, her eyes wide as she lifted her gaze to his.

'I—I did not know,' she stammered, suddenly feeling her cheeks and neck flare with the rush of hot colour and emotion that poured in a torrent through her, 'that he would be here...I thought—' She did not know what thoughts she'd had about Troye, for while she had never forgotten him she had tried not to remember.

Rupert hurried her along now, moving swiftly towards the privacy of the Raven chambers. As soon as the door closed he turned to her and said, 'I tried to tell you, earlier, to warn you, that Troye had returned to court.'

'How long has he been here?'

'About a year.'

'A year?' Her head jerked up and she stared at him. 'Why did you not write and tell me?'

'Because...' Rupert hesitated, anxious not to hurt his sister and yet mindful of the fact that she must face up to the truth '...because I feared that if I did you would not come to London.'

'But why did you not write a year ago and tell me he was here? Tell me that he was well and healed from his injuries?'

'Why?' he asked, his gaze direct and his voice firm, yet soft. 'Surely you harbour no feelings for him after all this time?'

Eleanor looked away, her fingers laced tightly together, suddenly feeling exhausted. She steeled herself and asked a question, the answer to which she dreaded, 'And his wife? Is she here too?'

Abruptly Rupert took two steps towards her and gripped her arms with both hands, staring at her keenly. 'Eleanor, do you not know?'

Alarmed at his reaction, she looked up at him with a frown. 'What do you mean?'

'His wife—she died. Two years ago. I wrote and told Mother. She wrote back and said that I was never to mention it to you. But I assumed that you had at least been informed.'

Suddenly it all became clear to Eleanor. The need deep within her, the patient and yet inexplicable insistence from her heart that she wait. And now, surely, at last the waiting was over. She struggled to free herself from Rupert's grasp and ran to the door, her skirts indeed billowing in her haste. She wrenched the door open, uncertain of where to go or what she would say, but her only purpose now was to find Troye and speak with him.

'Eleanor!' Rupert called out to her, running hard on her heels.

She took no heed, her feet drumming, her heart pounding as she ran down the corridor. But Rupert, taller and faster than his slender sister, caught up with her in a few moments and stopped her headlong flight with one arm about her waist. She cried out and struggled and fought against him, but firmly he dragged her back to her chamber and shut the door. Incoherently she shouted at him and tried to reach for the door handle and pull it open, but he blocked her path, grabbed hold of her by both shoulders and shook her until she was forced to yield.

'Stop! It will do you no good, Ellie. He is just as far beyond your reach now as he ever was years ago.'

Eleanor sagged, her chin dropping upon her chest as warm, wet tears glowed in her eyes. 'I would only speak with him. Comfort him.'

'It would make no difference what you say or do.' He held her as she leaned against his chest, patting her back as he would a child, and felt how slender she had become, how frail, 'His wife's death destroyed him. I am certain he will never love anyone again. Forget about him, Ellie, it will do you no good to yearn for him.'

Eleanor wept then, not for herself, not for a love that could never be, but for the wife that had been lost, and for Troye. She felt his pain and the moment it entered her heart she knew that she had never stopped loving him and she could never abandon that love again.

Rupert held her while she sobbed, and then gently wiped her face with his thumbs and murmured words of comfort and encouragement. She tried to absorb them, but the truth was they did not touch nor sway her, and when Rupert, with regret, departed to return to his duties, she sat in a chair beside the glowing hearth fire and stared blankly. She was still sitting thus when her parents returned, but she merely hid behind the excuses of headache and exhaustion. Her mother looked at her for a long moment, always able to detect the slightest falsehood, but whether she was aware or guessed at what ailed Eleanor, she made no comment and kissed her goodnight, withdrawing as Lord Henry impatiently called his wife to their bed-chamber.

Eleanor allowed the little maid to unlace her gown and dress her in a clean nightshift warmed with a hot iron. But when she made a move to brush Eleanor's hair she dismissed the maid and took the brush herself and climbed into bed. It soothed her spirit to stroke the swathes of hair. She lay awake for long hours and eventually fell asleep as the night-watchman passed along the embankment, swinging his lantern and calling out that all was well at midnight. As her eyelids drooped and dark lethargy dragged her down into the depths of sleep she resolved to heed her brother's words of advice and forget all about Troye de Valois.

In the morning, when Eleanor awoke and the little maid tugged back the heavy brocade curtains at the window, bright sunshine poured through the window panes and bounced shafts of white light off the gleaming floorboards. Eleanor sat up, blinking and stretching, looking at the bluest of clear blue skies, and her heart soared. All her intentions of the night before vanished, and she knew that she had to seek out Troye and speak with him as soon as possible.

With this ambition in mind, she wrote out a note and asked the maid to deliver it to the quarters of the King's Own. The maid was reluctant, but with the promise of a mark she hurried away to do as her mistress bid. Eleanor broke her fast on the curd tarts and warm milk the maid had left on a tray, and eagerly went to find her most becoming gown. She must look her best when Troye came to see her. She waited impatiently for the maid to return, and as time passed and her mother came in, greeting her good morn, urging her to dress if they were to visit London town and the markets before the lovely weather had waned, Eleanor began to chafe at the delay. It boded no good if the maid was taking so long to deliver her message to Troye, and receive his reply.

* * *

When she thought she could no longer hold off her mother's impatient nagging, at last the little maid returned. She whispered to Eleanor that the message had been delivered, but though she waited, no reply had been returned. Eleanor felt a blush stain her cheeks, vexed and embarrassed and puzzled all at the same time. Clearly, Troye had no wish to speak to her. But why? What harm would it do him to exchange a few words with her? Eleanor thanked the maid and gave her the promised coin, and then set about dressing and making herself presentable for the outing to the attractions of London town. Just as they departed, she murmured to the little maid that later she should go again to the soldiers' quarters and wait for an answer, but she impressed upon the quivering servant that by no means was her brother Rupert to know or interfere with her task. The maid looked doubtful and Eleanor faltered and wondered about the wisdom of her quest, but still, she could not turn her back on the path that for so long she had been set upon.

It was a tedious day that she endured, and she barely noticed the markets and streets, the sounds and smells that her parents found so fascinating. All she longed for was to return to the Palace and to rush to the little maid to hear when Troye would come to her.

This she did as soon as she set foot in her chamber, but, sorrowfully, the maid shook her head. Again, no reply had been forthcoming from Troye.

Eleanor felt her heart ache at this cruel rejection. She tried to put the matter in perspective—after all, it had been years since they last met and mayhap he had no idea who it was that wanted to speak with him. Or, she hastened to convince herself, Troye was mindful of her reputation and would not compromise her with a secret assignation. Aye, that was it, Eleanor smiled to herself, determined to believe that Troye was only doing what was honourable and best.

That evening they were to attend a banquet in the great hall and she would be presented to the King. Eleanor resolved to keep her eyes open for Troye and somehow find a moment to have a word with him. At her mother's urging she lay down to rest that afternoon and fell asleep with thoughts of finding just the right words and smiles and looks to approach Troye with. When she awoke the sun was setting in a blaze of apricot, pink clouds streaking across the sky. She roused herself from the warm quiet of slumber and chose a gown of midnight-blue that showed off her graceful curves and pale skin, a dark background for her auburn hair. About her neck she fastened one of her mother's gleaming gold-and-diamond necklets, which accentuated her slender throat and the fact that she was a woman full grown and no longer an adolescent girl. She felt confident that tonight her life would change, for the better: all that had once been lost would now be found.

Chapter Five

Since the death of his beloved queen, Eleanor of Castile, nine years ago, King Edward had morosely plodded on with dogged determination, concentrating his attention on making war with his neighbours in Scotland and Gascony. Now, as spring blossomed, it was rumoured that he had the urge to take another wife, the pleasures and the comforts of marriage being hard to resist for a man of his nature.

There were dozens of eligible ladies present this evening, under the watchful custody of their conniving relatives, as well as several foreign emissaries bearing portraits, all hopeful of making the most illustrious match in Europe.

The vast array of richly dressed ladies and gentlemen were quite a sight to behold. On the arm of her brother Eleanor stepped into the hall, following in the wake of their parents. The King sat upon an ornate chair on a purple-carpeted dais raised several steps high so that he might have a clear view as he looked down upon the crowd. Beside him his son, the young Prince Edward of Wales, a youth of but fifteen years, also sat, looking bored and embarrassed. Compared to his father, the prince held little in looks, nor the sturdy frame, to be a warrior—facts that were duly noted by his warlike sire, who did little to disguise his contempt for the boy.

Eleanor accepted a cup of elderberry punch from a servant and cast her eyes about in search of Troye. It was so crowded that she could see little except the people surrounding her. It was not long before a court official came to her father and whispered in his ear. With interest she watched as her father listened intently, and then darted a glance in her direction. Eleanor straightened and watched as her father came to her side, together with the courtier and her mother.

'You have been summoned to meet the King.'

Obediently she fell into step between her parents as they followed the King's messenger, and made their way through the crush of revellers to the dais at the far end of the hall.

Following her mother's example, Eleanor sank into a deep curtsy, her head bowed. Then they rose and she looked up cautiously, her thoughts stilled for the moment as she tried to summon the necessary emotions of awe and respect that she should have for her sovereign. He seemed very old to her, his hair snow white, although he was a big man, almost as big as her uncle, with long arms and legs. She did not like the way he perused her, with a sharp, assessing eye that roved over her as though he were studying the finer points of a horse. He did not meet her glance, nor speak to her, and then he turned to his son, leaning towards him as he whispered in the prince's ear. The boy looked at her with a fierce blush on his cheeks and Eleanor wondered what comment his father had made to cause such a reaction.

Her eyes wandered then, and noticed the knights that stood to attention behind and beside the King. They wore armour; once upon a time this would have been an unusual sight in a hall enjoying a banquet, but the continued attempts upon the King's life had left no one in doubt that all measures would be taken to protect him, even from his own subjects. Eleanor counted eight knights in all, four ranged on either side of the dais. They were identically and smartly dressed in scarlet tunics and blue breeches, mail vests and belted swords. They stood very still, except for their eyes, which moved with quiet intent constantly, searching the crowd, looking for any sudden or unusual movement or appearance. Her own glance moved from face to face and noted that some of them were quite handsome, and then her heart drummed in her chest and she caught her breath on a ragged gasp, as her eyes met those of Troye de Valois.

He eyed her impassively, with not the slightest spark of recognition or emotion. Knowing of the messages that she had sent him, she felt a blush flare on her cheeks. She stared at him, and wished that he would look at her, notice her, and it irked her that he seemed impervious to her presence. The night before she'd had barely a moment to look at him as they passed in the corridor, but tonight she had longer and it came again as a shock to see how he had aged. The light had gone from his eyes and though he was, and always had been, a good fifteen years older than she, he had never seemed like a man of mature years. Yet his silvered hair only made him more attractive to her, his lean, rugged face a portrait of the hardships he had suffered and yet would not reveal. She longed to reach out to him, to call his name, to touch his elbow, and whisper, 'I am here, I would listen, and upon my breast you may weep.' But, of course, she could do no such thing and she must remain as mute and remote as he.

Suddenly she became aware that her mother was tugging at her elbow. With a flick of his fingers the King had dismissed them, muttering to a confidant that one Eleanor in his lifetime was surely enough, and they were walking backwards, away from the royal presence. Well, thought Eleanor with sharp indignation, she would be slow to forget such a humiliating experience! It was with relief that she returned with her parents to the far end of the hall, where their friends waited, idly conversing with their neighbours as they watched the antics of a younger generation, whirling about in a *carol*.

Rupert confessed he was famished and together they wandered off in search of food. They found tables in a side chamber set with piles of roasted fowl and venison and boiled fish, pies and cheeses, as well as jellies and meringues and cakes to tempt the poorest of appetites. They returned to the hall with hands full and Eleanor stood with a roasted chicken leg in one hand and a cup of punch in the other. Uneasily she noticed the glances that came her way and leaned towards her father to whisper, 'Why are people staring? Do I have something stuck between my teeth? Or is my veil all askew?'

Lord Henry chewed on his hunk of venison, as he cast an eye over Eleanor in careful perusal, then he shook his head. 'I see naught amiss.'

He turned to look about the hall, taking note of the men who eyed Eleanor, some quite obvious in their interest, others a little more discreet and courteous. Over there stood Taddeo Visconti, the Italian nobleman from Florence, his eyes beneath shaggy brows dark and brooding. And beyond there was Neville Talbot. Against the wood panelling of the hall lounged Casper von Eckhart, with shaved blond head and icy blue eyes scrutinising Eleanor with a salacious look he greatly misliked. It dawned on him swiftly that these were all the fellows who had offered for Eleanor's hand, and he thought it best to make Eleanor aware of it.

Quietly, discreetly, he pointed out and named each one in turn, so that she would be on her guard. Eleanor was stunned, but wisely made no show of her feelings. This was why she had been brought to London, but the vague idea of marriage to some unknown gentleman and being confronted with the reality were two different things. She did not know what to think or how to react. Eleanor suddenly set aside her refreshments and grabbed her brother by his arm.

'Let us dance, Rupert,' she urged, 'let us enjoy our evening and not be glum.'

He smiled, eager to encourage this change of mood in his younger sister. For too long now the cares and woes of his soldier's life had been a burden upon his shoulders, broad and strong as they were, and he welcomed the light relief.

They joined a group of couples dancing a jig and gave themselves up to the music. Eleanor could not resist looking to see if Troye watched them, but he was soon lost to her view as she and Rupert moved further down the room. Her resolve was hindered by her emotions and while one moment she determined to put her feelings for Troye aside and enjoy the present company, the next she was unnerved by the attentions of the many young gentlemen who would pay her favour. She tried her best to give them due regard but again, as always, they could not hold her attention and it wandered towards the one who would always draw her, like a flower to sunlight—Troye de Valois.

He had left the King's dais and stood with elbows akimbo in conversation with another knight. She could bear it no longer; as soon as the dance ended she resolved to speak with Troye. She cornered a young pageboy and whispered a message in his ear, asking Troye to meet her in the rose garden as soon as ever possible.

It was not easy slipping away from the watchful eyes of her family, but she did so while Rupert was dancing with a pretty, fair-haired young girl whose blue eyes and shy smile disarmed him, and her parents had wandered away to pick on the fine fare laid out on trestle tables.

Her slippered feet tapped softly on the flagstones of the corridor as she ran, her gown clutched in both hands to free her ankles from the clinging folds of midnight-blue velvet. Glowing torches flickered amber light, in between dark pools, along the length of the corridor, until at last she came to the open door that led out into the courtyard that was grassed and set with lush beds of crimson and pink roses. On this moonlit spring evening the sweet and heady scent greeted Eleanor as she stepped down on to the grass, looking about her into the long shadows, wondering if Troye had received her message, if he would come, what she would say…

Suddenly a hand reached out of the dark and fastened on her elbow. She gasped and automatically made to pull away, until Troye murmured for her to be easy. She sighed in relief and turned to face him as he dragged her into a far corner, the stones of the wall warm from the sun despite the dark shadows of night. The moonlight fell upon his face and her eyes gazed upon his fine nose and handsome chin, but his expression she could not see. His hands had fastened on both of her elbows and she was startled as he shook her, ungently.

'What are you about, little girl?' he demanded in a harsh voice. 'You should not be sending me a message like that. Have you no care for your reputation?'

Eleanor stared up at him, aware of the warmth of his body, his broad muscular shoulders, of his hard fingers gripping the soft flesh of her arms, but she made no move to free herself. 'I—I merely wanted to speak with you. It has been so long—'

He snorted. 'Stop. There is no bond between us, so do not make a fool of yourself with confessions that I have no wish to hear.'

She gasped, shocked by the harshness of his response. But he had suffered greatly and she must make allowances, should she not? 'Nevertheless,' her voice was taut as she insisted, 'I recall the flash of sword blades very close to my head and I am eternally grateful and in your debt, for once upon a time you saved my life.' She leaned towards him and, greatly daring, she stood on tip-toe and pressed her lips to his rough cheek.

She heard his sharp intake of breath, but his reaction was unexpected. His fingers tightened even more and he thrust her back against the wall, gripping her wrists as his body leaned hard and heavy against her.

'What the devil are you up to?' he demanded in a rough voice. 'Are you indeed a wanton, Eleanor? Have you not heeded a single word of advice from anyone?'

'I did not mean—' protested Eleanor, but her words were cut short.

'I can see what is in your eyes, as they follow me about the hall. Is this what you want?' Troye demanded, grasping her chin between his fingers and tipping her face up.

He lowered his head and his mouth came crashing down on hers, her small cry smothered between his lips. His rough jaw scratched her tender skin and she could smell and taste musky maleness laced with wine. A small sound escaped from the constriction of her throat and she fought to free her wrists from his punishing grip. Then suddenly his hold loosened, his arms slid around her waist, pulling her body against him, and his mouth was now tender as he kissed her.

'I had forgotten,' he murmured, as he pressed his lips to her neck and for a moment breathed in the soft, sweet smell of her skin. His hands moved along her ribs and reached the swell of her breasts, covering them, feeling the weight of them cupped in his palms, his fingers expertly finding the nipples.

Eleanor gasped again and lifted her head, trying to see his face, his eyes, and murmured, 'What have you forgotten?'

'The feel of a woman.' His fingers smoothed down the curve of her back and gripped her buttocks, pulling her tight against him. She gave a little cry, her fingers clutching at his tunic. He realised her shock, that she had no experience of men and their lust—no doubt this was her first real kiss—and cursed softly.

Suddenly he released her and she fell back against the wall again. Her body was alive and on fire at his nearness, aching and trembling, so sensitive to every new sensation that his male fingers awakened where he had touched her, yet her mind whispered caution, for she knew well enough the boundaries that existed between a knight and a lady.

'Go back to the hall. Before we are seen,' he ordered. That was all he said. There were no sweet words of love or apology from Troye. Eleanor felt the sting of tears in her eyes. She sniffed, and, before she shamed herself further, picked up her skirts and fled.

Eleanor slowed as her feet pattered down the corridor and she found a shadowed alcove in which to tidy her hair and her clothes, to wipe away the taste of Troye's mouth on her lips and the hot sting of tears upon her cheeks. She could not let anyone see her in such a state, for questions would be asked and she had no intention of ever telling anyone what had passed between her and Troye de Valois. She stayed where she was for a long while, her mind whirling in confusion and pain and longing.

As she stood in the dark corner she could hear voices raised in heated argument as a couple walked by. She recognised the voices, they belonged to her mother and father, but instead of stepping forwards into the light and making herself known, some instinct made Eleanor shrink away, deeper into the shadows. She should not eavesdrop, and yet the words that reached her ears held her riveted to the spot.

'I cannot understand your reasoning, Hal! Surely by all that is holy it would be better to keep Eleanor here, in England, safely within the walls of Castle Ashton!'

Her father sighed. His back was turned to her, his hands on hips in that belligerent stance she knew so well. 'Do not argue, Joanna. My mind is made up. I do not care for the way von Eckhart reacted when I told him that I could not accept his offer. I think Eleanor will be safer if she goes to Aquitaine for the winter. And, if it is of any comfort, Remy agrees with me wholeheartedly. In fact, it was his idea.'

'Indeed!' snorted her mother, 'Well, then, I shall give the dolt a piece of my mind.'

'You are becoming hysterical. Becalm yourself.'

Eleanor was dismayed to see her mother stamp her foot, and hid a smile behind her fingers, freezing as her father looked about.

'Don't you dare speak to me like that, Henry Raven! I am not a silly chit to be ordered about—'

'God in heaven, I never in my life thought you were!'

'Tell the truth,' Joanna challenged. 'Tell me the real reason why you are sending Eleanor away.'

'I have—'

'Nay! The truth, Hal!' And this she instantly supplied for him, in a fierce whisper, 'The truth is that you are sending her away because she is mine, and not yours.'

'Nonsense!'

Eleanor frowned, a long-forgotten alarm bell dinging faintly at her mother's words.

'You are sending her away because she is Richard Blackthorn's and you fear what it is that she might become!'

'Stop it!' Her father's voice held a note of angry warning.

'Yet I carried her in my womb while he lay dead in the Welsh Marches, and she never even so much as laid eyes upon him!'

'Joanna, I beg you to stop. And lower your voice, for God's sake, these are things we do not wish to be overheard. Come, let us find Eleanor, she has been gone too long for a mere visit to the privy.'

Eleanor stepped away, goosebumps flaring in icy horror across her skin. The blood had frozen in her veins. What did her mother mean? Who was Richard Blackthorn? She remembered the tournament in London those many years ago and the puzzling words from her father as he had chastised her with a wooden spoon. She had feared then that her father was not her father, but the matter had been superseded by her un-requited love for Troye. Now, stifling a gasp of shock and disbelief, Eleanor shrank against the cold stone walls, her eyes wide and her mouth gaping. Her parents walked on by and returned to the hall. In the silence that was left in their wake Eleanor listened to the drumming of her heart and the quick, agitated gasps of her breath. What to do? She must find her brother, tell him what she had heard… Did he already know of this Richard Blackthorn? She felt sure that if he did he would not have revealed his knowledge, to save her anguish. Yet if he did know, now he could no longer protect her from the truth. She crept slowly and cautiously from her hiding place, looked up and down the deserted corridor and ran into the hall. She looked about, but could not see Rupert anywhere. At last she found the young lady he had been dancing with and she informed Eleanor, with regret, that Rupert had been called away to the armoury.

Eleanor was determined to seek Rupert out and together they would discover the truth, whatever that might be. She was not entirely certain where the armoury was located, but she hurried towards a less-frequented part of the Palace that she had a vague idea led to such places like the armoury. After a while of endless corridors she became nervous and turned back, anxious to reach the safe haven of her own apartment, to sit down to think. She would write a note and send one of the male servants, for the armoury was not a place that a female should go to. Eleanor realised that once again her sense of direction had been poor, as she traversed corridors that were unfamiliar and seemed to be leading nowhere near to her destination. When at last a gentleman came into view she stopped. The urgency of her quest and the shock of her recent encounters severely affected her judgement, for otherwise she would not have dared to speak alone with this man. But her words were already spoken by the time she recognised the German, Casper von Eckhart, he of the cold blue eyes and shaved blond head and who apparently had made an offer for her hand.

'Excuse me, sir, I am looking for my brother, Rupert Raven of Ashton, a lieutenant in the King's Own guard. Would you know where the armoury might be?'

The Hun looked down upon her upturned face, and smiled slowly.

Troye listened to Eleanor's footsteps, and her sobs, echo and fade as she ran down the stone-flagged corridor, back to the hall. He unclenched his fists and released his breath in a heavy sigh. He had no need for the adoration of foolish young girls, but he had no wish to inflict hurt either. He should not have kissed her in the way that he had, so roughly. He could still taste her soft skin against his lips. Quickly he turned; he should go after her, apologise, but on the steps he hesitated. His apologies would only be misconstrued and her hopes raised where no hope could ever flourish. For he could not love her, or any woman. To do so would only open the window to his heart and let the sunshine in, and in the cold dark place that was his heart all the pain now lost and buried would be found. To love again was something he could not do.

Instead of following Eleanor, he turned away from the beckoning light and noise of the crowded hall and sought solace in his own quarters, a chamber that he shared with four other knights. There he found Sir Lindsay Crawford lolling before the fire, a mug of ale clutched to his chest as he brooded upon the flickering flames and his own thoughts. Troye sat down carefully, in a wooden chair opposite, and murmured a greeting to his fellow knight.

Lindsay raised tormented eyes, 'What ho, not in the hall with all the frolicking damsels?'

Troye shook his head, and commented, 'Neither are you.'

With a dramatic sigh Lindsay confessed, 'I cannot look upon her fair face and know that she is not mine.'

Troye snorted and smothered his amusement. 'And which damsel has caught your fickle fancy tonight?' He knew well enough that Lindsay had a roving eye and no sooner had he charmed one lady than another took her place.

'Why,' retorted Lindsay, 'can there be any other maid in the kingdom as fair as Eleanor of Ashton?' He sat up straight, leaning towards Troye as he earnestly declared, 'She is so beautiful, so enchanting—'

Troye looked away, his stony gaze upon the hearth, 'Forget her,' he said darkly. 'She is beyond your dreams, and your means.'

'I hear her father is looking to make a match for her.'

'Indeed. A good match, not a disaster. You have nothing to offer her.'

'I have my self, and a true heart.'

Troye laughed, and reached for a mug, pouring himself ale from the keg upon the floor. ''Tis not enough. I think Lord Raven has it more in mind that his daughter is married to power and wealth. Not lovesick nonsense.'

'Love is not nonsense. It is everything. For without love what is man? Just an empty shell—' Lindsay realised his folly as Troye's face darkened and he turned away from him. 'I mean—'

'I know what you mean,' snapped Troye, and swiftly changed the subject, 'I mean to break in that new stallion tomorrow. Can I borrow your helm? Mine is at the blacksmith, having a few dents mended.'

They sat and talked about horses and weapons and war. They were joined by Sir Austin, and then by Sir Neville. A squire was sent to fetch another keg of ale and the gathering became raucous as the knights enjoyed an easy camaraderie. They knew each other well, both in battle and in training for battle, at the best of times as they indulged in the pleasures of life, and at the worst of times as they endured the hardships of war—injury and even death. But through it all Troye was silent, staring at the fire flames. His companions found nothing unusual in this, for all knew of the grief that plagued him and none would force him to be other than he was. But suddenly,

Troye rose and set aside his mug of ale. They looked at him askance.

'There is a matter I must attend to.'

Troye strode from the room, realising that he had done wrong by Eleanor and before the night was out he must make apology for his behaviour. He strode down the corridor briskly, intending to seek her out in the hall and discreetly manoeuvre her to a quiet alcove where they could speak in private.

Casper von Eckhart bowed and offered his arm as he smiled at Eleanor. 'Come, *fräulein,* I will take you to him.'

'Thank you.'

They fell into step and from the corner of her eye she cast a glance at him. He was not as tall as Rupert or Troye, but very broad and muscular. She could feel the corded strength of his arm beneath her hand. He seemed a most handsome gentleman, after one quick glance, but looking closer she detected something else…something that made her uneasy. It was not in the thin line of his mouth, nor in the piercing blue of his eyes, but all her instincts had suddenly sprung to life and alarm bells were ringing in her ears. She tried to make an excuse, to pull away from the arm holding hers, to pretend that she knew where to find Rupert, but he would not let her go.

'I protest, sir,' exclaimed Eleanor, finding her courage, 'let go of my arm!'

For an answer he merely pulled open the door of a nearby chamber and thrust her within, slamming the door shut behind him. Eleanor cried out, greatly alarmed. She drew herself proudly to her full height, cocking a brow as she tried to give the impression of bravado. They eyed each other in silence, both fully aware that his intentions were far from honourable. A flush of anger flared over Eleanor. Her lips tightened, and then she looked him in the eye and said in a cold, hard voice, 'I insist that you open the door.'

He shook his head and bowed to her. 'Apologies for the abrupt courtship, *fräulein,* but your father refused my offer of marriage. And I am not a man who takes kindly to refusal.'

He took a step closer to Eleanor and instinctively she took a step backwards. 'I do not know why, sir, but if my father has refused your proposal then it was for good reason.'

He laughed, a short, sharp, unpleasant bark. 'I fear he has made a grave mistake.'

Her heart hammered painfully and she tried to reason with him. 'I would advise you to release me. If you let me go now, I will not mention this…misadventure…to anyone.'

With hands on hips he simply stood, indifferent to her words, casting a glance along her slender form, from the top of her head down to the hem of her gown. 'At least you have a pretty face and figure. It will be no chore bedding you.'

A gasp of anger and outrage escaped from between Eleanor's lips. 'I would not lie with you if you were the last man on earth! I do not know you, sir, nor love you, nor would I ever consent to marrying you!'

Again that laugh that sent a shiver down her spine with its harshness. 'I do not require your consent, girl. For anything.'

'My God, sir!' exclaimed Eleanor, glaring at him and neatly side-stepping his advance, 'Your conceit is beyond belief! I can assure you I will not come willingly. If you think you can take me, just like that, against my will, then you had better think again. I will fight you, to the death if need be!'

He snorted, a derogatory, dismissive sound, as though he did not believe a word she uttered and clearly he did not believe that a mere slip of a girl could defy him. Not in his wildest dreams had it ever occurred to him that a gentle-born young lady would ever fight to resist him.

'If you touch me,' she warned, 'I will scream!'

At that he leapt towards her, intent on silencing her with a hand over her mouth, but before he could reach her Eleanor darted out of his way and opened her mouth on a piercing scream. She ran for the door, which he had not locked in his arrogance. He grabbed the flying swathes of her hair as she fled, jerking her backwards. She cried out at the searing pain, and then suddenly the door flung open and Troye burst into the room.

'Von Eckhart, let her go!'

Her cries turned to relief and the Hun released her so suddenly that she fell to her knees, doubled over as sudden weakness and shock sent waves of dizziness spinning all around her. There was a scuffle, several more people entered the room and she flushed as von Eckhart made protestations of innocence, claiming that Eleanor had led him on, that she was the one who was intent on seducing him. She hid her face in both hands, and began to weep for the shame of it all.

'Eleanor.'

She recognised the voice of her brother, as he stooped and lifted her from the floor. With a cry she flung herself into the safety of his embrace, and he folded protective arms about her as he confronted von Eckhart.

'What nonsense is this you are spewing, Hun?' Rupert demanded. 'Apologise at once, for 'tis clear that you are the one with evil intentions.'

Von Eckhart laughed. 'Is that so? Well, then, what was she doing here alone, with no escort? What was she doing earlier, in the rose garden, with de Valois? Seems like the little hussy just can't get enough—'

Both Rupert and Troye leapt towards the Hun, her

brother shouting his anger, Troye quiet yet firm as he ordered von Eckhart to be silent.

The Hun sneered at him. 'I am not one of your soldiers, Englishman, for you to order about. And you know well enough I tell the truth, for have you not this eve sampled the goods yourself?'

Troye felt colour flare beneath the dark hue of his tan, but even as Rupert looked at him questioningly he turned to the two guards who had entered the room, and jerked his head towards the door. 'Take him outside. Mayhap a breath of fresh air will convince him to tell the truth.'

A few sniggered, the implication being that the guards were to use a little more force than fresh air to convince von Eckhart. As he was dragged away, shouting his protests and claims of no wrongdoing, Troye turned his attention to Eleanor and spoke to her gently. 'Do not be afraid. Tell me what has happened here.'

Eleanor sniffed and wiped her nose and eyes with the back of her hand, but with so many people in the room, all of them men and eyeing her agog, she floundered and could not speak. She met Troye's eyes and the truth passed between them. They both knew that she had indeed behaved in an unladylike way this evening, and that he had responded in a manner most unlike a gentleman. But she could no more admit to the truth than he, and yet von Eckhart's version of events could not be allowed to stand.

While she thought furiously about what to say, the moment was only made worse by the entrance of her father. Lord Henry demanded to know what on earth was going on, and at the deafening silence that met his enquiry his all-too fragile hold upon his temper eluded his grasp. He exploded and his shouts were deafening as he grabbed hold of Eleanor by the arm and shook her soundly.

Both Rupert and Troye tried to intervene, and it took several bystanders to assist them in calming Lord Henry down and persuading him that it would not help matters for him to lose his temper.

Lord Henry clucked his tongue with frustration and rage, glaring at Eleanor. 'What is to be done with the girl?' he demanded, rolling his eyes around the company. 'Tell me, heh? Who amongst you has such a wilful, obstinate, wanton little chit for a daughter?'

There was an awkward silence, and then old Lord Charteris murmured, 'Well, my Maud was a bit of a goer in her day.'

As he hoped, his comment evinced amused chuckles, breaking the atmosphere and reducing Lord Henry's mood from rage to a slightly lesser degree of severe annoyance.

'My advice, Hal, is to take her to the King. Let him decide what's to be done. No doubt von Eckhart will make up a pack of lies to suit, but there is some question about what she's been up to with de Valois.

By gad, we've not had a mortal combat for ages! Just the thing to settle the matter of who gets the wench.'

'There's no doubt about who wants her, the problem is who should get her!'

'Enough.' Lord Henry glared at the speaker of this impertinent piece of advice, and with a sigh he agreed. ''Tis a matter for the king to settle.'

King Edward strode into the antechamber adjoining his personal suite, his noble, well-worn face set in a grim mask. He had retired early from the revelries, weary at heart, and took a dim view of being interrupted in his preparations for bed. But when his secretary had told him the nature of the brouhaha and knowing well Lord Henry's hot temper, he deemed it best to deal with the matter at once, before Lord Henry started stretching necks from the nearest oak tree. Hurriedly he had dressed in a richly embroidered brocade robe over his hose, nightshirt and slippers. Now he refused the offer of both a chair and a glass of wine as he turned at once amongst the bowing courtiers to survey the perpetrators of his displeasure. He cast his glance over the young Eleanor of Ashton as she stood with eyes downcast beside her father, Lord Henry. Separated by members of his guard stood Casper von Eckhart, known as the Hun. He could well see why this unflattering appellation was afforded the young man, his square, belligerent face, cold blue eyes and brutish behaviour affording him little sympathy.

'Well?' he demanded, in his usual, brusque, soldier's manner.

Lord Henry bowed, one hand fastened on the hilt of his sword, the other clenched into a tight fist. 'Your Majesty, this young man—' he indicated von Eckhart with one hand, unable to bring himself to even utter the cur's name '—has forced his attentions upon my daughter, Eleanor.'

At this von Eckhart sniggered and shook his head, as though the tale was a likely one. He was elbowed into silence.

'Further, your Majesty, I would have it known that von Eckhart made an offer of marriage for my daughter some weeks ago, an offer that I refused. I therefore deem him to be a danger not only to my daughter and my family, but to every other young English maiden and he should be refused the hospitality of England's most gracious court.'

'Indeed?' The King peered at von Eckhart, stroking his beard, recalling similar stories from other outraged fathers. But he must tread warily, for he had need of German mercenaries and could not afford to offend that nation at any cost. 'What have you to say for yourself, von Eckhart?'

The Hun shrugged, his mouth drawn down in a mocking line as he rolled his eyes, 'She made herself available. What red-blooded male would refuse such a pretty little thing? But I am willing to do the honourable thing and marry her.'

Lord Henry, Rupert and several others made snorts of disbelief and ridicule at this outrageous statement, and Eleanor looked up with a glimmer of fear in her eyes that did not go unnoticed by the King. Von Eckhart was eager to press his claim and, to his folly, he shouted, 'I was not the only one.' He pointed an accusing finger at Troye de Valois. 'Earlier in the evening I spied her with him, in the rose garden, kissing and letting him touch her all over!'

'Nonsense!' exclaimed Lord Henry.

Rupert hotly retorted, 'You are a liar, von Eckhart!'

'"Spied" being the operative word,' pointed out Lord Deverell, one of the King's confidantes. 'The fellow is a knave and should have his backside kicked out of London once and for all.'

'Hear, hear!'

The King lifted his hand, calling for silence, and his wishes were immediately obeyed. He looked at the guilty parties one by one, then spoke in a quiet voice. 'Eleanor, what have you to say? Were you in the rose garden with Sir Troye?'

Eleanor felt her neck and face glow hotly and heard the intake of breath from her father as her blush damned her to the truth. With eyes downcast, she nodded her head, and then, looking up swiftly at

Troye, pleading with her eyes for him to agree with her story, she defended them both. 'But nothing happened, sire. We are old acquaintances and merely passed a moment or two in greeting.'

'Indeed.' Edward restrained a smile for her courage in daring to lie to the King of England. He had no doubt, from the looks that passed between Eleanor and Troye, that they were more than 'old acquaintances'. Such daring could only spring from love. After a moment of thought, he announced, 'I will sleep upon this and in the morn my ruling will be made known. In the meantime, get you all to bed—the hour is late and enough excitement has been had by all. Except for him…' he pointed at von Eckhart. 'Get him to the Tower.'

Chapter Six

Eleanor spent an anxious and sleepless night, as did many others. After the escapades of the evening and the scolding from her father still ringing in her ears it was a relief, at last, to fall into bed and bury herself beneath the covers. She could not sleep, though, with all the thoughts that ran in circles through her mind.

The King would issue his decree on the morrow and she wondered with some apprehension about his judgement. Surely he would not believe a word that Casper von Eckhart had uttered? Her father had muttered darkly that the King would have no desire to upset the Germans. Indeed, he was eager to forge alliances with them, and he glared at Eleanor as he warned her that she had no one to blame except herself if she did end up being married off to the Hun. She shuddered at the thought of having to spend the rest of her life owned by such a man. She would rather die first!

And then her thoughts moved on to the conversation she had overheard between her parents. What did it mean? How could it possibly be true that her father was *not* her father? For a moment she doubted her own senses, that mayhap she had misheard, but as she remembered the name Richard Blackthorn, and her mother's words regarding him, she had no doubt that it was true. What did it matter? she asked herself, she had never known him and never would, if he had been dead all these years before she was even born. As far as Eleanor was concerned, Lord Henry was her father and she had too many other things to be concerned about to let this matter push itself to the fore of her bewildered mind.

Flooding every single thought and feeling and action of her mind and body was the remembrance of the moments she had spent with Troye, in the rose garden. The feel of his mouth and his body on hers. She could think of nothing else, for such sweet pleasure as she had felt in those brief moments had been everything that she had ever yearned for. And yet...not enough. She sensed that what she had experienced with Troye was only a taste of the delights that they could share, that there was more, more soft and sweet and satisfying than honey.

Hours later, at last, she fell into an uneasy, dream-muddled sleep.

* * *

When she awoke in the morning it was with a feeling of nervous anticipation. She dressed slowly, taking her time, and was anxious about greeting her parents on this morn. But when she went out into the ante-chamber only her mother sat at the table, staring blankly at the window and the framed picture of the Thames and London town beyond.

'Good morning, Mother,' Eleanor murmured as she sat down.

Joanna looked up from her reverie, and then smiled gently as she reached out and placed her hand on Eleanor's wrist, 'Good morning, my dearest child.'

In silence they waited while the maid set out on the table fresh baked bread and conserves, a dish of sliced cold ham and a jug of milk. They helped themselves and it weighed heavily on Eleanor to see her mother, usually so animated and full of the joys of life, this morn so downcast.

'Mother—' Eleanor swallowed her bread and strawberry jam, and sought to clear the doubts and anxiety that clouded the air between them, but her voice croaked on uncertainty. After taking a gulp of milk, she tried again. 'Mother, last night—' She looked at her mother's face, to gauge her reaction, but she seemed unperturbed. 'I—I overheard…you and Father were talking…is it true?'

Joanna turned to stare at Eleanor then, the colour ebbing from her face, aware that the moment of truth that she had sought these many years to avoid was upon her. But still she tried to avoid it, and feigned a puzzled frown.

Eleanor rushed on with impulsive boldness, 'Is it true that Sir Richard Blackthorn is my father? Mine and Rupert's?'

Joanna looked away, her glance falling down to the table. For a moment she thought of a number of lies that could, or would, maintain the charade her children had lived with all their lives, and then suddenly it seemed pointless, and such a relief to be free of the burden. She nodded, slowly, and then turned quickly to Eleanor and clasped her hand within both of hers. 'It is true, my dearest, but it makes no difference. I was very young when I married Sir Richard, and he was killed in battle when you were both still babes. To all intents and purposes your father, Lord Henry, is indeed your father, for he has raised you and loved you all these years.'

Eleanor was unable to speak for several moments, for the magnitude of this revelation was too great for her to comprehend. Yet her curiosity would not be stilled. 'Who was he? What was he like? Where did he come from?'

Here Joanna baulked, for she would always protect her children from knowing that their father was a wastrel and a knave. He had left her penniless and broken in both spirit and heart, until Lord Henry had rescued her from the ruins of her widowhood and shown her the true meaning of love. Carefully, she fabricated together bits of the truth, to make a whole, 'He was a knight in service to your grandparents, Lord Robert and Lady Margaret. His family home was in Kent, I do believe, a small village outside Canterbury called Long Howden. He said the mansion house of his mother, long since widowed, was called Peppermint Place.' She laughed slightly, ironically. 'A fanciful name if ever there was one, and we never went to visit. I never met his family, for we were married only a few years. So you see, my dear, you must not dwell on it.'

Eleanor looked at her, seeing her mother in a different light, and feeling as though her childhood had slipped away from her for ever. Now she must be an adult in an adult world—a world full of lies and deceit and violent passions.

Joanna, aware that her husband would soon return from his visit to Rupert in the guardroom, stroked Eleanor's forearm gently, 'We will not speak of this again.'

'Does Rupert know?'

'I will tell him.'

'Do you promise, Mother?' Eleanor insisted. 'It is not right that I should know the truth and he not.'

Her mother nodded, 'I will speak to him as soon as may be. Now…' Joanna rose from the table, brushing crumbs from her skirt '…let us go to the chapel. It will do us good to spend some time in prayer.'

Together they went to the chapel and prayed after the early morning mass. Eleanor's prayers were a disordered confusion of pleas and bargaining, promising God her complete faithfulness and devotion, if only He would save her from a life of misery. The door to the chapel creaked open and a pageboy came running to them, soundless on his little slippered feet. He leaned beside Lady Joanna and whispered in her ear. With a wordless glance at Eleanor she beckoned and Eleanor rose from her knees and fell into step with her mother as they returned to their apartment.

Lord Henry stood beside an ornate table placed near the window and the light glowing through the panes. On the table was a skein of scarlet ribbon, untied and discarded from the parchment he held in one hand. He turned and glanced at his wife and Eleanor as they came into the room, his face set in a grim line. They both stopped and looked at him, expectant, anxious for the news.

'Now, Eleanor—' Lord Henry's voice was firm yet gentle '—this may come as a surprise to you—

it certainly has to me! But I want you to remember that the King has your best interests at heart; indeed, for both of you—'

Eleanor felt her heart jump and her breath catch on a little quiver of alarm. 'Father—'

'I know he must seem very much older to you, but his experience and maturity is to be valued—'

'Hal!' exclaimed Joanna, goaded beyond her patience. 'For God's sake, put us out of our misery! Is it the King? Is Eleanor to marry the King?' When he shook his head Lady Joanna clenched her fist and pressed it to her drumming heart. 'Dear God in heaven, never say that he has chosen that vile German creature—'

'Father!'

Seeing her tension and her fear, Lord Henry hastened to make known the truth, 'Nay. Eleanor is to marry Troye de Valois.'

'What?' exclaimed Lady Joanna, a sudden frown creasing her brow, but her consternation was drowned out by Eleanor's shriek.

She grabbed hold of her mother by the waist and swung her in a giddy circle, then rushed to her father and flung her arms around his neck, kissing his cheek. Her elation and glee burst from her in little whoops of joy as she sang and danced around the room, the servants peeking in from the doorway to see what all the fuss was about.

Her parents stood there and watched, silent, amazed and utterly dumbfounded.

News of the King's decision soon swept through the palace. By late afternoon all of Westminster had heard the news. Lord Henry sent a summons to his prospective son-in-law to attend him in their private apartments. He also invited several friends—the Earl of Fairfax and Lord Charteris—as well as a bishop or two. He was determined to see the betrothal properly done, and, mindful of his daughter's wilful nature, deemed that a swift response to the King's order imperative.

Eleanor rushed to her chamber, summoning her maid, and made haste to dress in her best gown of ruby-red fustian, fastened with gold ribbons and girdle to match, her veil of the finest gossamer silk and crowned with her favourite gold circlet. Her hair gleamed like chestnuts, rippling loose and molten down her back. Her mother assured her that she looked very beautiful and it was with confidence that she stepped into the crowded antechamber on her father's arm, and looked up demurely at Troye de Valois.

He had not changed his dress and wore his soldier's doublet and breeches, his only concession to the occasion being that he had unlatched his sword. As she approached he looked at her, but there seemed to be no expression in his eyes or on his face. The steady thump of her heart turned to sudden little skips and she lowered her eyes in nervous confusion.

The Bishop performed the ritual of betrothal and confirmed to Lord Henry that the banns would be read for the first time this Sunday. Then they would be read for a further two more Sundays, and on the Monday following they would be married, here at Westminster. The documents were signed and the occasion celebrated with wine and cakes, the noise rising as guests chattered. The King called in and offered his hand to be kissed by both of the affianced. Eleanor curtsied deeply, and Troye bowed, each of them with fixed smiles upon their faces as the King made no bones about telling them how pleased he was with the union and that he considered it to be a good match.

Eleanor blushed, and tried to catch Troye's eye, but he was quickly snaffled by kindred knights eager to offer their congratulations. She kept glancing over her shoulder, hoping to gain his attention, frustrated by all the fussing of the ladies of the court as they gleefully made it their concern to advise her on all aspects of her forthcoming wedding.

All morning she hoped for a private moment, that Troye would endeavour to take her by the hand and slip away to some quiet corner. Of course, she did not expect instant adoration, but she would at least know that Troye was not unhappy about their betrothal. She must be patient, Eleanor reminded herself, *all good things come to those who wait.*

Troye did not stay long and returned to the armoury, many murmuring at what a fine fellow he was, so dedicated to his duty as an officer in the King's Own Guard. They congratulated Eleanor and it was some salve to her pride that Troye was so highly regarded. She could not be wrong about him, surely? Patience was a virtue, and though she felt that she had been more patient than any human being on earth over all these years of waiting, she bit her tongue and smiled, determined to summon the strength to be virtuous for a while longer.

They were to remain at court until the wedding day. Lord Henry chafed somewhat, reluctant to waste time kicking his heels in London, but it made no sense to journey four days homewards to Castle Ashton, only to pack and return shortly thereafter. He made best use of the time as he could, seeing to the purchase of new weapons and horses after the depletions of recent campaigns with the King to secure Wales. Lady Joanna decided that Eleanor had to have a new wardrobe, as befitted a married woman, and set about purchasing fabrics, all manner of haberdashery and employing seamstresses. There were a few occasions when the family met and all four went out on some jaunt, taking advantage of the fact that Rupert was close by so that they could all be together. Troye was invited to accompany them on a picnic aboard a barge on the Thames, but he declined, claiming his duties forced him to stay within the walls of the palace. Lord Henry promptly insisted that Troye attend them for dinner that evening and he duly arrived.

A table was set in the ante-room and food ordered from the kitchens. Rupert was on duty and unable to attend after his day out with them on the river, so Eleanor sat beside Troye and her parents sat opposite them across the table. She felt strangely awkward, and not all real, as though she moved through a dream, hardly able to believe that Troye was actually sitting next to her. She had no idea what to say to him and left it to her parents to direct the conversation, although she scarce absorbed a word and could only listen to the entrancing tone of his masculine voice.

They discovered that his home was far to the north in York. His mother was a lady from a good family in Luxembourg that ran a thriving wool import-and-export business. Troye's father, recently deceased, had been a titled gentleman, there was a manor house and some land, his parents had taken over the wool business and expanded it from York, but Troye was at pains to stress that he was not a wealthy man. There was an awkward moment or two, in which Lord Henry smoothly assured Troye that Eleanor would not come to him empty-handed. Eleanor felt a red-hot blush flare over her cheeks and neck, both angry and resentful at being discussed like she was a chattel of some kind, and mortified that Troye's only interest in her seemed to be financial.

At the end of the meal her parents deliberately found an excuse to leave the room briefly, leaving Troye alone with Eleanor for a few moments. She stood beside the open window, gazing out at the glowing amber and pink clouds streaking the evening sky, a soft breeze cool as it wafted across the lawns from the river. Despite being sure that the golden light and the breeze were flattering to her, Troye made no move to take advantage of their solitude. He stood on the far side of the room, one arm raised as he leaned against the fire hearth and stared down at his boots with great fascination.

Eleanor sighed, and resisted the temptation to call out, to draw his attention, for that would not be ladylike. She glanced over her shoulder again, and this time their eyes met as she discovered that he was looking at her, with an almost puzzled expression upon his face. She smiled tentatively, and he smiled gently in return, but before she could encourage him to speak her mother returned, bearing a tray of chilled mead and fresh spiced fruit cakes. Troye declined both, however, thanked them for the meal, glanced briefly at Eleanor and announced that he must depart and inspect the change of guard.

'Well, it's been very good to spend some time with you, Sir Troye,' said Lady Joanna as she set her tray down and she offered her cheek for Troye to kiss in farewell, 'and we look forward to meeting your mother when she attends for the wedding.'

'Alas,' apologised Troye, 'my mother lives too far away to make such a journey. But I will send a messenger with word of the marriage.' He came then to Eleanor and kissed the finger of her left hand that he had set his ring upon, bowed to her father and then departed.

As the door closed and the footfalls of Troye's boots faded down the corridor, Lady Joanna sighed. 'That man is certainly very pleasant. What a lucky girl you are, Eleanor!'

'Indeed.' Lord Henry sighed, with a doubtful note in his voice. 'He was not terribly forthcoming about his family circumstances. And York is not too great a distance for his mother to make the journey to attend such an important occasion as her son's wedding, surely? Mayhap it has something to do with the fact that he's been married before. I was hoping that he would set our minds to rest regarding his first wife.'

'Father!' exclaimed Eleanor, her heart giving a sudden lurch of anger and alarm. 'Don't you ever dare to ask him such a thing. It is none of our business, surely?'

Her parents exchanged a glance, and murmured soothing sounds of agreement, although in the privacy of their chamber they discussed the matter in whispers, both anxious that Troye's first marriage would become a hindrance to his second, and a source of pain to Eleanor. Clearly it was not a matter that she wished to face and for now they were content to sweep it under the carpet. It seemed there was little else they could do, without causing offence to both Eleanor and their son-to-be.

A few days before her wedding her aunt Lady Beatrice arrived, accompanied, of course, by her husband Sir Remy and baby son Tristan. Eleanor was surprised and delighted, embracing them and laughing her joy as they all met together in a house just inside the West Gate that Sir Remy had rented for the occasion.

'We only just received the news and came at once.' Lady Beatrice smiled, hugging her niece fondly, laughing as Eleanor exclaimed again how she could hardly believe they were here. 'Do you think I would miss my only niece's wedding?'

'Well…' Eleanor shrugged, looking at the baby '…I didn't think you or Tristan would be able to make such a long journey.'

Lady Beatrice laughed. 'Well, we did! Now, then, what are you going to wear on your wedding day?'

Lord Henry and Sir Remy grinned at each other and left the ladies to their dilemmas while they went outside and discussed more manly matters. As the light faded, Lord Henry gathered up his womenfolk, anxious to return to the Palace before nightfall and the dangers of London streets were upon them. Eleanor was reluctant to leave her Aunt Beatrice, for often-times they had been closer than Eleanor was to her own mother, but Beatrice promised that they would be at the Palace of Westminster bright and early on the morrow, and they would accompany them to church. It was the final Sunday for the banns to be read and then preparations would go ahead with all speed for the wedding ceremony on Monday morning.

Eleanor had not seen or spoken to Troye for nearly a week. She accepted that his duties kept him very busy, and if truth be known she was a little anxious about spending too much time with him before they were married, afraid that she would be rash and say or do something that would discourage him. She had strange dreams at night, in which she ran through swirling mists trying to find the door to the chapel, knowing that she was late for her own wedding and unable to find her way. Over and over she had this dream, and she would wake sweating and with a stifled gasp of fear. Eleanor realised that she wanted to be Troye's wife so much that she feared that even the smallest hindrance might prevent it. Please God, she prayed, please let nothing stand in our way. She had no other thought, except to make it to the altar and that Troye would be standing there, waiting for her.

At last, the great day dawned. She rose early and ran to the window, pulling open the heavy brocade curtains. It was a grey, dismal day that greeted her eyes, and she peered up at the sky anxiously, hoping to see some glimmer of light. Instead, a fine drizzle of rain misted the glass panes and Eleanor sighed, swallowing her disappointment. No matter, she told herself firmly, the sun might shine later. She crossed the room to the oak coffer where her wedding gown was laid out, ready and waiting. She ran her fingers over the silver-blue brocade, the sleeves fastened with silver ribbons, and a silver girdle for her waist lay on top of the gown. Her hair would be loose, as befitted an unwed maiden. She had bathed the night before with rose soap and her hair and her skin smelled fresh, soft and clean to the touch.

Eleanor went back to bed, curling up and hugging her excitement to herself, until the maid arrived with a hearty meal to break her fast and a beaker of warm, cinnamon-spiced milk. Eleanor tucked into fresh-baked crusty bread and a slice of honey-roasted ham, chewing thoughtfully as she wondered if the flowers picked for the circlet upon her head were still fresh. As she finished eating her mother entered the bedchamber, followed soon after by her Aunt Beatrice. They both gave her an embrace and kiss, wishing her well and much happiness on this special day, and Eleanor glowed, hardly able to contain her joy and eager to dress and be on her way to the chapel.

'No need for haste,' laughed Lady Beatrice. 'It is the custom for the bride to be a little late.'

'Why?' asked Eleanor, wide-eyed.

'Well,' her mother mused, 'a husband must learn from the beginning that he can never take anything for granted when it comes to a wife.'

'Oh, surely not,' gasped Eleanor, 'It is my duty to honour and obey.'

'And it is the same for him.'

As her aunt brushed out her hair and her mother fastened and tweaked the many dainty little silver ribbons on her gown, Eleanor stood patiently and waited while they dressed her. Her new cream stockings felt like gossamer and her pale blue slippers soft and soundless upon her feet.

'I have always thought it most strange,' mused Eleanor, as her mother placed the garland of pink rosebuds, daises, almond blossom and forget-me-knots on her head, 'why a husband is called son-in-law by the parents…would that not then make him my brother?'

'Oh, tush!' exclaimed Lady Joanna, 'Don't be too clever, my girl. A man has no patience for a wife whose intellect may be greater than his.'

'But surely that would be to his advantage?' Eleanor demurred. 'To have a witty and talented wife?'

'Some may see it as so...' her mother replied slowly, looking to her sister-in-law for assistance on this one.

'But most,' supplied Lady Beatrice candidly, 'would see it as a threat to his manhood and even interpret intellect in a woman as an inclination towards cunning and manipulation.'

Lady Joanna nodded her agreement and both her mother and aunt proceeded to offer her advice on the pitfalls of marriage and the management of husbands. Many marriages were arranged ones; indeed, it was rare that couples married purely for love. But, Lady Beatrice was eager to reassure her niece, this did not mean that love could not grow. Troye de Valois seemed a man of good and honourable character and there was no reason why they should not be happy as man and wife. Eleanor smiled to herself, knowing in her heart that she had loved Troye for so long that the fact their marriage had been arranged was of no consequence to her. Carefully, with delicate words and no great detail that might shock or alarm Eleanor, they made known the secrets of the marriage bed, much to Eleanor's embarrassment. With this intimate information echoing in her mind, and a final adjustment of a ribbon here and a lock of hair there, they went to the antechamber, where her father and brother were waiting.

'You look very beautiful, Eleanor.'

Her father kissed her cheek, as did Rupert, and then they proceeded to make their way to the chapel. Eleanor glanced to the windows lining the corridors, overlooking the river, but it was still grey and damp. She was cheered, however, when they entered the chapel: it glowed from the golden light of hundreds of candles lit on every stand available and rose petals were strewn on the path she trod towards the altar. There were many guests, standing on both sides of the church, but Eleanor knew few of them. She curtsied to the King and his young son, acknowledging the great honour of his attendance, and smiled at her Uncle Remy as she spotted him to her left, his wink reassuring the nervous flutter in her heart as they approached the altar. Would Troye be there? She was afraid to look…mayhap he had taken it into his head to jump on his horse and gallop away as fast as he could…

Her father came to a halt, and she had to raise her eyes. Her bridegroom was there, standing broad-shouldered and handsome. His dark eyes roamed over her, his glance approving. She looked at his mouth and remembered how it had felt when he had kissed her… She blushed at the thought, and Troye smiled, noticing the pink colour stain her neck and cheeks. Her father gave her a little nudge and she stepped towards Troye. He took her left hand in his and together they turned to face the Bishop.

The vows were spoken, Troye's voice firm and unwavering, Eleanor's very soft; she was surprised by the quaver in her voice and the very slight but noticeable tremble in her hand as it rested in the palm of Troye's. She looked up at him, from the corner of her eye, and suddenly she realised, with breathtaking alarm, that she doubted her feelings of love. Why, she hardly knew this man! When had they ever had a proper conversation? How was she to know what his likes and dislikes were, if his beliefs in God and the universe were the same as her own? Had she any evidence that he would be a kind and gentle husband?

It was the most inconvenient and inauspicious moment to consider such things, and she stood there mutely as the Bishop droned on. She stared wide-eyed at the stained glass windows of the chapel, swallowing with painful difficulty, and the colour draining from her face as she swayed slightly on a wave of nausea and dizziness. She half-turned to find her mother, to seek the aid and protection of her father, as she had always done all her life. But she felt frozen to the spot, with all the people watching and fearful of making a fool of herself upon this great occasion. Then she felt an arm circle her waist, and she glanced up as Troye leaned towards her. His fingers gently pressed the soft flesh between her ribs and hip, he smiled at her, and in that moment she sighed with relief. His gesture did much to reassure her, yet, demurely, confused by so many emotions, she cast her eyes down. But Troye's arm remained, supporting her, warm and strong, until at last the ceremony and the mass was at an end, and they emerged from the chapel as husband and wife.

King Edward had generously ordered a lavish feast be laid out in the great hall and the wedding guests followed the newly married couple down the corridors. It was a noisy, cheerful throng that traversed the walkways, for there had been little of late to celebrate. What with a succession of wars with the Scots and France, and the death of the much-beloved Queen Eleanor, a cause to celebrate the nuptials of Troye de Valois, the King's champion, defender of the King's life and hero of many campaigns, was welcomed with pleasure. That he had suffered a personal tragedy—one that he refused to discuss, thus there was little known about it—only endeared him more greatly to the King and his court.

The King naturally took pride of place at table, but close to him sat Eleanor and Troye, her parents, Rupert, her aunt and uncle, and the evening was a most enjoyable one. Mayhap it was the strong Burgundy wine that went to her head, but she felt all her nerves evaporate as she shared her trencher with

Troye, and he cut morsels of roast goose and venison for her to eat. The cook came out from his kitchen and proudly presented the newlyweds with a cake, a towering and impressive concoction of spun sugar, cream, almonds and crystallised violets. The King urged them to take the first slice together, and Troye rose from his seat, retrieved his dagger from its sheath on his belt and cut a small sliver. He then leaned down and fed it to a blushing Eleanor, who laughed and wiped the messy crumbs from her lips. The hall cheered and thumped fists on tables as they urged her to do the same for her husband, and she rose on trembling legs, as Troye gave the slim handle of his lethal knife to her. She leaned forwards, her hair dangling, and managed to slice a piece without too much trouble. The guests were vociferous as they chanted and clapped, watching as she rose on tip-toe and pressed her cake-laden fingers to Troye's mouth. He seemed not at all fazed, neither embarrassed nor spurred to silly antics as many a bridegroom had been known to do. He gazed at Eleanor with steady eyes, and opened his mouth, his teeth and tongue scraping the morsels of cake from her fingers.

'Troye,' called out his life-long friend, Sir Austin, 'your wife has her hair in the cake. Be a good husband, and clean it up for her!'

This ribald comment was met with risqué comments and advice, and Troye, bowing to the company at large, solemnly took the skeins of auburn hair in one hand, and licked off the sugar and cream. This sensual act broke forth shouts from the male guests that rattled the very rafters, quickly followed by the disapproving tut-tutting and rib-poking from many wives, sympathising with Eleanor's obvious embarrassment.

The King diverted attention by ordering the musicians to play. He led Lady Joanna out in the first dance, urging Troye to follow with his bride. Eleanor thought this must be what it felt like to be drunk, as her senses reeled. She placed her hand in Troye's and they proceeded to pass through the intricate routine of steps of a *carole*, never touching except for their hands. His eyes were often on her, though; she could feel the heat of his glance on her lips, her neck, her breasts. His fingers felt warm, strong as they clasped and twirled her about, the beat of the music a heady rhythm. Into her mind came the knowledge that her mother and aunt had passed on to her while they had dressed her for the wedding, and she swallowed as her throat constricted at the memory and a faint dew of sweat beaded her forehead. The marriage bed still awaited them, and she could not help but wonder what it would be like. Please God, let me not faint out of sheer joy!

As the company enjoyed the music, the dancing, the food and wine, Lady Joanna discreetly indicated to her cousin, Lady Beatrice, that it was time for Eleanor to withdraw. They took the opportunity whilst the gathering was well occupied with other pleasures to take Eleanor away, and thus avoid the rude revelries that wedding guests so enjoyed. Under strict instructions from their womenfolk, Lord Henry and Sir Remy restrained any that espied the departure of the blushing bride.

The ladies returned to the apartment that she had left only that morning. Once her parents had returned to Somerset, she and Troye would occupy the rooms as a married couple in their own right. This being her wedding night, she would much rather have had a chamber that was far distant from her parents, but Troye occupied military quarters shared with other soldiers, and her bedchamber was the only offer of privacy available. With trembling fingers she removed the wilted wreath of flowers from her head, and set them gently aside on a table. Then she stood with arms held out as her mother and aunt undid the many ribbons of her gown. She bent and removed her stockings and slippers, standing naked as her mother slipped a shift of the softest, whitest linen over her head. The fragile straps and thin material did little to hide the curves of her slender body and she shivered slightly.

'Into bed with you,' her mother murmured, tucking the covers around Eleanor. She leaned down and kissed her forehead. 'May this night bring you much joy and happiness, my sweet Eleanor.'

Lady Beatrice offered her a hug and a few words of advice that left Eleanor blushing, then she lay there as they left the room and closed the door. She wondered how long she would have to wait. After a while she sat up and decided to draw the curtains around the bed, just in case Troye was accompanied by over-enthusiastic and curious wedding guests. Then she lay down again, pulling the covers up to her chin, replaying in her mind the events of the day, smiling, rejoicing in the knowledge that she was now Lady Eleanor de Valois.

Her eyelids were beginning to droop when at last she heard a commotion, but it was contained within the antechamber. She listened with ears finely tuned, until at last she heard the click of the door as it opened, and then a clunk as it was closed and barred. She heard the thump of booted feet, and then she struggled to hear anything at all, finally discerning the chink of metal as a belt was discarded, the rustle of clothing falling to the floor, the splash of water. And then she started as suddenly the bedcurtains parted and a warm body lifted the covers and slid in beside her.

'Troye?'

'Aye.'

She felt an incredible wave of warmth emanating

from his body, and she need have had no fear about any awkward hesitation on Troye's part, or not knowing what to do because of her own inexperience. He took command and reached for her at once. In the dark she sensed his head lower as he searched for her face, and then the delicious warmth of his lips on hers. He slid the straps of her shift from her shoulders and quickly removed the barrier of linen between them. It was the most pleasant sensation she had ever felt, to have Troye's naked body touching hers. She felt the soft hair of his chest brush her breasts and was surprised at how much hair covered his chest, tapering down to the flat, hard planes of his belly. Her hands reached out and fastened on his shoulders, feeling the strength and smoothness of his muscles moulded beneath her hands.

He kissed her deeply, with quiet concentration. And while she gasped and shivered, and moaned at his touch, he made no sound. He cupped his fingers to the female curves of her buttocks and pulled her hard against him, pressing the length of his body against hers. His kisses continued, on her face, and neck, her shoulders and then his fingers reached down to capture the woman's mound between her thighs, pressing firmly, all the while kissing her, his tongue in her mouth. He rolled her over on to her back and parted her thighs, his fingers stroking gently, seeking her entrance. His mouth broke free of hers and he lowered his head to her breast, finding her nipple with his tongue and sucking on it. She arched and groaned with the sensation of pleasure, and while he gave the same attention to her other breast, he still made no sound.

He spread her thighs wider and mounted her, his manhood probing and eager, a hot lance that reared impatiently to possess her womanhood. She tensed slightly as his hands slid under her bottom and he pulled her closer, his hips on top of hers. The brush of his chest hair on her breasts was exquisite, but then all sensation was concentrated in that one place and her mouth opened on a soundless, wordless cry as he penetrated with one hard thrust. She had not expected a man to be quite so big and felt him stretching her virginity, breaking it, and thrusting deeper into the molten core of her body.

'That feels so good,' he murmured in her ear, and she was a little taken aback, at the sound of his voice, his matter-of-fact words that seemed to hold no hint of romance or passion.

Instinctively, she wrapped her arms around his strong back and held on while his hips plunged back and forth, and she stared up at the canopy of the bed, a little bemused. At last he stopped, kissed her forehead, and then rolled away to one side and was soon asleep.

Eleanor lay awake for some while. Unbidden, and

despite her struggle to resist them, tears came and she too rolled on to her side and tried to go to sleep. What had she expected, the sensible part of her demanded, while her heart, that foolish and fragile creature, wept with disappointment? Was the failure hers? Or had her aunt exaggerated about the pleasures of coupling? True, he had not hurt her except for a brief moment and she had expected that, but she felt sure that there should be something more. Troye had not uttered a sound, and while her own skin had been on fire and dewed with aroused sweat, his body had felt cool to her touch. Mayhap she had not pleasured him enough for him to make any noises? Or it was not the same for a man as it was for a woman? With these unsettling thoughts in the back of her mind, Eleanor at last fell into an exhausted, unhappy sleep.

Chapter Seven

In the morning Eleanor woke to find herself alone. At first she wondered why this seemed strange, as she had slept alone all her life, then she remembered that yesterday she had married Troye de Valois. And last night he had bedded her. She sat up and reached for her shift, covering herself hastily, aware that at any moment her mother would come in to inspect the sheets. She thrust aside the covers and swung her legs out of the still-warm bed, glancing back over her shoulder at the rusty stains that were ample evidence of her virtue. And her undisputed right to call herself Troye de Valois's wife. She hesitated for a moment, as she remembered the events of the night before. Her tears were spent, and she was left only with a feeling of numbness in her heart, and an uncomfortable ache between her legs. She was still sitting thus when the door opened and her mother entered the room.

Lady Joanna smiled at her daughter, her enquiry soft and tactful. 'You are well this morning, child?'

Eleanor nodded her head, and gave in to a watery smile. 'Except I am not a child any longer, Mother.'

'Aye,' Lady Joanna agreed, yet she sensed that all was not well. It so rarely was on the first occasion between husband and wife. Eleanor was now a woman full grown and married, and as her mother Lady Joanna felt it was not her place to pry into the intimate details of Eleanor's marriage. If Eleanor wished to discuss the matter, she would. For now, all her mother did was pat Eleanor on the shoulder and chivvy her out of bed so that she could extract the bottom sheet. The King's secretary and several ladies of the court waited eagerly in the ante-chamber for proof that Troye and Eleanor were well and truly wed.

They were well satisfied and discreetly departed while Eleanor bathed and dressed.

By the time she emerged from her chamber there was only her father there, staring out of the window at another grey day. He turned as he noticed her presence, and as he often did he opened his arms for her greeting.

Eleanor hugged her father, but though his silence was an invitation to her confidence she was reluctant to discuss such a personal matter as the loss of her virginity. She moved away and began to take great interest in several swans that padded on the green lawns.

Casually, as he pretended to peruse a letter upon the table, Lord Henry asked softly, 'He has treated you well?'

'Aye. Oh, do look, Father, are not those cygnets the prettiest little things?'

He peered over her shoulder and through the thick panes of glass, nodded and muttered his agreement. Then, clearing his throat, he announced, 'Now that the wedding is done, your mother and I must make haste to return home.'

Eleanor whirled. 'Oh, Father, surely not so soon?'

'We have been gone nigh on four weeks. Things will fall to rack and ruin, the servants pilfering and the neighbours encroaching on our grazing, if I am not there to make sure they do not take advantage.'

'But—'

He held up his hand, checking her flood of protests. 'You have a husband now, Eleanor. It is to him you must look.'

She subsided, visibly sagging as she mutely realised the truth of her situation. Her husband owned her—all her goods, all of her body, and even her soul if he so wished. He could do what he wanted with her, love and cherish her if he so desired, or ignore her and have no care for her feelings in any matter. Such was the lot of a wife.

Lord Henry noticed the obstinate little pout that set his daughter's lips, the squaring of her delicate shoulders and the little flick of her head that sent shimmering waves of auburn hair rippling like a silk pennant down her back. With a small shake of his head and raised eyebrows, he hoped to God that the King realised what he had let Troye de Valois in for!

By midday her parents had packed their trunks, their horses were saddled and waiting in a courtyard; their plan was to meet with Sir Remy and Lady Beatrice by the West Gate and travel homewards together. Eleanor waved them goodbye, at her side her new husband who, at last, had made an appearance, his apologies thin to her ears as he claimed 'duties in the armoury' had forced him to rise early and kept him busy all morning; this was an expression that she was soon to become very familiar with.

As she called a final farewell, waving until she could no longer see her parents as they disappeared beyond the palace walls, she felt alone and bereft. Tentatively, she asked Troye, 'Will my lord join me for the midday meal?'

He opened his mouth, about to refuse, and then glanced at her wan face and relented. 'Aye.'

They returned to the chambers that Eleanor had shared with her parents, which had now been set aside for the newly married couple, as Eleanor could not be expected to reside in the military quarters Troye shared with others. A servant had laid out platters of cold meat and yellow cheese, fresh bread and a flagon of wine. Eleanor sat down, and wondered if it was her duty to serve Troye, but he helped himself to food and made no comment or insistence that she do so. They ate in silence, and she wondered what his thoughts were, and should she voice her own? She searched her mind, but could not find anything to say. She felt…empty.

From the corner of her eye she watched his hands, his lean brown fingers, and remembered that they had touched her skin, the most intimate parts of her body, and she had found much pleasure in his touch. But the other part… Suddenly his hands had stilled, he laid his knife to one side and her eyelids flew up as she lifted her gaze to him. He was staring at her, with those dark, impenetrable eyes. The light falling through the small panes of the window shaded his lean face and his silver-gilded hair. Her eyes examined his handsome nose and beautiful mouth, the upper lip a controlled line over the fuller lower, hinting at the passions of his nature. And yet, last night, even in her innocence she did not think there had been much in the way of passion.

'You are well this morn?' he asked, awkwardly, almost gruffly, glancing away, swallowing a chunk of bread and reaching for his goblet of wine.

Eleanor laughed softly, with a little defiant shake of her head. 'That is the third time I have been asked that exact question!'

'Indeed?' He washed his hands in a bowl of warm water, then glanced at her keenly as he cleaned his knife on a cloth and sheathed it. 'And what has your reply been, twice so far?'

If it was not for the note of amusement in his voice she would have flounced angrily from the table, hardly able to contain her injured feelings any longer. But as he smiled, she smiled too. 'That I am well.'

'Hmm.' He looked at her for a long hard moment, not a man given to many words, all his life having applied stern discipline to his thoughts, words and actions. He floundered now, aware that he had not bedded his second wife in quite the same manner as his first, but this was a matter he could discuss with no one. He rose and went to the door, hesitating a moment as he looked back at Eleanor, sitting alone at the table. 'You have…things to occupy you?'

Eleanor nodded her head. 'Aunt Beatrice brought my tapestries and calligraphy.'

He nodded, eager to be away and about his 'duties', but still hesitant to leave her. 'I could speak with Lady Denys, if you are in need of female company. She was a lady-in-waiting to Queen Eleanor and will introduce you to the other ladies at court.'

She shook her head, and hastened to assure him that she was well content with her own company. He murmured a farewell and closed the door, as much relieved as she to part. But instead of working on either tapestry or the Bible transcripts, Eleanor retired to her chamber and lay down upon the bed, her mind in a whirl. There were too many thoughts, unfamiliar ones that she had never dealt with before, and though she tried to wrestle with them and put them in their place, she could not. Suddenly she felt very tired, and pulled up the covers as she fell into the warm, welcoming arms of slumber.

When Troye returned at dusk, after a hard afternoon breaking in one of the most vicious and stubborn stallions he had ever encountered, yet promised to be the most courageous and reliable of destriers in battle, he opened their bedchamber door to find Eleanor still asleep. The long sweep of her molten hair fell across the edge of the bed, as she slept curled up on her side. For long moments he stood gazing down at her, and then closed the door and took himself off to the soldiers' quarters that he had until recently shared with the other knights.

There he ordered a bath and scrubbed the mud and sweat from his body, paying attention to the maroon lesions on his calves and forearms that the stallion had inflicted with his teeth. As the bath was taken away by his squire he dressed and sat down by the fire with a tankard of ale, his feet up on a small stool.

The door opened and Sir Lindsay came in, brushing

off dust and straw from his tunic. He was taken aback as he saw Troye sitting in front of the hearth.

'What the devil are you doing here?' he asked, with frank incredulity. 'Should you not be with your wife?'

'She's asleep. I did not wish to disturb her.'

Sir Lindsay grunted, not at all pleased with this piece of information. He thought life vastly unfair that Troye had won the hand of the only worthy maiden at court, and did not even appreciate her. His ire made his next remark less than chivalrous. 'So what have you done to the poor girl to leave her so exhausted?'

Troye shot him an indignant glance, followed by an obvious glint of warning, but remained silent. Sir Lindsay took the hint and went off to clean himself up for the evening meal in the great hall, eager to find a new object for his affections. Some moments later Sir Percy and Sir Ronan came in; though they too were surprised to find Troye there, they made no comment and welcomed him, as they settled down to discuss the best way to proceed with the feisty stallion.

'Be sure it's a tricky one,' bemoaned Sir Ronan. 'In Ireland I've seen many a good stallion ruined by having his spirit broken. You need to show him who is master, and yet still allow him to be the proud animal that he is.'

Troye agreed, and the talk moved on to other

matters and problems that had arisen in the daily life of the King's Own. He quite forgot the passing of time, as he accompanied the knights to the hall and sat down to eat his evening meal, as he did most evenings, unless he had been sent on duties that required his presence elsewhere. As the night wore on, he wondered at the many glances that came his way, and then Rupert Raven, a junior officer who had no business speaking to him in the first place, came and sat down beside him on the bench. Rupert conversed cautiously for a few moments, and then said softly, 'I must confess, sir, I am surprised to see you here.' He hesitated, and then asked, awkwardly, 'Eleanor—she is well?'

Troye stared at him for a moment, suddenly realising that she would be awake by now. He rose so swiftly he knocked over his goblet of wine and tripped over his own feet. Some laughed with amusement as he hurried from the hall, but Rupert frowned and felt uneasy.

Eleanor sat at the table by the window, much as he had left her after their noon meal together. Except now it was dark, and the room was full of shadows as two or three candles flickered. She looked most dejected as she sat there, picking at the carcass of a roasted pullet with little enthusiasm. He closed the door and came towards her, enquiring carefully as to how she had fared in his absence.

Eleanor, having acquired her father's temper by nurture if not by nature, exploded. She jumped to her feet and hurled a chicken leg at his head. It missed, largely due to her poor aim and Troye's agile ducking.

'If this is how you mean to treat me, Troye de Valois,' she cried, 'then—then I wish I'd never married you!'

'What?' He seemed perplexed, but was not about to let her have a childish tantrum at his expense. 'I have surely done naught that could possibly displease you.'

She snorted. 'Done naught indeed!'

'Calm yourself—'

'No! I will not calm myself!' Eleanor stamped her foot now, and reached for anything that she could grab from the table, hurling grapes, lumps of cheese, apples, at him. 'How dare you go off and leave me here all alone!'

'Stop screaming like a fishwife.'

At that Eleanor loosed a shriek that made both their ears ring and she grasped a wooden platter, certain that this would inflict slightly more damage than grapes, but as she raised her arm to take aim, he rushed at her. Troye caught her about the waist, forced her to relinquish the platter and, mindful of his earlier discussion on the taming of wild animals, swept Eleanor into his arms and carried her to their bedchamber, kicking the door shut behind him.

He bore her to the bed and flung her down, lowering himself on top of her before she could jump up. He flinched as she grabbed a handful of his hair and tugged viciously, the nails of her other hand reaching up to scratch his face.

'You vixen!' he exclaimed, grasping her flailing arms by both wrists and firmly holding her down. 'Stop now, or you will hurt yourself!'

She glared at him, frustration and disappointment provoking her anger. Troye straddled her hips and held her thrashing body between the muscular bulk of his thighs. As she struggled to free herself the bodice of her gown slipped from her shoulder and the hem of her skirts rode up past her knees. Suddenly she was aware of the maleness of his body, the masculinity of his broad shoulders, strong arms and musky smell. She ceased to struggle and lay back, her bosom heaving as she panted for air. He looked down at her, his glance falling to her lips as they parted, and down further, to the high full mound of her straining bosom. He released one of her wrists and boldly placed his hand on her breast, mastering her with his touch. When she made no move to protest or resist he leaned down and kissed her.

Eleanor gasped, and relaxed, her lips parting as his tongue teased and probed. His jaw worked as he deepened the kiss, pressing his body down on hers, nudging her legs apart so that he lay between them.

It seemed to her that they lay just so for ever, kissing and kissing. He manoeuvred her bodily into the middle of the vast mattress, lifting her skirts up higher, pushing them past her waist. Eleanor realised then what he was intent on, and she pressed her hand behind his neck, her other hand sliding down his back, settling on the taut muscles of his buttocks. Every muscle of his body felt so hard and lean, she gloried in the feel of him, entranced by his masculine strength. As he fumbled with the laces of his breeches she hoped that this time would be better, and she would not be left feeling…discontented.

She thought he would undress her, tenderly kiss her breasts and her body, and take off his own clothes, but while he had kicked off his boots at some stage, he was still fully clothed as he spread her thighs and lowered himself between them. Eleanor tensed, accepting the hot, hard thrust of his manhood into her body, eager to please him, and yet vaguely aware that he made no effort to please her. He thrust, his eyes closed, as though he hardly noticed her existence, and again he made no sound. It did not seem to take very long, for which she was grateful, as she was still tender from the night before. She sensed that his joining with her was no more than male mating with female, an act of simple pleasure, not love, and she experienced again that empty feeling of numbness. There was something she needed to know, to think about, but what it was she had not yet discovered. When he had finished and withdrawn, she pulled down her skirts and rolled on to her side.

He rose from the bed and began to strip off his clothes, dropping them carelessly on the floor. He went to the water jug and bowl set on a coffer in one corner of the room, and washed. Eleanor watched him, his back to her, the sleek, taut muscles of his body bulging and rippling at his every movement. He was very beautiful to behold. She turned away then, and began to tug at the laces of her gown, shrugging it off and climbing into bed dressed in her shift. She curled in one corner and waited. He blew out the candles one by one, then, naked, climbed into bed and pulled the covers up over both of them.

''Tis a chill in the air tonight. Most like we will have rain on the morrow.'

'Aye,' she quietly agreed.

'Goodnight, Eleanor.'

'Goodnight…Troye.'

He was soon asleep, lying on his back, his breathing becoming heavy as he relaxed into deep slumber. Eleanor rolled over and faced him, her eyes gazing up at him and his bulk as he lay warm and heavy beside her, the hairs of his legs tickling her skin, but she could see nothing in the darkness. They were so close, and yet she could have been miles away for all the notice he took of her. At last, she snuggled her cheek into the palm of her hand, almost touching the muscular curve of his upper arm, and fell asleep.

Spring eased into summer and though the days were warm Eleanor felt little warmth as they settled into a version of married life that left her disappointed, lost and unhappy. She had nothing to compare it with, except her parents' own marriage, which to her mind had seemed full of warmth and affection and laughter. When the solitude of her own company became too unbearable she sought out the ladies of the court. The welcome into their circle was a cool one, for she held no great rank, her acceptance only in deference to her husband, although some pretended friendly intentions and were happy to cozen up to her out of a need to feed their insatiable appetite for gossip. Eleanor was no fool and when she resisted all attempts to draw from her intimate details of her marriage, the ladies drifted away and she was left alone again.

One blazing hot afternoon Eleanor walked along the riverbank, safely within the Palace grounds, and settled down to catch a cooling breeze from the Thames. Troye was away on some errand to do with the King's Own and had said he would not return this evening. Left to her own devices, Eleanor pondered on the strangeness of her life. She missed him when he was not here…and yet when he was she still felt lonely. Impatient at her own weakness she blinked back the sudden sting of tears.

Idly she plucked at blades of grass and gazed at the river and the boats, the thatched and red-tiled rooftops, and the many church spires of London town. She watched while an ornate barge ploughed upriver, the oars dipping and rising with a steady rhythm, silver droplets glinting as the water splashed. Realising that it was the King's own barge, swathed with ornate awnings to shade him from the sun and decked with guards both fore and aft, she followed its progress. Gliding gracefully to the jetty, the barge came to a halt and the King alighted, striding up the steps and across the lawn in that brisk manner he had. He turned his head slightly, and looked to the river with idle interest, and then he spotted Eleanor and he faltered, changed course and walked towards her.

'Good day, Lady de Valois,' he called out in greeting.

Eleanor scrambled hastily to her feet, and sank into a deep curtsy, her head bowed. The King urged her to rise, and with one hand beneath her chin raised her face to look at him. He noticed at once the tell-tale spiky lashes fringing her reddened and damp eyes. It had not escaped his attention that Eleanor was much alone, and seemed a pale shadow of her former self.

He waved away the officials and courtiers who always hovered close to his elbow, and they retreated. The King leaned towards Eleanor and asked, in a gentle tone for his usually gruff voice, 'Tell me, child, what it is that ails you? Is Sir Troye unkind to you?'

Eleanor felt her cheeks flush with colour, embarrassed beyond measure. It was not for a wife to criticise her husband, and yet once she had lied to the King and could not bring herself to do so again. 'Your Majesty,' Eleanor whispered, 'he is my husband and I would be loyal and faithful to him, but I fear…he does not love me…as I love him.'

There! She had said it, voiced at last the terrible thought that had been harboured at the back of her mind all these many weeks. Yet to her amazement the King's response was to chuckle, hook his arm through her arm, and they began to stroll along the riverbank as he spoke, musing aloud.

'Marriages are not made for love, my dear. They are for security and heirs and assets. When I first met my Eleanor, I was little impressed. Yet we were married for thirty-six years and I loved that woman more than life itself. And she loved me. Love does not always spring forth like a fountain. Sometimes it is more like a gentle stream. But…' here he sighed, and looked about as he frowned '…I own that you have not had a fair chance. Sir Troye has too many duties at court to pay time and attention to his duties as husband. But never fear, that is a matter I will attend to at all speed. Now, come with me and let us have some refreshments.' He mopped his brow with a fine white handkerchief. ''Tis a hot day indeed; no doubt we will have a storm tonight. What say you to a cup of cold lemonade?'

There was indeed a storm that night, and Eleanor lay alone in the great four-poster bed and listened to the boom of thunder and crack of lightning that licked across the roiling sky like a serpent's tongue, followed by the noisy downpour of rain. She did not think she would sleep at all, and was still awake when the bed-chamber door opened and Troye came in. She sat up, with a small cry of pleasure and surprise, and climbed quickly from the bed, tip-toeing on bare feet as she ran to him. He greeted her briefly, soaked to the skin and his hair plastered wet and shiny to his head. Rivulets of raindrops ran down his face and Eleanor exclaimed her concern, as he stood there sodden and shivering.

'Look at you…' she reached for his belt and un-latched it with unsteady fingers '…you should have waited till morning before returning.'

He said nothing, only watched her with hooded eyes, as she worked quickly to help him remove the cold, heavy weight of his wet clothing. When he stood naked she fetched a linen cloth and began to rub him dry, but then he grasped her wrists and forced her to stop. He pulled her close as he bent his head and looked her in the eye.

'The King summoned me to return at once. I was

ordered to report to him as soon as I came in, and, though 'tis well past midnight, I obeyed. The King has ordered me to take a leave of absence from court and return home. He says I have neglected my wife. Have you been running to the King with tales of woe?'

His voice was dull and flat, and he still shivered slightly, standing there naked, his skin brushing hers as she only wore her shift. And yet, despite the warmth of her body, and her longing to put her arms around him and hold him close to her heart, she did not dare to touch him. Between the two of them stood an invisible barrier.

'I—I…' She faltered, uncertain what to say. 'I have not complained, or told tales, but I am…unhappy… and others may have noticed.'

He frowned, his grasp on her wrists tightening, 'Unhappy? What do you mean?'

She shrugged and lowered her eyes, unable to look him in the eye as the cold hard truth threatened to drive a wedge between them.

'Well—' he let go of her, suddenly, and she stumbled '—thanks to you we have a long journey on the morrow. We ride for York as soon as you are packed. I will not stay another day at court when you have made such a fool of me.'

He strode to the linen press and pulled out clean clothes, shrugging them on quickly, pulling on his boots. Eleanor watched, dazed and confused. He barked his instructions at her as though he were speaking to one of his subordinates.

'We leave at dawn. I suggest you start packing your things now, as will I.' He went to the door, and looked back at her over his shoulder. 'I am going to the armoury to assist my squire, for it is no easy task. I will sleep there for what's left of the night. Be sure that you are ready when I return as soon as day breaks.'

The door banged shut behind him and Eleanor stood there for a few moments, bewildered. How dared he speak to her like that! She hovered between the desire to run after him and make protest, and tears. But no, she told herself firmly, she must not give in to either temptation. It would do her no good to argue with Troye, for a man could not love a woman he was constantly at war with, and it would do her no good to weep. Instead she hurried to pull out her clothes, slippers, cloak, hairbrush, a precious few bars of rose-scented soap, her books and tapestries, a basket of needles and thread, and make them all ready in linen bundles ready for the morrow.

They departed as the sun rose in the east, simply dressed so as not to attract attention upon the roads, and accompanied only by Troye's squire, Dylan. Troye intended to make swift time with Eleanor riding pillion, rather than the entire party being at the mercy of her riding her own horse, or a slow-moving cart to convey her. Their wedding gifts and Eleanor's chattels for her new life as a married woman would be sent after them by wagon, together with Troye's precious armour and the more cumbersome of his weapons such as crossbow and mace; he and his squire were only lightly armed.

Troye vaulted astride his excited horse and quietened the creature before reaching for Eleanor as her brother lifted her up. He settled her pillion behind him and her slender arms slid around his waist, above the leather belt latched with sword and dagger. He felt the fragile bones press against his ribs, her body a slight weight leaning against the strong bastion of his back.

'Fare thee well,' Rupert bade them, from where he stood upon the steps, 'and don't forget to write to Mother, she will want to know how…things…are for you in York.'

'I will.' Eleanor smiled gently, reaching down with her fingers to clasp his. He kissed them and reluctantly they let go of one another, as Troye called a brusque goodbye and spurred his horse onward.

Once they had left the cobbled streets of London behind them the roads were muddy after the recent rain, the horses slip-sliding on the deeply rutted tracks. Above them the trees crowded with thick leafy green canopies and the land was in full summer bloom, the fields rippling with crops; there was a sense of tranquillity as most of the hard labour for harvesting would not begin for several more weeks.

Towards late afternoon it began to rain again and they made slow progress as the horses plodded with heads down. It was cold and uncomfortable, and Troye rode with care, making sure his squire kept close to his flank, frustrated at the slow pace. As Eleanor's shivering intensified Troye decided to call it a day and stopped for the night at Berkhamsted, where they took refuge for the night safe within the castle, a stronghold of the King. Troye was well known and courteously welcome, although he did not hold sufficient rank to be afforded a private chamber. He and Dylan would sleep in bedrolls on the floor of the great hall, and Eleanor was assigned a cot in an elderly gentlewoman's chamber. The tension between her and Troye was taut as a bowstring and Eleanor was eager to be alone with her husband, to talk with him, but he seemed just as eager to avoid her. She pondered on this, her gaze dwelling on him as they sat at the table in the hall and ate their evening meal. Was it her imagination, or did Troye deliberately look away every time their eyes met? When he rose from the table she rose too, and hurried after him.

'Troye?' she called.

He halted in his tracks and turned towards her with

a slight frown. 'I am going to the privy. There is no need for you to accompany me.'

Eleanor felt her lips tighten and the flush on her cheeks flagged her temper. 'I am sorry if I have angered you—'

'I am not angry,' he replied, with a thunderous frown that belied his words. 'Go you to bed. I will see you in the morn.'

'Very well,' Eleanor retorted. She would not beg him for his favour, and she turned sharply on her heel and flounced away towards the spiral of stairs that would lead her to her bedchamber for the night.

Troye watched her go, his own emotions in turmoil. He had not asked for this marriage, and he certainly never felt any desire to bed a woman when the one he truly desired could not be his for the taking. He could not help resenting Eleanor for the emotions she was reawakening, and for not being the woman he truly loved. That night he lay awake and restless, brooding on this marriage that had so unexpectedly been forced upon him. In the chamber above stairs, Eleanor lay awake too.

The next day they rode onwards, stopping only briefly to water the horses and partake of a meal at an inn along the way. The land was awash with bands of robbers, some of them mercenaries who had failed to secure war and coin for their services, as well as migrants of all sorts, ranging from expelled Jews to merchants taxed into bankruptcy. Troye was wary about fellow travellers and falling victim to any desperate marauders.

That evening Troye had hoped to make the castle at Bedford, but the light faded too quickly and Eleanor wilted, hungry and thirsty, her arms aching from clinging to his belt for many hours, day after day. They came to a village scarcely a few miles from Bedford, and Troye guided his horse into the yard of the Black Swan. He hired a modest room and his squire, Dylan, would sleep close to the horses in the stables.

Troye avoided Eleanor, keeping himself busy supervising Dylan in the stables until he was sure that Eleanor would, by now, be bathed and dressed in her nightshift and abed. When he returned to the chamber, he found Eleanor asleep, the remains of a meal upon the table by the fire. He helped himself to half a roast chicken, bread and a thick wedge of apple pie, sitting in a chair in front of the warm glow of the fire, one booted foot crooked against the hearth. He ate, drank wine, put aside his weapons and his boots, and lay down upon the floor, wrapped in his cloak, to sleep fully dressed, with one ear on alert. Such was the life of a knight.

He was almost asleep when a sharp knock on the door stirred him. With silent care, so as not to wake

Eleanor, he padded on bare feet to the door, his sword grasped in one hand.

'Who goes there?'

''Tis I.'

Troye unlocked the door and held it ajar, frowning at his squire, not at all pleased by the disturbance. 'What is it?'

'Master,' Dylan whispered with an urgent tone to his voice, 'there is sickness here. We must move on.'

He had noticed several people coughing and spluttering with sneezes, but thought nothing more of it. With one glance over his shoulder at Eleanor asleep in the bed, he replied, ''Tis too late now to seek shelter elsewhere. We must abide, but stay you away from the others, and I will not leave this room tonight. We do not eat here in the morn, but be ready with the horses to depart as soon as daylight breaks.'

'Aye, master.' Dylan nodded his head in agreement, and then retreated from the festering inn to the stables, which, to his mind, represented a better and safer bed for the night than within the walls of the inn.

The next morning they slipped away before anyone else was abroad and Troye hoped that they would not be affected by any ills. The weather had cleared and he was eager to press on. They had a long journey north ahead of them and he reckoned it would take the best part of six days, so on this the third day he forced the pace. Eleanor made no complaint, though her backside ached, and she was often thirsty as the sun blazed hot and burning from a cloudless corn-flower-blue sky. Troye scarcely spoke a single word to her, despite the long hours they spent with her arms wrapped around him as the horses trotted and cantered and walked mile after many mile. He made it clear that he resented this journey and he was in no mood for forgiveness.

Late that afternoon they came across several horsemen gathered at a crossroads. Troye and Dylan exchanged glances as they skirted them. Troye took careful note of their armour and the language they conversed in—Flemish—and he needed little convincing that they were mercenaries. He urged his horse into a canter, hoping to put some distance between them and such dubious characters.

They kept to a steady canter for as long as possible, until the horses were blowing hard and needed to rest. They came to a halt by a river, dismounted and let the horses cool before allowing them to drink. Eleanor stepped away into the concealment of nearby bushes to attend to her needs, and Troye sat upon a fallen tree trunk, talking with Dylan about the proposed march next spring on Scotland. They had been on campaign there before—the fighting against the ruthless Scots had always been bloody and vile…

Into the clearing trotted the four Flemings they had seen earlier, and Troye placed a cautionary hand on Dylan's wrist as the boy would rise at once with sword drawn. Troye, however, murmured for him to be still, and he watched with an impassive face as the gang halted before him. He thanked God that Eleanor had disappeared into the woods and hoped that she had sense enough to stay there.

The mercenaries milled about in a threatening manner on their horses, spurs jingling, and one of them, whom Troye took to be the leader of this sorry band, called out a greeting. He was a pock-marked, dirty-looking individual, with lank hair and unshaven jaw. Troye merely nodded a response, eyes narrowed.

'You have a woman?' the mercenary asked in rough-accented English.

Troye said nothing, just stared at the fellow.

The Fleming tried again. 'We have gold. We pay for her.'

Troye rose slowly to his feet. 'She's not for sale.'

The Fleming laughed. 'All women have a price.'

'Not this one.' His hand settled on the hilt of his sword. He calculated the odds and wished he'd armed himself with more than just his sword and pavade.

Dylan rose too, and perhaps there would have been a fight, except from the other side of the river a party of travellers came, fording the shallow water and calling out loudly as they advised and encouraged one another over the rocks and swirling water to reach the far bank.

'Good day.' A jovial, ruddy-cheeked fellow built like an oak tree beamed, tipping his staff in friendly greeting to the group, unaware that violence had been imminent.

'Good day.' Troye replied loudly, 'Have you come far, sir?'

'Aye, indeed.' The fellow halted, as Troye had hoped, leaning on his staff and ambling into a long-winded account of his day's journey from Newmarket. The Flemings, having lost both patience and the odds, spurred their horses onwards and crashed through the river, galloping up the far bank and disappearing over the brow of the hill.

Eleanor emerged then, peering cautiously from behind the trees where she had hidden. Troye spotted her and beckoned. His arm slid around her waist, a possessive gesture that was not lost on the party of travellers, farmers and their wives, as they gathered about.

The big fellow introduced himself as Watt, and pondered, 'Them fellows looked like trouble.' He nodded his head in the direction the Flemings had taken.

'I fear you may be right,' Troye agreed.

'You are welcome to join us.'

'Thank you, but we are going north.'

Watt offered his hand. 'God speed.'

Troye and Eleanor both murmured their thanks, and then they mounted up and rode onwards. But Troye did not follow in the wake of the Flemings, for fear of ambush. He knew the roads and paths well—for had he not traversed them many times over the years? He circled around, and diverted to Warwick.

The master-at-arms of Warwick Castle was a personal and very old friend. The Earl of Warwick, William Beauchamp, had fostered them both many years before, and now Troye, together with his wife and squire, were made welcome for the night. They lingered there for a day, to be sure that the Flemings had cleared the area; Troye also announced that the horses were in need of respite. Eleanor was much chagrined as she wondered if he had even considered that she too might be in need of rest, but she was too tired to challenge him on the subject and loathe to aggravate already frosty relations.

They set off again on the next bright morning, heading north for Leicester. But the weather did not hold; by afternoon it rained and a chill wind blew from the north, making matters very unpleasant for travellers on the roads. They spent another night at an inn, sleeping in a common room as all the private rooms were taken. It was an agonising night that Eleanor feared would never end, with her and Troye both sleeping in a narrow cot, Dylan on the floor stabling their horses. The air was close and fetid, and here too several travellers seemed unwell.

It worried her there was sickness in the land and she murmured her concerns to Troye. He brushed them aside with a few brisk words, yet at the end of another day's hard riding he sought refuge for the night at a monastery. Eleanor shared his hope that the monks kept a clean house and at least they did not have to share the bare cell assigned to them for the night with others.

Troye washed and removed only his boots and belt, unlatching his sword and dagger, placing these on the floor close at hand as he lay down on the bed. She followed his example and washed only her face and removed her shoes, but also her gown, which was damp—this she laid out to dry on the back of a chair. She sat down on the edge of the bed, glancing over her shoulder at Troye as he lay on his side. How she hated his silence, his back turned to her! Reminding herself that she was his wife, gently she laid her hand on his hip. His eyes opened and he looked at her hand. She felt the colour rise hotly in her cheeks, uncertain as to how to approach him.

'Is it very far still to York?' she asked, her voice soft.

'One day.'

She could think of nothing else to say, so she lay down, wriggling and trying to make for herself a comfortable spot on the hard, narrow bed. The covers were thin and rough, so she pressed herself against the warmth of Troye's body. It had been several weeks since they had last coupled, and though she found little pleasure in the act, she knew instinctively that it was a bond between husband and wife, which, if neglected, would be easily broken. She bit her lip, a puzzled frown creasing her brows, trying to think how to ask him without sounding like a harlot. Instead she thought actions would speak louder than words. She rolled over, facing the broad width of his back, snuggling against the taut curve of his buttocks, her hand stealing over his waist to settle on the flat, hard planes of his abdomen. She felt him tense.

'Troye…'

'What?'

'I am sorry, if I have angered you…'

'I am not angry.'

She almost laughed at that, at the strange feeling of *déjà vu* as they repeated a previous conversation, for it was obvious from his manner and his taut body that he harboured ill feelings of some sort, and had for some while now. Her heart ached—she only wanted to share with him her love, to pleasure him, and comfort him. Greatly daring, breath tensely held, she let her hand move down, stroking the bulge of his manhood, dormant and yet powerfully masculine to her exploring fingers. She unlaced his breeches and slid her hand within, cupping the twin orbs of his male parts, never having touched him before. She felt his shoulders move as he drew in a breath, but he did not refuse her touch. Her fingers moved upwards, and she explored all parts of him, squeezing and stroking, until with a groan he rolled over on to his back and pulled her on top of him. He lifted the hem of her shift, pushing it up, and his hands grasped her hips, positioning her female sex on his male. He closed his eyes, his hands reaching up to grasp her breasts and squeeze them. Her breath came in quick gasps, yet she felt too far from him and uncomfortable, her thighs stretched as she kneeled astride him. She had not known that it was possible in this position… She felt heat flare across her skin as she leaned down and kissed him. He let her, opening his lips, and she slid her tongue within his mouth, kissing him deeply. His body moved beneath her, straining and pushing, his hands on her hips manoeuvring her back and forth to match the rhythm of his movements. She thrilled to feel, for the first time, the heat in his skin, and then with one hand he grasped himself and guided his aching manhood to find the entrance to her body, inserting himself, thrusting, pushing. He felt very big and Eleanor gasped, arching back, resisting the bulk that stretched and invaded the tiny confines of her womanhood. She would have pulled away, but with a small growl he held her tight and thrust hard inside her. As his movements became more frantic she felt heat and pleasure flare between her legs, startling her with its fierceness. She dug her nails into his shoulders, rose and fell with him, for the first time experiencing the power of being a woman. She looked down at Troye, this muscular, powerful man, this knight and soldier of the battlefield, and gloried at his weakness. She leaned down and brushed her nipple against his mouth; he turned his head and grasped it with his lips, opening his mouth and closing it over the heavy flesh of her breast, sucking with a firm motion. Pleasure seared Eleanor and she clutched at Troye's shoulders as he sat up, grasping her buttocks, in one fluid movement turning her until he was on top. His knee spread her thighs wide and he lunged with his hips, again and again, his fingers stroking her thighs, her softly-haired mound, silently urging her to take him. She did, swinging her hips in a frenzy to match his, her head arched back, until she felt a hot, aching need growing and straining. She thought she would burst with the pleasure of it, but then he stopped, having satisfied himself, and quickly withdrew. She stared at him, aching and wet with his seed and yet unfulfilled.

In a choked voice, mystified and yet sure that there was more, she pleaded, 'Troye…?'

He looked at her then, with hard eyes, his glance lowering to her spread legs, to her womanhood, and almost with reluctance slid his fingers into the moist, tender space he had claimed for himself. He stroked her, and she shuddered, tender from the force of his possession and finding no pleasure in his touch. She pushed his hand away, confused and hurting in more ways than just physically. At her rejection, he shrugged and turned away.

'Get some sleep, Eleanor. We rise early, as soon as day breaks.'

Eleanor put her shift to rights and lay down on the pillow beside him. Her heart beat very hard and the heat of desire ebbed away to be replaced by the sudden, white-hot flare of anger. She stared at Troye, as he lay with his back to her and his heavy breathing gave evidence of his swift retreat into sleep. For a moment she was greatly tempted to shake him awake, to shout at him that he had no right to treat her like a whore, pleasuring himself as and when it suited him. Yet she feared to confront him, feared to hear the words spoken aloud from his lips that would confirm her suspicions that their marriage was doomed. Once again, she forced herself to keep silent, and closed her eyes, hoping that sleep would soon rescue her from the torment of her thoughts.

Chapter Eight

On the morrow they reached the Vale of York. Through a haze of misty pink, as the glowing gold orb of the sun lowered, they could see the vast bulk of the Minster silhouetted on the far horizon. To the right were the smaller outlines of St Mary's Cathedral and York Castle, and in between the thatched and shingled rooftops of the houses. Surrounding the city stretched golden limestone walls, banked by a high grassy mound that dropped into a steep ditch. Troye and Dylan discussed the merits of York's fine defences, but they did not enter the city by any of the four stout barbicans.

'It looks like a fairy tale from this distance,' said Troye, 'but within the city walls the streets are narrow and difficult to ride through. We would do well to avoid the noise and the stink.'

Eleanor looked at the golden vision of York, doubting his word and thinking how like Troye to ruin all the romance of this, her first glimpse of her new home, but all day she had been plagued by a headache. She made no comment, longing only to lie down in a cool, dark place.

Troye's family home was in the small village of Fulford, a mile or so from the city walls. They rode up to a large timber-framed manor house, two-storied, the walls plastered and painted white and the windows paned with small leaded squares. It was set on a knoll and partly hidden from the road by oak and ash trees. Yet these details she scarcely took in, barely able to lift her head from where she leaned between Troye's shoulder blades, a pillow that yielded little comfort. For Dylan, too, it had been a day best forgotten, with his master snapping and snarling at every opportunity; it had not gone unnoticed by Dylan that his master hardly spoke a single word to his lady wife. As a mere squire it was not his place to remonstrate, but it was no easy task for Dylan to bite his tongue. He, too, was heartily glad to reach their destination.

As the weary travellers halted the front door opened and several people crowded on the step as they looked out curiously.

'Troye!' A tall woman, dressed in linen wimple and gown, her handsome features and dark eyes easily betraying her identity, called out his name.

He dropped the reins of his horse and vaulted down, leaving Eleanor slumped precariously on the back of the unattended animal. Quickly Dylan dismounted and came to assist her in doing the same, holding out his arms for her to jump down into. Eleanor misjudged slightly, and the horse shifted just as she was about to descend, so that the slender Dylan was hard pressed and, with a smothered groan and grunt, they both fell to the ground.

Troye exclaimed angrily and pulled Dylan to his feet with one hand and Eleanor with the other, applying little gentleness to either. Eleanor brushed the dirt from her skirts and hands, feeling the colour rise in her face as the woman asked who they were.

'Mother, this is Dylan, my squire, and this…this…is…my wife, Eleanor,' he introduced them to each other in a brisk manner. 'My mother, the Lady Anne.'

Eleanor dipped into a curtsy, her eyes lowered as the two servants crowding at Lady Anne's shoulder failed to smother their gasps of surprise.

'Well, you'd best come inside.' Lady Anne peered in the gloom of dusk, but could see little of her son's new and unexpected bride. She gathered her skirts in both hands and, in a firm manner that reminded Eleanor much of her son, she ordered her servants to go on and light the lamps. 'And tell cook we have extra mouths for supper.'

Dylan departed under Troye's directions to the stables at the rear of the manor house, and Eleanor was sorry to see his familiar face depart. Though he had said little to her on the long, exhausting journey from London she had sensed his sympathy and his quiet presence had been a buffer between her and Troye. Now, she would be alone with him and his family. What would she make of them? More importantly, what would they make of her?

As soon as she walked over the threshold of the de Valois family home, Eleanor sensed an atmosphere that she had never encountered before. She wondered why, and blamed it on her headache and sore throat, for she was sure by now that she had succumbed to sickness. But she did her best to smile for Troye's mother, to answer her questions as politely as she could about her family and her home in Somerset, as Lady Anne led them to a settle before the hearth in the main hall. A maidservant came in with a tray and Eleanor drank thirstily of cool wine, but refused the honey cakes offered.

'And when did this marriage take place?' Lady Anne asked her son bluntly, as she poured wine and crumbled a cake in her palm.

'A month or so ago.'

'And you did not think to write and invite your mother to the wedding?'

'There was no time,' replied Troye in an evasive tone, unlatching his sword and laying it to one side, 'but I wrote with news of the event.'

'I have not received any missive.'

Troye shrugged. 'I did have my suspicions that the messenger was not trustworthy. 'Tis likely he pocketed the silver and never left London.'

Lady Anne surveyed her son with sceptical raised brows, and then turned to Eleanor, glancing at her with shrewd eyes. In a more gentle tone than the one she had used with Troye she asked, 'And now my son has dragged you all the way from London in a matter of six days, sat on the back of his horse? No doubt you are exhausted.'

Eleanor smiled weakly, her voice rasping painfully as she whispered, 'Indeed, Lady Mother.'

'You may call me Lady Anne. I much prefer it.' Lady Anne rose from her chair, a slight frown on her brows. She went to Eleanor and placed a cool hand on her forehead. 'Why, child, you are burning up!' She glared accusingly at Troye over her shoulder.

He replied with an aggrieved glare of his own, ''Tis not my fault if there was sickness on the road.'

Lady Anne tutted under her breath and called for her maidservant. 'Meg, bring warm and cold washing water to…the master's bedchamber.' For a moment she looked at Troye, and then at Eleanor, as though in some doubt, and then again at Troye. 'Will you… she…have that chamber?'

He shrugged and nodded. 'There is no other.'

'I will take it, and you may have mine.'

'Nay.' Troye's reply was short and sharp. ''Twill make no difference.'

'But—'

They stared at each other for a very long moment, it seemed to Eleanor, and she rose to her feet, puzzled, anxious that no fuss be made because of her. 'I am sorry if I have caused you inconvenience—'

'Tush, child.' Lady Anne turned to Eleanor, and then cried out in alarm, 'Troye! Quickly, catch her!'

The room seemed to spin in dizzy, whirling circles as Eleanor felt a wave of heat rush at her. One moment she felt Troye's arms fasten about her waist, and the next her feet lift from the ground. She was vaguely aware of a swaying giddy motion as he carried her up the stairs, the thump of his booted feet on wooden floor boards, the creak of a door as it opened, and then the blessed relief of cool linen…and no more.

For several days she drifted in and out of consciousness, her body burning with a scorching fever, hair and skin drenched in sweat as she fought to overcome the sickness that attacked her. She had nightmares, and strange dreams. Sometimes she thought she heard the voice of a child, at others a dog barking, and though she was sure she called out for Troye, she was just as sure that he did not come to her. She cried and sobbed and begged…but still he did not come…she could not hear his voice, or feel the touch of his fingers…he was lost…drifting…and so was she.

A bright glare woke Eleanor. She turned her head, very slowly, towards the light. For a moment she resisted, a desire so strong pulling at her to sink back into the dark oblivion of sleep, but some unknown, unseen force tugged and pulled with steely determination to bring her out of the fog and into the light once more. She could see a window, and beyond it white snowflakes fluttered against a grey sky. Outside all was covered in a thick layer of snow, the stark bare limbs of the trees dredged sugar-white. For a long while she lay still, watching the snow drifting silent and serene from the winter sky.

Then she heard the sound of a dog barking, followed by laughter—a charming, happy, feminine laugh. She lifted her head from a thick pillow encased in stiff white linen, and looked out of the diamond-paned window.

A girl stood outside, a slim girl of medium height with dark hair swirling around her waist. She wore a burgundy gown and a dark blue velvet cloak. She was very beautiful. Eleanor sat up, on one elbow, and stared at the girl, drawn to her for some inexplicable reason. She pushed aside the bedcovers and padded barefoot, in her nightshift, to the small square window and knelt with one knee on an ornately carved oak coffer set beneath it, topped with a cushion. Leaning against the mullion-panes, she peered out, hardly noticing how cold the glass felt beneath her palm.

The girl laughed again, and turned towards the dog, a small spaniel that gambolled in the snow and cavorted around her skirts, playfully picking up and dropping a stick for her to throw. Eleanor could see that her skin was almost as pale as the snow, unblemished, suffused with the soft rose hue of a blush induced by the freezing weather, her breath pluming in a delicate mist upon the air as she laughed out loud. She called to the dog in a language Eleanor did not understand. The girl's eyes were a very dark brown, fringed with thick, dark lashes. Her nose was straight and delicate, her mouth a dusky, dark pink and well shaped, the bottom lip full and generous. The girl swung round, her skirts swirling across the snow, and for a brief moment looked directly at Eleanor. She felt the urge to tap on the window, to call her attention, but the girl looked away and ran across the garden and behind a bay hedge, the dog following after her with a wild thrashing of his tail and eager yapping.

With a small cry Eleanor turned quickly from the window and ran to the door. She tripped over the edge of a carpet laid upon the darkly polished wooden floor. Her knees banged hard as she fell, her body clumsy from so little use in the weeks past. But she scrambled up and continued. She had to find the girl, had to speak to her. She wrenched at the wrought-iron door-pull and ran out into the main hall of the house…her bare feet crunched on the icy snow….

'Eleanor!'

A voice called out, she struggled, and then suddenly she was awake, staring about her in wild confusion, panting, realising that she had been dreaming and yet… She gave an incoherent cry as she looked about. This was the very same room that had been in her dream, but when she turned her head and looked out of the same window there was no snow. It was still summer, the grass was green and the trees full of leaves, the sky blue. There was no fire in the hearth, but there was the coffer under the window, and she could have sworn that she had never been here before, had never seen this room before…was she going mad? She stared up at the woman leaning over her, a high-born lady judging by her dress. Eleanor peered at her, trying hard to remember. The woman spoke her name and then a maid came pattering into the room, staring at her with curious eyes, and the lady, her mistress, said, 'Fetch my son.'

The maid ran off to find her master, bursting with excitement to be the bearer of glad tidings. Her booted feet pattered on the wooden floorboards as she ran from room to room in search of him. But she could not find him.

In the kitchen she tugged at the broad sleeve of their cook. 'Master Jarvis, where be our young sir? His lady is awake!'

He frowned, pink jowls wobbling as he turned, and looked out the window across the yard. 'A wagon came in, not long ago. He may well be up at top barn, overseeing the unloading.'

Without a word of thanks the little maid veered off, hair and cap all flying as she ran, picking up her skirts, pounding and slipping and sliding across the treacherous ground of the rutted track that led to the storage barns and pens to the rear of the manor house. There, to her relief, she found Troye, and she burst upon him, pulling and tugging, her explanation a garbled shriek of words he could barely grasp. But instinct knew that there could be only one source of such consternation. Without question or doubt he turned away from his task of checking the bales of wool ready to be shipped to Holland and ran to the house, his long, muscular legs leaving behind the maid as he outpaced her stumbling trot.

Eleanor sat up in the bed, pushing back the long swathes of her hair, her eyes skimming about the room, taking careful note of the dark furniture, the canopied bed, the coffer under the window. How familiar it all seemed and yet she was sure she had never been here before... She looked up at the woman, and remembered, a slight smile breaking on her lips as she murmured, 'Lady Anne.'

Her mother-in-law sat down on the edge of the bed and took one of Eleanor's hands into both of her own, clasping them gently yet with firm assurance.

'You had me worried there for a time, child.' Lady Anne was about to say that she thought it a cruel twist of fate that a second daughter-in-law should lie ill in the same bed as the first, but then she doubted the wisdom of it, not knowing what Troye had told Eleanor. So she merely smiled gently. 'How do you feel?'

'Weak as a kitten.' Eleanor smiled.

'You have been very ill. But I think the worst is over.' Lady Anne pressed her fingers to Eleanor's cheek. 'Aye, you are cool now.'

Eleanor smiled, and nodded her head, sagging back against the pillows and turning her face towards the window. Lady Anne rose and departed from the room, saying she would return with a tray of food, promising that she would find little morsels to tempt Eleanor's appetite and build up her strength.

'Thank you,' Eleanor murmured, but as the door closed and she was left alone she again stared out the window, and at the coffer placed beneath it, strangely drawn to both.

She listened to the sounds of the house, the creaking floorboards, the distant voices, the birds singing in the trees, and the sound of her own breathing, the steady thump-thump of her heart. There was something…she could not be sure what…but something that made her heart ache and her soul weep hot tears of sorrow… She smoothed the palm of her hand over the coverlet of the bed, glancing up at the emerald-green canopy of the great tester bed. This bed…had he lain here with…her? The thought caused a knife-sharp ache to pierce her heart and she sat up, trying to push back the covers, but she froze as the door clicked open.

Footfalls echoed on the floorboards and the tread was so familiar to her that she scarcely had to turn and glance over her shoulder at him. Such was the emotion felt within her that tears stung her eyes as Troye approached. Somehow she had feared that she would never see him again, never touch him, or kiss him or tell him how much she loved him… Her teeth caught at her bottom lip as he came to a halt beside the bed, and slowly she raised her eyes to his.

'I am told you are much recovered?'

He spoke in that calm, clear voice that betrayed no emotion and yet touched her deeply just by its timbre. His enquiry, though, was hardly the tender concern of a loving husband, and the tears burned even sharper in her eyes. She turned away, so that he would not see them, and simply nodded her head. She made much of trying to push aside the covers, and he came and easily lifted them aside. Eleanor swung her legs out, and placed her feet carefully upon the cool, dark wooden floorboards. Her legs felt wobbly indeed as she rose, and Troye reached out and placed his hand under her elbow. She smiled her thanks and then, taking a few hesitant steps, walked to the window.

He walked with her, and stood close at her side as Eleanor squinted against the light, looking to left and to right. She could not resist the temptation and asked him, as casually as she could, 'There has not been snow, has there?'

Troye stared at her, as though she were mad indeed, supporting her with one hand under her elbow, 'Indeed not, 'tis the hottest summer we have had in a long while. Why do you ask?'

Eleanor glanced down at the coffer, and then she shook her head. 'No matter. I had strange dreams.'

''Tis common with delirious fevers.' He followed the line of her gaze and abruptly urged her back to the bed. 'You are weak still, you need to rest.'

Eleanor could hear Lady Anne and the maid she called Meg as they came up the stairs, and though she longed to ask him the many questions in her mind, they both turned from the window and hurried with almost guilty haste to return Eleanor to the bed.

For the next few days Eleanor gradually felt her strength return, as did her sense of smell and with it her appetite. She looked forward to when Troye would come to see her. Once he sat on the coffer under the window, staring at her with an expression on his face that she could not quite fathom.

'How are you feeling today?' he asked, his hands clasped between his spread knees, his eyes not quite meeting hers.

'I am much recovered, thank you.' Eleanor smiled at him then, and patted the edge of the bed, feeling that he was far too distant and too formal. 'I am not contagious.'

At her insistence he rose from the coffer and perched on the edge of the bed, and she held out her hand to him. He took it into the warmth of his and she drew strength from his strength, and yet she sensed his reluctance.

Blushing a little, she murmured, 'I miss you, Troye. This bed is far too big for just one person.' She smiled, adding a soft little laugh to hide how earnest her loneliness.

His glance strayed to the window, unable to find the words to admit that he had not been able to bring himself to sleep in this bed with her, the bed that he had shared with his first wife.

'You must take as much time as you need to recover,' he prevaricated, 'you don't need my snores keeping you awake.'

'I like your snores.'

'Indeed?' He returned his glance to her, drawn by her smile and amused tone.

'Aye, I find the sound very comforting.'

He laughed, not believing her for a moment, pressing his point further by adding, 'And 'tis very hot at the moment. I'm sweating like a pig all night long.'

The thought of Troye lying beside her, hot and sweating, was more tantalising than she could bear, so demurely she lowered her eyes, with a slight smile and accepted that today she would not win this argument; but there would always be tomorrow. After a few moments of idle conversation, she freed her hand from his and let him go. He rose and at the door turned back to look at her. Their eyes met; Eleanor smiled gently, but her encouragement was not rewarded. Troye left and went about his business. With a sigh Eleanor snuggled down on to the pillow, still tired and weak and perplexed about how to bridge the widening gulf between her and Troye.

By the end of the week Lady Anne encouraged her to dress and go outside to get some fresh air. They strolled together in the garden, and then sat upon a stone bench beside a fish pond, not far distant from the house. The golden light of late afternoon slanted across the grass and trees, the air sweet with roses and honeysuckle. Eleanor turned her face to the sunlight and closed her eyes, basking in the warmth and the soft sense of peace. She was aware of Lady Anne sitting beside her, watching her, though she pretended not to. Eleanor opened her eyes and turned her head, a question in her eyes.

Lady Anne merely patted Eleanor's hand as she leaned back on the bench. 'What has he told you?'

Eleanor looked away then, a chagrined smile turning down the corners of her mouth. There was no need to pretend. They both knew what her mother-in-law alluded to. Eleanor shook her head. 'Nothing. He has said nothing.'

'Come…' Lady Anne rose '…do you feel strong enough for a short walk?'

'Indeed.' Eleanor welcomed the opportunity to stretch her legs and to escape the confines of the house.

They followed a path between a high hedge. Eleanor had a peculiar feeling as though she had been here before. She remembered the dream, the one that had seemed so real, and the girl playing with the dog—they too had turned this way. Lady Anne led her along the banks of a river, the green delicate fronds of willow trees leaning down to weep into the cool, dark waters. After a short distance she turned away from the river and followed the path towards the village of Fulford. There was an inn and a blacksmith and several cottages, but on this dry afternoon there was no one about, all able bodies out in the fields beyond helping to reap the harvest of oats, wheat and barley. A church stood beyond a stand of copper beeches thick with dark brown leaves. The lych-gate creaked as Lady Anne opened it and they entered holy ground, their shadows mingling with the shadows thrown by gravestones on the grass. Eleanor followed her to a corner sheltered by trees and a hedgerow of wild rosehips and hawthorn. There was one small stone beneath the boughs, and here Lady Anne halted. Eleanor brushed aside the damp tendrils of hair that clung to her brow, tired from even this slight exertion, and looked down, reading the carved inscription:

Isabeau de Valois
Beloved Wife
Loved and Cherished For Ever

For a long moment all she could do was stand and stare. Here at last, she was confronted with all that stood between her and Troye. Again she read the inscription, each word and her tender age burning painfully into her senses, and then Eleanor murmured, 'She was a mere score years. My age.'

'Aye.' Lady Anne folded her arms in a resigned gesture, glancing up to the sky, to the heavens, to a God she felt sure had deserted them on that dreadful day. 'She was a young, beautiful woman.'

'He loved her.'

'Aye.'

'How…what happened?'

They did not look at each other as she asked, and she was not sure if Lady Anne would reply. She had no right to ask, no desire to stir pain that lay dormant.

'She slipped and fell, on an icy winter's day just before Christmas, and hit her head.'

Eleanor didn't know what to say to that, all sorts of thoughts and questions running riot through her mind. She searched for something, some starting point for a matter that was so simple and yet too vast for her understanding. She asked as carefully as she could, 'How did they meet one another?'

'Isabeau was a Jewess; her father was a banker whom my husband sometimes borrowed money from when shipments were late. They had known each other since they were children. My husband used to take Troye with him into York, to visit the merchants, and sometimes the Jewish banker, Leo Samuels, in Jubbergate when finances were tight. Now and then I would go too, and we would see her sitting there, writing in a book, helping her father to keep his accounts. She always had a little dog and sometimes we would let the children go out in the yard and play with him while we talked business. Of course, Troye was older than Isabeau, and at first he grumbled, but her mother baked delicious sweet biscuits or poppy-seed cake and he made good use of Isabeau to purloin generous portions.' Lady Anne smiled gently at the memory. 'She was a very pretty child, so…serene, and clever. Yet always she was kind, and amusing—I remember how she made Troye smile. And her laugh was the prettiest sound.' The remembrance of happy times made Lady Anne's face light up fondly, but her eyes soon clouded over as other thoughts intruded. 'But then the King expelled all Jews from the kingdom. My husband took pity on them and gave the Samuels shelter, while they made arrangements to pack up and go to the Netherlands. It took some time and Isabeau and Troye spent a lot of it together, too much. They fell in love. Troye asked Leo Samuels for permission to marry his daughter, but he refused. He had betrothed her from birth to another, a Jew, a scholar of their faith. Her father insisted that Isabeau would go with her family to Antwerp and she would marry this…other man. So they ran away, and married in secret; then, when he thought it was safe, Troye brought her home to live with us here. My husband passed away shortly after that, and I welcomed Isabeau, loved her as the daughter I'd never had. Who could not love Isabeau? And then…' here Lady Anne's voice hardened as she struggled with the terrible truth and she fought the sorrow that threatened to overspill '…the King recalled Troye to Court, and after a year of banishment he could not refuse to return and make his peace with the King. Isabeau was expecting their second child, so she stayed at home. It was winter, we went out for a walk with Toby, her little spaniel, but along the way she slipped on some ice and fell.' Lady Anne was silent for a long moment, and her throat worked painfully as she struggled to control the emotions that threatened to drown her voice. 'Down there—' she pointed back, to the opposite direction from which they had come, the shorter, quicker route from the manor house to the village, but one that she could not bear to tread '—by the river. She had no more than a small bruise on her forehead. None of us thought anything of it. But God in his great wisdom chose to take our fair Isabeau. I found her in the morning, lying still and pale in the bed, as though she were asleep.'

Eleanor stood transfixed, head bowed, staring at the gravestone, part of her trying to imagine the woman who now lay beneath the ground, nothing more than dust to dust. The other part of her cringed and wanted to flee from the terrible, painful thought, not only of a woman so greatly loved, but one who should still be alive. The thought made her weep, soundless tears coursing down her cheeks, grieving for a woman she had never known and yet one who so greatly influenced her life that she might well have been living and breathing at this very moment.

'Did Troye tell you any of this?'

Eleanor shook her head, sniffing and wiping her damp nose with the back of one hand.

Lady Anne shook her head in disapproval of her son's reticence. 'Pardon me for asking, child, but I am perplexed as to why he married you.'

Eleanor lifted her head then, pain tearing at her heart and opening the floodgates for more tears, 'You mean, why did he marry me when he still loves her?' She nodded towards the gravestone and sobbed, her eyes a bright glitter of unshed silver, 'On the orders of the King. Why else? Troye would never do anything except his duty.'

Picking up her skirts in both hands, Eleanor fled from the churchyard, running blindly as she sought to escape the truth and the pain that would now haunt her for ever. She ignored Lady Anne as she called out after her, and ran on, but in her weakened state she was soon forced to stop, gasping for breath, sinking down on to her knees on the path by the river. She lay there and wept, her heart aching inside of her with all the love that could never be: not only her love for Troye, but the love shared by Isabeau and Troye, so cruelly and unjustly ended. A shadow cast itself over her, and she yielded as Lady Anne gently urged her to rise and guided her back to the house.

In the cool dim shadows of the bedchamber, Eleanor sank down on to the bed and confessed to being worn out. She was greatly relieved when Lady Anne withdrew and left her alone. Her tears had spent themselves and she felt numb, empty, as though the very heart had been torn out of her. How would she survive this? How could her marriage be anything except a sham and a lifetime of loneliness and disappointment?

The afternoon waned, the golden light easing into the dark shadows of evening. She could hear the servants setting the table in the hall below, and she was sure she could hear the small, thin voice of a child, the patter of tiny feet. She remembered Lady Anne's words, that Isabeau had been carrying their *second* child…so there was a child…but Troye had seen fit to keep them apart… Why, indeed, would he hasten to introduce her? A stepmother was as welcome to a child as a toothache, and she had no doubt that if Troye had his way they would never meet…yet to be fair, Eleanor grasped at straws, she had been ill and no father would endanger his child with another's sickness.

Eleanor turned over on to her side and gazed at the window, but it was dark now and she could see nothing. Then her glance fell to the coffer, and the cold hand of curiosity stirred and urged her to sit up. She rose from the bed and fumbled in the dark to find a candle on the table by the hearth, tiptoeing out into the hall and lighting it from a rush lamp, and then just as stealthily returning to her chamber and closing the door. She padded on bare soundless feet to the coffer and knelt.

Eleanor unlatched the clasp; the lid was heavy and creaked as she lifted it slowly, her breath tensely held somewhere in her throat. She glanced nervously over her shoulder, some instinct making her tremble and fear Troye's wrath. Whatever was contained in this chest, it was not something that Troye would share with her. He would not allow her questions, so she would have to find her own answers. And so she convinced herself of the justice of her quest as she propped the lid against the wall and held the candle closer.

A smell of camphor and lavender rose to invade her nostrils. The chest seemed to be packed with clothes. She recognised the burgundy gown and dark blue cloak. Beneath them, at the bottom of the chest, lay what she could only surmise to be wedding gifts—silver candlesticks, goblets, sewing needles, and a pair of velvet slippers. Eleanor recoiled from investigating further. She could hear hoofbeats outside, and Troye giving instructions to Dylan as they arrived back from a trip to the bonding-house in York. Her heart began a nervous drumbeat. Gently, carefully, she tidied the contents, and then her fingers touched the hard edge of a picture frame and she could not resist. Holding the candle closer, she pulled out a small painted portrait, a miniature, framed in gilt.

Goosebumps flared over her forearms. She stared at the beautiful, still, silent, serene image of a lovely face, dark eyes, dark hair, pale skin, perfect nose, lush, petal-soft mouth…the girl in her dream!

Isabeau de Valois.

For long moments she stared, and then she heard the main door open, and Troye call out a greeting to his mother. She could not hear the words of their conversation, but now she hastened to put away the portrait and close the chest, some instinct urging her that Troye would not be pleased to find her snooping. She could hear his footsteps ascend the wooden stairs and she hurried to sit upon the edge of the bed, busying herself with shaking fingers to pull on her hose.

The bedchamber door clicked open and Troye looked around it. Seeing Eleanor was awake, he came in. He watched for a moment while she reached for a hairbrush and stroked it through the long skeins of her auburn hair. A distant memory stirred within him of…*her*…sat upon the edge of their bed brushing her hair, after they had… He forced the memory away, and stared hard at Eleanor, who had neither the smile nor the glow of a woman well content and satisfied.

'You look tired,' Troye commented, noting the dark circles and puffy redness of her eyes. 'You must not try to do too much, too soon.'

She lifted her wary gaze to his, and forced a smile. 'I would not have your mother think I am lazy.'

'No one thinks that of you.' Troye turned away, always ready to retreat at any mention of personal matters, 'Supper is ready.'

Eleanor rose and slipped her feet into her shoes, straightened her gown, and he held the door open as together they left the bedchamber.

In the hall below the long refectory table of dark oak had been set with trenchers and a bowl of steaming chicken stew. Lady Anne sat in her customary place at the head of the table and Eleanor took her seat to the left, while Troye sat opposite on his mother's right. Had it been so with Isabeau? Eleanor wondered as she sat down.

Mother and son conversed in an easy fashion as they each helped themselves to food, their talk mainly of the wool business and the weather and their neighbours. Eleanor listened, but it was all unfamiliar to her and she made no comment. With head bowed she ate in a desultory fashion, a nauseous wave of homesickness sweeping over her as she wondered what her parents might be doing and how they fared at Castle Ashton. She reached for the round loaf of bread and tore off a chunk, dipping it into the gravy of her stew and chewing with little enthusiasm. Is this how it would be, for all the days of her life? She raised her eyes and looked at Troye, seeing him in a different light now that she knew about his wife. Anger almost flared as some sensible part of her rushed to declare,

'*You* are his wife!' Yet her heart, which had never been overly keen on sense, knew full well that she was not. She watched him as he talked and imagined how he must have felt when news reached him of Isabeau's death. The hairs on her forearms flared and she shivered, all too aware of the pain and the shock that he must have felt.

Feeling her gaze upon his face Troye turned, and halted in his conversation on the merits of the High Sheriff and whether they should have him to dine. 'Is there aught amiss?' he asked Eleanor, noting her pale face and how quiet she had been. 'Do you feel unwell?'

Eleanor shook her head. 'Nay.'

'You have not said a word all evening.'

Lady Anne laid her hand upon Troye's wrist, a discreet yet warning gesture. 'Well, we are much remiss in that we have talked of nothing that Eleanor would be able to make comment upon.'

'I am happy to sit and listen,' Eleanor murmured.

Troye observed her downcast eyes. 'I must go into York on the morrow. If you wish, you are welcome to accompany me. You have not yet seen the city. The market and the cathedral may interest you.'

'We will go together,' Lady Anne brooked Eleanor's hesitation. 'I need to see the cobbler about my winter shoes. Come now, child, have a slice of this plum cake. Fresh from the oven it is, and just looking at you, all skin and bone, we need to feed you up if you are to be strong and healthy again.'

Eleanor had little choice but to accept the wedge of cake, and delicious it was, smothered in fresh cream. She smiled as Troye complained at the thick wedge that his mother had cut for him, sadly aware that even to watch him eat was a guilty pleasure. He wiped cream and cake from his mouth, laughing as he refused a second helping. He scraped back his chair, 'I am off to see what Dylan is up to.' He glanced at Eleanor in parting, 'Until the morrow.'

She realised then that he was bidding her goodnight, and the thought of another night without him sleeping by her side was unbearable. From the corner of her eye she watched as Lady Anne went to a basket in a far corner to fetch her embroidery, and while she was gone she hurried after Troye as he reached for his cloak.

'Troye—' She halted him with one hand upon his arm, and then coloured profusely as she stumbled on the words of her request.

'What is it?' he asked, glancing down at her with a frown.

'I—I—' She glanced over her shoulder, and then whispered, 'Where have you slept these nights past?'

His face closed and he swung his cloak about his shoulders, giving himself a moment to consider his reply, which was, to her frustration, rather vague. 'I have been comfortable enough.'

She looked up at him then, blushing with a rosy hue. 'I have missed you.'

He made no comment and she was forced to make herself clearer. 'I am well enough for you to return. If you wish.'

'Do you want me to?'

'Aye.'

'Then so be it. But do not wait up for me.'

He strode away then, but it was with a happy glow that Eleanor spent the evening quietly darning his lambrequin, a cloth hood worn beneath his chain-mail coif. She sat and thought about the pleasure of having him return to her bed, and that it would be a good opportunity to ask about the child. She was sure that Lady Anne would have been willing to tell all, to introduce the child, but it was clearly obvious that she was under instructions from Troye not to. And yet she had her curiosity about Isabeau, much aware that Lady Anne had been fond of her.

'Lady Anne?'

'Hmm?' She looked up as she bit off a thread.

'Tell me about…Isabeau.'

Her question was only met with silence, as Lady Anne rummaged through her silks for a particular colour with great attention.

'Was she pretty?' Eleanor persisted.

Lady Anne squinted at a needle as she threaded a dark shade of green. 'Aye. Very pretty.'

'Was she…fair?' Eleanor blushed at her deception.

'Nay. She had dark hair, and dark brown eyes.'

'Was she…tall?'

'Nay, she was a little thing, smaller than you.' Lady Anne gave her a hard, shrewd look with eyes as dark as Troye's, peering into the depths of Eleanor's soul as if she would pluck out the truth by the mere force of her gaze. 'Now listen to my words, and heed you well. The past is a dangerous fellow—he can charm and beguile and poison, when in fact he has no existence except in our minds. Live for today, Eleanor. Forget the past. It can only hurt you if you allow it to stay with you.'

Eleanor blushed. She set aside her sewing and, rising from her chair, murmured, 'Lady Anne, it is not I who has trouble with the past.'

She bid her goodnight, retiring to her bedchamber and taking with her a candle and her anxious thoughts. With great care she attended to her ablutions, washing with rose-scented water and brushing out her hair until it shone, soft to the touch. She chose a delicate nightshift, tied with pink ribbons, and then climbed beneath the covers of the bed and lay there to wait.

After a time, bored with staring up at the tester's canopy, she began to say her prayers, but her mind wandered and once again it returned to the thought uppermost: Isabeau. Again she wondered if Troye had shared this bed with her—it seemed very likely, but she questioned the wisdom of asking him such. What difference would it make? If he replied aye, then what could she do? Ask for a new bed? That would be unlikely! She had a feeling that though the de Valois manor was well kept and well run, they were not as wealthy as her own family. She chewed on her lip, surmising that she could appeal to her father to use her dowry for a new bed, and then smiled at the complete fool she would make of herself with such a request. The fact was, Isabeau had been here, but now she was gone. And Eleanor had to make the best of it. She rolled over on to her side, facing the door, wondering how late it would be before Troye returned. She sighed, her eyes closing, and though she tried to force them apart it had been a tiring day. She relaxed, burrowing down beneath the covers, snuggling into the pillow. It was a very comfortable bed indeed…

A sudden draught and the feel of cold flesh against her warm skin woke Eleanor. Troye murmured an apology as he climbed into bed, naked and cold. Half-asleep, Eleanor lifted her arms and slid them around his broad back, urging him closer to her warmth. In silence, he complied. She held him, the masculine scent of his body tingling in her nose, awakening her senses. The muscles of his arms and shoulders bulged, firm and hard, the planes of his chest and midriff lean against the softness of her breasts and her woman's body. He sighed, relaxing in her embrace, pressing the roughness of his jaw into the smooth crook of her neck. They said not a word to each other, and yet she sensed his need. With the fingertips of one hand she stroked the back of his neck, encouraging him.

Fumbling almost like a callow youth, his lips moved across her face, seeking her mouth. He kissed her, his hands sliding down her back to grasp her buttocks. She made a sound, one of pleasure, without words trying to convey to him that she loved the way he kissed her and touched her. Eleanor pressed her body closer to his, her aching nipples taut against his chest, enjoying the rough tickle of the dark hairs that matted his torso. She could feel his arousal, pressing into her, hard and strong.

With bold fingers Troye quickly removed her shift, tossing it aside and running his hands over her naked body. She moaned and groaned with lusty pleasure, hoping that he would echo her, but he was silent, as always. She felt heat on her skin at his touch, and though his manhood was hot as a fire-poker, his back was cool beneath the palm of her hand. Into her mind came an insidious thought, an image, of him and *her*…making love…Troye calling out her name… She drew back, but it was too late, Troye was intent on reaching his goal.

He rolled her over on to her back and parted her thighs, moving to a position of dominance as he mounted her. She lay back, accepting him as he thrust into her body. He rose and fell, plunging faster and faster, and though his breath came slightly louder against her ear, he made no sound, no cries of pleasure, nor of love. She held on to his broad shoulders as he moved above her, in the dark unable to see his face, but certain that his eyes were closed, lost in his own world, a world that he would not allow her to follow him into. She enjoyed the feel of him and the power of her own body to give him pleasure, and yet she still yearned for more as his movements stopped, and she could only guess that he had done that inexplicable and mysterious act that left her moist with his seed. A small sound of disappointment escaped from her throat, and he raised himself on to his elbows. Though he, too, could not see her face in the dark, he looked upon her.

'I'm sorry,' he murmured. 'You…are not…well enough yet?'

She hesitated with her reply, wondering at the wisdom of making an issue of something that she had no knowledge of in the first place, and for some strange reason she felt that Troye must not take the blame for her lack of satisfaction. Indeed, in her innocence she considered the fault to be her own.

'I am rather tired,' she hedged, and softened her

words by stroking his face and kissing his cheek. 'But it is my duty to let you...have your way, is it not?'

Troye snorted, well aware that duty and passion were not compatible, and yet had their couplings ever been anything except duty?

'Eleanor—'

She had no wish to discuss the matter further. Turning on her side, she bid him, 'Good night, Troye.'

Chapter Nine

Eleanor woke to the sound of birds twittering their sweet chorus in the trees. The sun rose very early and she expected, as always, to find herself alone, but as her senses gradually awakened she felt the warmth and heaviness of Troye, lying asleep alongside her. Remembering how he had been with her during the night, she was loath to face him in the cold light of day.

Eleanor hunched over, curled on her side with knees drawn up, lying on the edge of the bed as far from him as possible. She closed her eyes and tried to go back to sleep, but a rooster crowed outside and below she could hear the household stirring—the cook, Jarvis, clattering pans, the soft voice of Meg conversing with Dylan. However much she longed to, escape into slumber eluded her.

Troye stirred then; she heard his deep even breathing alter and she sensed that he was awake. He sighed and stretched, and then she felt the mattress move as he leaned towards her. His hand gently touched her shoulder.

'Eleanor,' he whispered, 'are you awake?'

'Hmm,' she replied drowsily, not turning to face him, but his hand insisted and reluctantly she rolled over. Opening her eyes a little, she was met with the sight of his broad, muscular chest and shoulders towering above her, his long legs close to her own, yet not quite touching. The warmth and strength of his body was very seductive to her senses, she could feel her breasts ache in response, and further down, in that mysterious place between her legs, still damp and aching from his possession, she throbbed with a sudden stab of desire.

Troye studied her face, and her downcast eyes. It pained him to see the unhappiness written so clearly on her features, and yet he could not help but be the cause of it. Awkwardly, he murmured, 'Last night…' He struggled to find the words to express the thoughts and emotions that hammered like an unwanted visitor on the door of his mind. 'It was no good for you, was it?'

It was on the tip of her tongue to agree with him, but she refrained, wondering at this change in Troye. He had never bothered before to speak of intimacy. Confusion warred with hope, and she hardly dared to lift her eyes to his, uncertain of what she would find written there.

'Eleanor,' he spoke softly, yet his voice firm and clear, 'I know I have not been the best of husbands to you, and I do not mean to be so harsh. I am sorry. I cannot help but be the way I am—of that I warned you.'

A sigh escaped from between her lips, as hope faded and disappointment crushed her heart yet again. She nodded, unable to speak a word, fearing that if she did all that was now held tight and fast within her would burst forth in a torrent. He would only refuse to face anything other than his own sorrow and shut her out.

'I promise that I will never again…take you, if you are unwilling.'

Her eyelashes flew up and she stared at him, the cold hand of fear gripping her. 'What do you mean?'

He sat up, pushing aside the bedcovers as he swung his legs to the floor. 'I mean you need have no more worries. I will refrain from…marital relations, unless you should have a need for it and ask me to, um…' he hesitated delicately '…bed you.'

Eleanor almost gave a cry then, watching his beautiful body as he walked across the room and reached for his clothes, pulling on his breeches. He did not want her for his wife to love, and now he did not want her as a woman to hold! Her humiliation and disappointment was absolute.

'We will go to York mid-morning. You are well enough to ride, or shall I ask Dylan to drive you in the cart?'

'Nay,' Eleanor croaked, then cleared her throat and tried again. 'I can ride.'

'Good.' He fastened his tunic and tugged on his boots, reaching for his belt and sword, latching these about his waist as he smiled at her from the door. 'I will see you anon.'

As soon as the door closed, Eleanor buried her face in the pillow and smothered the great sobs that tore from her, racked with a bout of weeping that left her drained and disconsolate. At last, the tears spent, she lay there and wondered how on earth she could manage to drag her body from the bed. Even to rise and dress was too much effort, let alone ride a horse the mile or so to York and spend all day with Troye and his mother. I cannot do it! Eleanor declared to herself, wiping her face and nose with the back of her hand. She imagined herself telling them excuses, anything, that she felt unwell, and staying here in the bed. Or, her resilient mind plotted further, while they were gone she would pack and run away! Aye! She could not live with this agony, it could not go on. She would leave…but for where? York was so very far from anywhere, she would never be able to ride alone on the roads for six days to reach London.

Eleanor subsided. Good sense told her it was impossible. This was her life, there was no other. She had no choice but to stay and endure the pain of being married to a man who did not love her, as she loved him. Mayhap it would not hurt so much as the years passed by. She would become accustomed to the pain and, like Troye, cease to feel anything at all.

Meg came in then, with a soft knock upon the door, bearing a tray set with a mug of warm milk spiced with nutmeg and honey, and fresh-baked curd cheese tarts thick with raisins. The maid greeted her and set the tray down, and Eleanor thanked her as she sat up in the bed and donned her shift.

'Meg, I would bathe. Please bring the tub and lots of hot water. 'Tis a warm morning and I would take advantage of it.'

'My lady.' Meg bobbed a curtsy and hurried off to the kitchen to set water on the boil and call to Simon the house-serf and Dylan to bring the bathing tub upstairs.

The water would take some time and Eleanor made no hurry. She ate the tarts and drank the milk and then went to sit upon the coffer beneath the window and gaze out at the flat Yorkshire landscape. It was colder here, and very open, compared to the rolling hills and dales of Somerset. Had Isabeau sat here too? No doubt she had been well content. Eleanor heaved another sigh and reached for her brush, applying it to her hair, which she then tied with a wide ribbon in a knot upon her head.

A knock rapped on the door and she called enter. With grunts and sighs Simon and Dylan manoeuvred a beaten copper bathing tub into the room, no light weight, and set it down before the hearth.

'Would my lady be wanting a fire?' asked Simon, wiping the sweat from his brow.

Eleanor smiled and shook her head. 'Nay, 'tis warm enough.'

His relief was almost palpable. 'Very good. We'll be bringing up the water now, if my lady is ready?'

'Aye. Thank you.'

It took five trips each by Dylan and Simon to empty steaming copper jugs of water into the tub, and Eleanor felt much obliged for their exertions. She gave them her thanks and then dismissed Meg, assuring her that she could manage on her own. She wanted to be alone and lie in the warm water for as long as possible before it cooled, without the hovering maidservant to intrude upon her troublesome thoughts.

Eleanor untied the ribbons of her shift and let it fall to the ground about her ankles, stepping out of the soft folds of linen and into the bathing tub. With a sigh and a shiver of pleasure she sank down into the hot water. It felt wonderful and she relaxed into the water for some long moments. Then she reached for a bar of rose-scented soap and stood up, lathering it between her hands to wash her body.

Below in the hall, Troye waited impatiently. He was ready to ride for York, yet his mother informed him that Eleanor was making use of the bathing tub. With a frown he mounted the stairs and went up to their bedchamber to chivvy her along. As he opened the door he was all of a mind to give her sharp words, yet the sight that met his eyes quite took his words, and his breath, away.

Eleanor stood naked in the tub of water, the golden morning light streaming through the window and gilding her pale skin with an apricot glow. He could not help but look at her smooth, graceful back, tapering down to a narrow waist and the feminine curves of a bottom that was smooth and exquisite to his male gaze. Her hair was tied up and displayed the slender beauty of her neck and shoulders. He stood back and closed the door almost completely, but not quite, riveted by the sight of her body and realising that he had never seen her naked before. Always it had been dark or she had been covered by clothing when he had availed himself… Abruptly he turned his mind away from the memory of their coupling, and yet he could not help but stare when Eleanor half-turned. He gazed at her breasts as with the palm of her hand she soaped them, cupping and circling the small yet high mounds of firm flesh and dark pink nipples. Her hand moved down over her flat belly and lathered the dark patch of maidenhair between her legs. He felt heat rush through him, desire as he had not felt for a long while rising fiercely in all parts of him that were male. For a moment he was tempted to stride through the door, lift her from the bath and throw her down upon the bed, slaking his lust with the soft womanliness of her body. He had the right to, as her husband, she was his, to have and to hold, and yet… He closed the door carefully, aware that he was breathing hard and that a faint dew of sweat moistened his brow. He had promised her that he would not touch her, unless she asked him first, and somehow he doubted very much that she would. For a moment he stood there, staring at his boots, confused, perplexed, and then he turned away and went downstairs, treading softly.

Lady Anne looked at Troye as he passed, at the grim set of his mouth and the faint hint of colour beneath his tan. She smiled to herself, and made much of having lost a lace for her boot, calling for Meg to bring another. Troye grunted and sat down upon a chair, fists clenched on his knees, staring blankly at the cold grey stones of the empty fire hearth.

'Is Eleanor ready then?' asked Lady Anne casually.

Troye cleared his throat before replying, 'Not quite.'

'I will send Meg to hurry her up.'

'Aye. The day is passing.' Troye rose abruptly from his seat, saying that he would be out by the stables checking that Dylan had the horses ready.

Lady Anne nodded, as Meg handed her a spare bootlace and she spoke quietly to the little maid, 'Meg, go and see to Lady Eleanor. Make sure she is dressed in her prettiest gown and her hair is not tied back in a wimple—'

'But—' Meg was aghast that a married lady would go abroad with her hair loose, but she bit back her words as Lady Anne hushed her.

'And then fetch your cloak, Meg, for you will accompany me this morn.'

Delighted, Meg dipped a curtsy, excited at the prospect of a morning in York. In the master's bedchamber she found Eleanor washed, dried and slipping on her underclothes. Meg persuaded her to wear the green gown that looked so becoming with Eleanor's auburn hair, and brushed her hair out until it gleamed. She wove two thin braids on either side of Eleanor's temple and fastened them with gold ribbons.

'There, my lady, you look a bonnie lass.'

Eleanor smiled, somewhat bemused by Meg's ministrations.

'The master be waiting.' Meg promptly reminded her, sensing that Eleanor was about to question this sudden interest in her appearance, and the maid hurried away to fetch her boots and cloak, greatly looking forward to the outing, especially as the handsome young Dylan would go with them. She had been in love with Simon for many months but he was rather slow in his courtship—mayhap a little jealousy would hasten him along, or indeed Dylan might well prove to be the man for her.

The horses waited at the front door, and Dylan had chosen a quiet grey palfrey for Eleanor, a sweet little horse who gently nuzzled her palm as she approached and took the reins from Dylan.

'They say her name is Luz. They bought her from a Spaniard and she's a fine creature, my lady. Her mouth is light as a feather and fit for a queen. You'll have no trouble with her.'

Eleanor smiled, stroked the pink nose and looked at the dark brown eyes of Luz. 'Thank you, Dylan. Would you give me a boost up, please?'

The squire looked to his master, uncertain, as it was Troye's place to assist his wife into the saddle, but Troye seemed much occupied with his own horse and tightening the girth. Dylan linked his hands and Eleanor placed her booted foot into them. With ease he threw her light weight up into the saddle, and Eleanor settled herself. While she sorted the reins Dylan vaulted on to his own horse, and leaned down to haul the maid Meg pillion behind him. Eleanor smiled as she noticed Meg blush and the way her arms settled around Dylan's waist. He gasped and gruffly begged her to loosen her grip. Once Lady Anne was settled on her own horse, a thick-set dun gelding well accustomed to his mistress, they set off on the short journey to York.

They followed a path from Fulford alongside the River Ouse, fording it where it was shallow. On the far bank they rode past the Bar Convent and entered the city by the Mickelgate Bar. The arched stone gateway was set with gate and portcullis, ready at a moment's notice to be closed in defence of the city, and the stout bartizans well positioned for archers to shoot their arrows through. It was guarded by several yeomanry soldiers, who checked all those who entered York, wary of Scots and Jews and lepers. Troye leaned over in his saddle towards Eleanor, quietly telling her not to look up, for there had been an execution recently and the head of the man guilty of rape and murder was displayed on the inner rampart, above the Bar.

Eleanor obeyed, and touched her heel to Luz as Troye urged the horses onwards down the cobbled road of Mickelgate. The Spanish horse proved true to her name and was indeed light. It was a pleasant day, sunny with a few clouds scudding against a pale blue sky and a soft breeze lifting the heat of summer; Eleanor felt her spirits lift. But with the breeze came the stench of the tanners and the dung heaps and the fish market alongside the quay on the river.

They crossed the river again over the Ouse Bridge and rode down the narrow streets until they came to a halt in Marketskyre. Here it was decided that Dylan would wait with the horses, much to Meg's chagrin as Lady Anne bade her to take her basket and follow her to the Butcher's Hall, where she would place an order for the feast to be held in honour of Troye and Eleanor's marriage.

Lady Anne gave to Eleanor a list of spices that she wanted, and another of ribbons and threads from the haberdashers. They agreed they would meet on the steps of the Minster one stroke after the noon hour. Troye urged Dylan to keep a good watch on the horses and not to wander away, to which his squire had great difficulty replying in a civil tone, aggrieved to miss out on accompanying the pretty little Meg about her errands.

Eleanor fell into step with Troye, who guided her along the narrow lanes to the first port of call, the haberdasher's. He waited outside while she went in and selected the items that Lady Anne wanted, pleasantly surprised by the choice and quality offered to her by the shopkeeper, a local lady who made polite enquiry and bade Eleanor welcome at the news that this was her first visit to York. With her purchases neatly wrapped in a square of felt, Eleanor bade farewell and went out the low door way into the street, where she found Troye conversing with a portly gentleman.

She stood at his elbow and waited, slowly becoming aware of the gentleman's stare. She looked up, and then Troye too paused as he noticed the direction of his companion's stare. Briskly he introduced them.

'Sir Malcolm Rix, High Sheriff of York, my lady wife, Eleanor.'

With great gusto Sir Malcolm bowed and kissed her hand as she offered it in polite acknowledgement of their introduction. 'Why, 'tis a great honour, my lady, to welcome you to our fine city, and what a privilege to meet such a beautiful lady. 'Tis lucky indeed you are, Sir Troye.'

'Quite.' Troye bowed, and then, grasping Eleanor's elbow, he led her away, almost with unseemly haste, it seemed to Eleanor.

She glanced back over her shoulder as Sir Malcolm called out, '*Adieu,* Lady de Valois, until we meet again at the wedding feast.'

Eleanor smiled, and almost stumbled on the rough cobbles, glancing up at Troye as he scowled and pulled her along. 'Is aught amiss, my lord?'

'The old lecher,' grunted Troye beneath his breath. 'He's had three wives already and killed them all. He'd do well to keep his eyes off the wives of other men.'

For several moments Eleanor was puzzled and a little embarrassed by Troye's reaction. Was he ashamed of her? She felt an angry flush colour her cheeks and neck and before she could stop herself, she had exclaimed, 'Mayhap my lord would prefer it if I wore a sack over my head?'

He glanced down at her, a speculative gleam in his

dark eyes at this possibility, and then, realising her jest, he replied, 'Don't be facetious.'

Eleanor tossed her head, jerking her arm free from his grasp. 'Well, I am very sorry that you are lumbered with such an ugly wife!'

Troye stopped in his tracks, and then, to her great surprise, he began to laugh, a soft, throaty sound that had been little used these few years past. 'You silly goose. I am sure you well know that you are a comely woman.'

'But—' Eleanor almost exploded at this insinuation that she was fishing for compliments, and it took great restraint on her part not to poke him in the ribs.

'I would prefer, however, if next time you go into the city your hair is covered. Such beauty is not for every Tom, Dick and Harry to look at.'

He had resumed his brisk stride and as they walked Eleanor suddenly realised, with a little glow that was most pleasant indeed, that Troye was jealous! Her heart suddenly lifted and the day seemed bright and full of hope. She much enjoyed the way Troye guided and protected her with his arm about her shoulders as they passed through the crowded streets, pushing aside any unsavoury characters that came too close. They walked out of the narrow confines of the shambles and made their way to the stall in the market where the spice seller had set up his wares. It did not take long to purchase cinnamon and nutmeg and mace, but in the square beyond they met several people who knew Troye of old and introductions again had to be made. Eleanor at last felt like their marriage was almost real, as he introduced her as his 'lady wife'.

Making their way to the Minster, they stopped to watch mummers performing a play in Sampson Square. It was all to do with fertility and was somewhat lewd, but Eleanor welcomed the way it made Troye smile, though her cheeks were quite blushing as they left the crowds standing about laughing and revelling in the story.

York was graced with over fifty churches, and now as one past the midday hour struck many bells clanged. The great, golden bulk of the Minster rose ahead of them and Eleanor waved as she spotted Lady Anne waiting on the steps.

'Where's Meg?' asked Eleanor. 'She is not lost, is she?'

'Nay…' Lady Anne smiled '…but I feel rather tired and I have sent her to fetch Dylan with the horses. It is so very hot today. Troye, I was not able to see the linen merchant, he has been delayed. Would you be so kind? He's not paid for the last shipment to Holland and I am not of a mind to convey any more for him until he does. They say he will return after dinner. Mayhap you and Eleanor could partake of the noon meal while you wait. Meg and I will return home, with Dylan.'

Troye turned to Eleanor. 'You may return home as well, if you wish. If you are tired?'

'Nay, I am very well,' assured Eleanor.

And Lady Anne added to her part in the scheme, insisting, 'I thought you might wish to show Eleanor around the Minster. Such a fine cathedral it is and people come from miles around to worship here. The shrine of St William draws many pilgrims.'

Eleanor craned her neck and looked up at the high walls so beautifully and ornately decorated with intricate stone work, murmuring that she would very much like the opportunity to pray at such a famous church. Dylan rode up then, with Lady Anne's horse on a lead rein and Meg pillion behind him. Troye was not best pleased to discover that the expensive Luz and his own destrier Merlin had been left in the stables of a nearby inn, and that he would have to pay a few marks for the services of the liveryman who kept a watchful eye on them. He sighed and muttered; his mother chided him for making fuss of nothing, but he had no choice other than to accept the situation, though he did so with little grace.

Lady Anne, fearing for her well-laid plan for Eleanor to spend some carefree time with her husband, sweetened the deal with an offer to fetch the horses at once, leaving Eleanor and Troye free to stroll home, for it was no great distance. This appealed to Troye even less and he waved his hand, dismissing the subject and urging his mother to make tracks homewards and take her rest.

'And be sure that Troye does not forget to feed you, Eleanor,' called Lady Anne as they wheeled their horses and set off for Fulford.

Eleanor smiled, waving as they departed and feeling a little nervous as she stood alone with Troye. She glanced cautiously up at his face, noting that his scowl had not lessened and inwardly full of trepidation for the afternoon. Clouds covered the sun and the wind lifted, whipping her cloak and her hair back. She shivered in its chill, and then asked softly, 'Shall we go inside?' nodding with her head towards the Minster.

'Aye.' He took her arm and together they mounted the steps and went in through the side door.

Eleanor looked about with great interest. She had never seen such a vast expanse of nave before, rising up to stained-glass windows set high above.

'The outside walls are some ninety feet,' supplied Troye in a quiet voice, 'and the interior is over five hundred feet long.'

'Indeed,' Eleanor murmured in reply, taking little heed of these facts and struck only by the painstaking workmanship and the wide, open, yet lofty space of the cathedral. It was very inspiring and she paused by a wrought-iron stand that held many candles. Here the faithful and the lost prayed for their tribulations, and Eleanor felt drawn to do the same. She knelt, and folded her palms together in prayer.

Troye stood to one side, looking away, for he had lost all faith in God. The death of Isabeau had robbed him of any notion that God was loving and just, for where was the justice and the kindness in taking Isabeau? Yet he turned and looked at Eleanor as she knelt, her head slightly bent and her eyes closed as she prayed. The flickering of many candles cast a gentle glow over her profile, gilding her auburn hair with a burnished halo. She looked angelic indeed, and yet his thoughts were far more intimate, as he remembered how she had looked naked, bathing, and how her body had felt lying beneath him... But these were not decent thoughts to have within the walls of a church, and he admonished himself harshly. Abruptly he walked away and went out into the sunlight.

Eleanor was lost in her own thoughts as she prayed. Within her mind she pleaded, 'St Jude, worker of miracles, please pray for me. St Jude, helper of the hopeless, pray for me, who am so alone and helpless. Amen.'

For a long while she stayed upon her knees, laying at God's feet all the pain and difficulties that her love for Troye had brought into her life, and begging for assistance. ''Tis too much for me to bear alone, O Lord. Please come to me in my present and urgent need. Amen.'

She opened her eyes then, crossed herself, and rose from her knees. She looked about, but could not see Troye. She would have liked to stay longer in the peace and grandeur of the cathedral, but, fearing that Troye might have abandoned her, went in search of him. Assuming that it was all too much for him, she rightly went to the main doors, out into the bright afternoon and down the steps, looking to left and to right. She found him leaning against the walls, eyes closed, waiting, though she doubted whether it was with any patience. She went up to him, and gently touched one of his arms, folded across his chest.

His eyes opened, and he looked down at her. Within their dark depths she saw much pain, and with a smothered moan she stood on tiptoe and reached up to kiss him, her arms sliding around the bulk of his shoulders as she urged him into the comfort of her embrace.

To her surprise, he yielded. His arms went around her slender back and they held each other. She pressed her cheek to his, the roughness of his shaven jaw harsh against her smooth skin, and then moved her head and blindly, tears crowding her eyes, found his mouth. She kissed him, with a gentleness that conveyed warmth and love and solace. His lips felt cool beneath her own, and did not respond to the pressure of her lips. Then, when she feared there was no hope, he relaxed, his hand sliding up to support the back of her neck as he opened his mouth to accept her kiss of comfort.

Aware that they were in a public place, she broke free, and whispered, 'Troye?'

'Hmm?'

'I am sorry about Isabeau.'

She felt him stiffen in her arms, his muscles bunch and bulk as he grasped her arms and held her away from him, stooping as he glared into her eyes. 'What do you know of Isabeau?'

'I—I…only what your mother has told me.' Warily she cringed, reluctant to recall the past and yet shrewdly aware that if they did not acknowledge it, talk about it, feel it, then the past would always stand as a barrier between them. 'Please do not be angry. Surely I have the right to know?'

'The right to know?' he demanded, giving her a little shake. 'Nay, you have no right. 'Tis none of your business. And I do not care for you to say her name.'

Eleanor gasped, shocked by the harshness of his words, and the pain they inflicted upon her inner heart. Yet her love for him was true and she could understand that he spoke out of his own pain, and not out of any need to be cruel to her. Instead of holding fast to him, she let go, bowing her head as she murmured an apology.

Troye felt the coolness of the wind swirl between

them as Eleanor stepped away, and as he looked upon her bowed face, her eyes hidden from him as her tear-spiked lashes swept down, he felt a twinge of remorse. He had often treated her harshly, like a bull stomping about in blind rage at the brutal pain inflicted on him. It dawned on him slowly, through the haze of his own sorrow, that there was no honour and no need for his manner to be so harsh towards Eleanor.

He placed thumb and forefinger beneath her chin and raised her face to him, smiling gently. 'Come, let us find some dinner. I don't know about you but I am starving.'

With great effort Eleanor summoned a fragile smile in return, and gladly placed her hand in his proffered one, as they turned away from the vast walls of the Minster and plunged into the narrow streets of the shops and merchants crowding alongside. Troye mused on a suitable place for their midday meal, aware that many of the public houses were full of rough peasants and soldiers and harlots, but Eleanor insisted that she was happy to purchase pasties and they could find a quiet spot to eat their meal *al fresco*.

They found a vendor in Coney Street and bought fresh-baked meat pies, and several smaller apple tarts, the pastry golden and crumbling and fragrant with cinnamon. Then Troye led her to a sheltered corner near St Mary's Abbey and they sat upon the grass to eat their meal.

Eleanor sat cross-legged like a girl, and Troye stretched out beside her. She laughed as dark gravy spilled from his meat pasty, and wiped his chin with her sleeve. He thanked her, and they ate in companionable quiet, making casual comment upon the weather and Eleanor's impressions of the city of York. After-dinner lethargy set in and they lay on the grass in the warm summer sunshine, and Eleanor hoped that her fervent prayers would be answered. For a short while at least Troye did not shut her out.

She was greatly tempted to seize the moment and ask him about the child, but then she feared to spoil the day with another bout of anger, so she held her tongue. At his urging she rose from the grass and followed him as they went to the linen merchant on the quay. She sat on an upturned barrel and watched the dark green, fast moving waters of the River Ouse slide by, while Troye went inside and talked business.

'Good day to you, pretty lady.'

Eleanor looked up as a shadow cast itself over her. Her eyes met shrewd black ones that darted about, inspecting Eleanor keenly, as well as their immediate surroundings. The nut-brown skin, hooped gold earrings and tiered skirts made of multi-coloured squares identified the woman as a gypsy, and she held out to Eleanor a sprig of white heather.

'For luck,' murmured the gypsy woman, with a beguiling smile.

Eleanor knew full well that to refuse white heather from a gypsy would only invite curses and bad fortune, so she reached for the leather pouched attached to her girdle and withdrew the smallest coin. She pressed it into the gypsy's hand and took the heather, hoping it would be enough to satisfy her and she would quietly depart, for Eleanor, like many English, had no great trust or fondness for gypsies.

For a moment it seemed that the gypsy would depart, but then she paused and picked up Eleanor's right hand and turned it over, gazing at her palm. She looked at Eleanor with eyes full of ancient wisdom.

'Aye, 'tis as I thought, my pretty little lady. You carry a great burden, yet your heart is steadfast and true. There is much pain—' She looked up quickly, as did Eleanor, at the sound of a deep male voice from the doorway of the building behind them.

'Be off with you!' called out the linen merchant. 'We'll not be having your sort round here to hassle good folks.'

'Fear not, all will be well,' the gypsy whispered urgently as she made to flee. 'Pain will turn to pleasure, if you remain patient and loyal.'

'Wait!' Eleanor sought for another coin from her pouch, and furtively pressed it into her palm as Troye and the linen merchant approached, the latter shouting and looking about for a weapon to belabour the gypsy with.

They exchanged a glance and a smile, and then Eleanor turned as Troye placed his hand on her shoulder in a protective gesture.

'Did she cause you any harm?' he asked, his eyes following the flashing heels and skirts of the gypsy woman as she ran away down the quayside. 'You should have called me.'

'Nay. Indeed, it was most interesting.' Eleanor smiled, recalling the words of the old Romany and tucking them away in a safe place in her mind, to be mulled over later.

Troye nodded, satisfied after a quick glance from head to toe that Eleanor was safe and sound, and then he turned his gaze to the lowering sun. 'Let us make for home. It has been a busy day and you look tired.'

Troye made his farewells to the linen merchant, and then led the way to the inn where the horses had been stabled. He was impatient to collect Luz and his own beloved Merlin and make sure that no harm had come to them either; Eleanor could not help but wonder if she rated above or below his concern for his animals. It had indeed been an eventful day for her and suddenly she longed to leave the noise and stench of the city and return to the peace and quiet of home. Eleanor acknowledged with a smile how quickly she had accepted the manor house in Fulford as her home.

The horses were lively, trotting out with tails held

high and snatching at the bit, their noses lifted and ears pricked as they scented home and the promise of a bucketful of feed. Luz pranced coyly beside the powerful destrier Merlin, forcing Eleanor to take a firm hand as the Spanish mare jibbed and broke into a canter without permission. When Eleanor pulled her back, Luz almost reared up on her back legs and she was hard pressed to keep her seat.

'Can you manage?' asked Troye with a frown. 'Let me put a lead rein on her.'

Eleanor laughed, and shook her head. 'She means no harm. I can manage her well enough.'

'Do not fall.' Troye scowled, giving Merlin a sharp reprimand and pulling him away from the overexcited Luz.

'I won't. I've been riding since I was a child.'

'Indeed.'

Eleanor glanced up at him, noticing his frown, and suddenly remembered Isabeau. She had taken a fall, and died. It was natural that Troye should fear such things happening again. Instead of enjoying the high spirits of Luz, she made it quite clear that her behaviour was not acceptable. Immediately the Spanish horse settled and dropped her nose, trotting along with docile submission. None the less, Eleanor was relieved when they reached the manor house and turned into the stable yard. Dylan came running out, Eleanor kicked her foot out of the stirrup and made

ready to jump down, but instead of the squire, Troye
came to assist her.

Troye was taller and more muscular than Dylan and
she had no qualms as she jumped down into his arms.
He held her for a moment, their eyes meeting, and
then he set her down upon her feet.

'Thank you,' she murmured. 'It has been a very
pleasant day.'

He bowed, and smiled, and they both turned at the
sound of raised voices, one most matronly and the
other a high-pitched squeal. Around the hedge
dividing the stable yard from the gardens came
running at full speed a small child, her skirts lifted in
both hands and a spaniel leaping at her side.

'Come back here, you little scamp,' panted the
woman, who Eleanor concluded must be the nurse.
'You know full well you are not allowed—'

'Papa!' shrieked the child, and flung herself into
Troye's arms.

The stout nurse came to a halt, her wimple flapping
and her cheeks quite reddened and wobbling from the
unaccustomed exercise. She clucked her tongue and
made an apology to Troye, her eyes sliding away in
a most guilty manner as Eleanor tried to bestow upon
her a smile.

'No matter.' Troye leaned down and caught the
child about her tiny waist, throwing her up in the air,
much to the little girl's giggling delight. Then he

settled her in the crook of his arm and turned to Eleanor. 'There is someone I would like you to meet. This little baggage is my daughter, Joan.'

Chapter Ten

The child stared back at Eleanor with doe-brown eyes, her long dark hair neatly braided into a single plait, tendrils escaping about her pretty little face.

Eleanor smiled, but when she reached out to touch the child on her hand she wriggled and kicked to be free of Troye's clasp. He set her down on her feet and at once she went to the dog, clutching his collar and holding him protectively to her. Eleanor recognised them both, the features of the little girl were the same as the woman in her dream and in the portrait, and the little dog, she was sure, must be the same spaniel.

Troye cleared his throat, feeling awkward, uncertain how to explain Eleanor's presence, nor her position in their lives, having little understanding of it himself. He proceeded with the facts, and naught else. 'Joan, this is my wife. You may call her Lady Eleanor.'

The little girl pouted and hugged her dog with one

plump arm around his neck, and though Eleanor made to protest at so formal a title, by what other name could she be called? The child already had a mother, one that was much loved, and she had no wish to usurp that.

She bent at the waist and held out her hand to the little girl. 'How do you do, Lady Joan? I am very pleased to meet you.' Joan stared at her solemnly, hiding her hands behind her back, so Eleanor knelt on one knee and fondled the silky golden ears of the spaniel, who welcomed her gentle touch, wagging his tail and licking her hand, 'And what is the name of your companion?'

'He's Toby…' she glanced up at her father '…he's a very good dog.'

'I'm sure he is.' Eleanor smiled, her frown directed at Troye and his mild snort of exasperation.

Joan looked up at Eleanor, seeing in her childish innocence only a lady who was fair and kind. Toby reached out with a black twitching nose to sniff at Eleanor's legs. He thumped his tail and the little girl grinned. 'Toby likes you.'

Eleanor patted the dog's head and then stood up. 'Shall we go inside? I believe Meg will have some nice cool milk for us to drink.'

Joan hopped up and down at this pleasant thought, and then fell into step with Eleanor as they turned towards the kitchen door, 'And cinnamon biscuits. Me helped make 'em.'

'Hmm…' Eleanor smiled '…my favourite.' As they walked she wondered at Joan's age, guessing that she must be at least five.

As if sensing her query, Troye murmured, 'She was a honeymoon baby.' He stood back and let Eleanor and his daughter enter the house ahead of him, following in their wake into the hall and standing by the fire hearth to watch as Joan ran to her grandmother. Lady Anne sat in a chair by the light of a window with a pile of linen on her lap, sewing a new shift for the fast-growing young Joan.

The tableau of his mother, his wife, and his daughter was one so familiar to him that he felt the stirring of an ache in his chest. The pain of it was so great that he turned away and stared down at the cold, grey, silent stones of the hearth. But he could still hear them. His mother's even, stoic tones, Joan's piping, breathless chatter, and the soft voice of Eleanor. He listened to her voice, so gentle and sweet, yet aware there was a note of uncertainty. How could he have ever doubted that Eleanor would be anything except kind to his daughter? And how could he have doubted that to see another woman act as mother to Isabeau's child was going to be anything less than agony?

Glancing across the room, Eleanor noticed his stricken expression, and guessed the reason why he had kept Joan from her all this time. Her heart ached as she realised that he had not intended to hurt her by denying her the privileges of stepmotherhood, but only to protect himself from pain.

'Troye?' Eleanor took a step towards him, but he turned away from her.

He felt like he couldn't breathe, that his heart and his lungs and his ribs were so constricted with a physical pain that he would surely die. Abruptly, without saying a word to anyone, he walked from the hall.

'Troye!' Eleanor called, and would have run after him, but Lady Anne urged her to leave him be.

Troye went outside, into the garden, and breathed in great gulps of cool evening air. But still that was not enough. The hurt was burning and raw in his chest. He ran then, through the stable yard, and along the riverbank. His legs pounded, rising up and down, his hands thrashing aside long fronds of grass and reeds growing alongside the path. He ran and ran until he was far from the manor and too exhausted to run any more. His feet shuffled wearily as he slowed to a walk, little realising where it was that he went, until he came to the gate of the church yard. He moved as if in a dream, and went to the far corner where few ever paused. Panting and sweating, he flung himself down on the ground beside her grave, one word escaping in a choked whisper from his throat.

'Isabeau.'

Even after all this time he missed her so much. He dreamed of her at night, dreams so vivid and real that it seemed he held her in his arms, only to awaken to reality and the grief that left him cold and empty. He raised his eyes to the inscription on the headstone, and vowed to Isabeau that he would always love and cherish her. And yet, he remembered the nights with Eleanor in his bed, and the pleasant afternoon that he had just spent with her in York, when he had almost forgotten his grief. Now he felt racked with guilt. How could he ever love anyone except Isabeau?

Lady Anne bade supper be served without Troye. It was the custom for Joan to eat with her nurse in the bedchamber the two occupied in the furthest wing of the manor house, but in the absence of her father Joan begged to sit up at the table, and Lady Anne saw no reason to demur. Eleanor smiled gently at the child as she insisted on sitting next to her, and watched her with big eyes throughout the meal. They spoke little and Eleanor struggled to put on a brave face. At its end the nurse came and carried her away, Joan little protesting as she yawned and laid her head on the broad shoulder of her nurse, sucking her thumb and waving to Eleanor as they climbed the stairs.

Eleanor waved and called goodnight, and then turned to the table and helped Meg to clear the dishes.

Though the maid protested, Eleanor sought to find any little task that would keep her busy, for if she was to pause for even a moment, and dwell on Troye, then her resolve would break and she would start to panic at Troye's continued absence.

On this summer evening the light stayed until quite late. The servants finished in the kitchen and took themselves off to their own rooms behind the pantry, and together Eleanor and Lady Anne sat in companionable silence. The windows were open and they could hear the evensong of blackbirds and a cuckoo. When it became too dark to see their sewing, Eleanor lit a candle and at Lady Anne's request she took down the family Bible from where it was kept on a shelf and opened it upon her knee, drawing the candle a little closer to see the small, handwritten words.

'Read to me Corinthians, chapter one, verse thirteen.'

Eleanor rifled through the pages, until she found the passage Lady Anne wanted to hear.

'…if I speak in the tongues of men and of angels, but have not love, I am only a resounding gong or a clanging cymbal. If I have the gift of knowledge, and if I have a faith that can move mountains, but have not love, I am nothing.' Eleanor's voice slowed and faltered. She felt the thick burn of tears in her eyes and throat and nose, but she swallowed them back and carried on. 'If I give all I possess to the poor and surrender my body to the flames, but have not love, I gain nothing. Love is patient, love is kind. It does not envy, it does not boast, it is not proud. It is not rude, it is not self-seeking, it…is…' Eleanor's voice cracked then, as tears flowed freely and dripped down her cheeks '…it is not easily angered, it keeps no record of wrongs. Love does not delight in evil, but rejoices with the truth. It always protects, always trusts, always hopes, always perseveres. Love never fails.'

She sobbed on the final words, and in defeat pressed her face into the palm of her hand. Lady Anne rose from her chair and went to her. She patted Eleanor on the shoulder and hugged her close to her midriff in a gesture of comfort. She did not try to stop Eleanor's tears, but let her weep. Then, as she quietened, sniffing and gulping, Lady Anne asked gently, 'Do you love Troye?'

Eleanor nodded, unable to speak.

'Then be patient. Be kind. He punishes himself now, for what happened to Isabeau, and his heart is broken into a thousand pieces. It's been a few years, but mourning has no allotted time span. He misses her still, he cannot accept that she is gone, but one day the truth will become reality. He will come to you then and he will need your love.'

'How can I be sure of that?' Eleanor sobbed, hardly believing that such a thing could be possible. 'It may be that he will never want me.'

Lady Anne shrugged. 'How can we be sure of anything in this life? I know 'tis hard to find faith and little comfort on lonely nights, but try.' She stooped and kissed Eleanor on the top of her head. 'Troye will not be home tonight. Go you now to bed.'

Eleanor looked up then, on the tip of her tongue the fearful question as to where Troye would be, and anxious that she wait up for him. But she was exhausted, both emotionally and physically, and she nodded her head in agreement and rose from her chair.

Lady Anne watched as Eleanor climbed the stairs, her fragile shoulders bowed and her footsteps slow and weary. With a sigh Lady Anne turned then, and called to Dylan, who waited in the shadows, as he always did.

He came forwards now, into the light. 'My Lady?'

'Go to your master. See to it that he makes his way safely home.'

Dylan bowed, knowing full well that he would find Troye at the castle in York, where he sought the company of other knights, or if not there, then in one of the city taverns, most likely the Golden Fleece. He went on foot—it was a pleasant evening and no great distance, and less chance of being set upon by thieves and ruffians if he left the horses in their stable.

Times were quiet and the city gates stood open, yet were still guarded. He crossed the bridge and went first to the castle, but no one had seen Troye that eve.

Dylan made his way through the narrow cobbled streets to the Golden Fleece. He found Troye sat in a snug at the back of the tavern, with his head bowed over a mug of wine. His master had never had a great fondness for the vine, and usually it didn't take long for him to become drunk. Dylan sat down and unwrapped his cloak, glancing sideways.

'What are you looking at, boy?' growled Troye, taking another swig of the strong Burgundy that made his tongue curl but dulled, in a small measure, the pain that ached within him.

'Naught, sir.' Dylan leaned his elbows on the table and glanced about, taking note of the other customers and any potential troublemakers. It was busy and noisy with yeomanry who would march as foot soldiers with the King to Scotland.

Troye grunted. 'I suppose my mother sent you trotting after me.'

'Aye. She knows well enough you gone off to get ratted.'

'Watch your tongue, boy. I'm sufficiently unratted to give you a lesson in respect for your master.'

Dylan's eyebrows rose and he cast Troye a sceptical glance. He nodded at the mug of wine. 'How many have you had, my master?'

'Too many to count, and too few to make a difference.'

'Have you had any supper?'

''Tis not food in my belly I want.'

'We had good fodder this evening,' Dylan mused with a tone of fond remembrance. 'Chicken and ham pie, with stewed apples and plums in custard for afters. Lady Anne keeps a good table.'

Troye scowled and hunched over his wine, clicking his fingers at the innkeeper as he ordered another skinful. It was brought over by a maid, a loose woman with low-cut bodice and coarse features, who was not averse to supplementing her income in the alley behind the tavern. She leaned over Troye, her eyes inviting as she made sure her full breasts displayed plenty of cleavage.

Dylan gave her a shove. 'Clear off.'

The barmaid pouted and flounced away, throwing over her shoulder an aggrieved glance at Dylan. But he cared nothing for the tender feelings of a harlot, and was much more concerned with getting his master home before the hour waned and all manner of ill stalked the midnight streets.

''Tis a warm and comfortable bed that awaits you, sir,' he dropped the gentle hint.

Troye grunted. He would not confess to his squire that it was the comforts of his bed that kept him away. Yet he found he had no taste for more wine. Rising abruptly, he tossed a few coins upon the table. Dylan followed, taken aback by this sudden departure and apparent change of heart.

As soon as the fresh night air hit Troye's lungs, so did a violent nausea. He doubled over in a nearby gutter and lost the contents of his stomach, reeling as Dylan assisted him on the long walk home. But once there he could not face climbing the stairs, nor Eleanor asleep in the bed that once he had shared with another. Instead he slept in the kitchen, rolled in his cloak beside the warm hearth and the fire that never went out, watched over by the faithful Dylan.

In the morning, he rose and went out into the yard to dip his head in a bucket of cold water, shaking it off and stretching in the cool morning air. Then he returned to the kitchen and sat down at the scrubbed and scarred table as Jarvis the cook and Meg the maid tiptoed around him.

'Bring me something to ease the parch in my throat,' he snapped at anyone luckless enough to be within earshot.

Without a word Jarvis plonked a jug of milk in front of his lord, and turned swiftly away. Troye grimaced as he drank the warm liquid, and contemplated whether he would do best outside in case his stomach rebelled. Just as he rose his mother appeared in the doorway, and her glance was enough to make him sit down again.

Lady Anne folded her arms about her waist and fixed her son with a stern glance. 'And what do you have to say for yourself this morn?'

'Good morning, Mother.'

She clucked her tongue, with a little shake of her head, both of them knowing full well the meaning of her words. She took a few steps forwards, and placed her hand on Troye's shoulder. 'How long will this go on?'

'What?'

'How long will you punish yourself?'

He scowled and ignored her.

'It's been years, Troye. Nothing you do will change the past. Nothing will bring Isabeau back—'

'Don't!' he warned.

'I cannot sit back and say nothing, watch you tear yourself to pieces. And what of Eleanor? The poor child has done nothing to warrant such treatment. She loves you, you know.'

'Be quiet, Mother,' Troye all but snarled, rising from his chair, shaking off her restraining hand. 'Leave me be.'

'Troye—' She followed him as he marched out into the stable yard, but checked him with one firm hand on his forearm. 'You must take responsibility for your wife. If you cannot live with her in affection, then this marriage must be annulled. Eleanor is a lovely young woman—'tis a cruelty to condemn her for life to a loveless marriage. Do you have no feeling for her at all?'

He closed his eyes, for a moment, and then walked

away from the manor house, to the garden, where it was more private and he could be sure they would not be overheard. Lady Anne followed, and waited, as he struggled to find the right words, to sort through the tangle of emotions in his mind and his heart. At last, in a low, anguished voice he said, 'It is not that I have no feeling for Eleanor. Indeed, she is much like Isabeau, sweet and gentle and pretty. But it hurts, Mother, it hurts too much. And I feel guilty. How can I stop loving Isabeau?'

Gently Lady Anne stroked his cheek. 'A part of you will always love Isabeau. That is as it should be. She was your wife, she is Joan's mother. But that was then, and this is now. You are not the same man that you were then, and there will never be another Isabeau. If you were to love another it would be in a different way, and you should feel no shame or guilt for that. Don't punish yourself for feeling happy. Your marriage vows were made until death do you part. There is no sin if you were to love again.'

Troye stared at her. There was much for him to consider in her words, too much for his consciousness to understand. Yet he nodded, and she let him go. They went their separate ways—Lady Anne returning to the house and chivvying her household into its daily chores, and Troye to rouse Dylan and set about his duty in training the young lad to knighthood.

* * *

For several days they went about their business as though life was idyllic and there was no torment, yet of them all it was Eleanor who was the most anguished by the atmosphere clouded with tension. At night she slept alone, and during the day she tried to exhaust herself by keeping busy.

A week after her pleasant day in York with Troye, which no doubt he had found to be not to his taste, judging from his avoidance of her, Eleanor rose as usual and sat on the coffer by the window. She stared out idly, her brush in one hand, hardly able to find the energy to sweep it through the long length of her hair. But she looked up at the jingle of harness and the clop of horses' hooves. Below Troye swung two bulging saddlebags on Merlin's back, and then vaulted up into the saddle. He glanced up and saw Eleanor. Their eyes met. Eleanor felt her blood run cold and she rose from her seat, leaning towards the window. But before she could open it and call out to Troye, he raised his hand in a gesture of farewell, wheeled Merlin about and rode off.

With a small cry, she ran to the door; it opened before she reached it and Lady Anne checked her headlong rush.

'He leaves me!' Eleanor cried, staring up at her mother-in-law, confused and distraught.

'Hush, now, do not overset yourself. Aye, he leaves, but not for long. He goes to Antwerp to deliver a shipment of wool and linen. We have had some trouble with the Brabants and Troye goes to deal with it. Have no fear, he will return in a week or so.'

'He did not say goodbye!'

Gently Lady Anne stroked the tendrils of hair from Eleanor's brow. 'Aye, but forgive him for that. He is as much troubled as you are. It will do you both some good to have time apart.'

Eleanor could not agree with her sentiment and abruptly tore out of Lady Anne's arms and returned to her seat by the window. She sat down and stared out at the empty space where only a few moments ago Troye had been. She would not see him for a whole week! How would she survive? What would he do while he was gone? Would he find other women to console himself with? When he returned, would the separation have done him so much good that he would want it to be permanent? All these thoughts and many more ran riot in her mind, yet she sat silent and still, her face pale, her eyes dull as she stared blankly.

Lady Anne was much concerned at the effect on Eleanor. Matters of the heart were always a great strain even on the strongest person, and to her mind Eleanor seemed increasingly fragile. She felt the answer was to keep her busy, and most especially that Eleanor and Joan should spend much more time together. After all, as her grandmother, Lady Anne was not growing any younger and the child would need the presence and guidance of a lady in her life as she grew up.

Briskly Lady Anne brushed her hands together and stepped towards the door. 'Now, there's much to be done and I am no longer as young or agile as I was. Meg, bless her, does her best, but I would welcome another pair of strong hands to help me. The butter needs churning, if you are willing?'

She looked at Eleanor expectantly. Her smooth, patrician features belied the age that Lady Anne claimed, but Eleanor realised, with a blush of shame, that her mother-in-law must be in the twilight of her years as Troye neared middle age. Manual labour was not something Eleanor was used to, having always had servants to perform any task she ordered, but now she welcomed the respite of chores that would distract her from her thoughts.

'Aye, my lady,' Eleanor whispered. 'I am willing.'

The day passed quickly, in the coolness of the small buttery alongside the kitchen. Her shoulders and hands ached as she helped to churn the butter and to skim the previous day's curds, placing spoonfuls in muslin and hanging it up from the rafters for the whey to drip out. Lady Anne spoke little, directing Eleanor in a quiet voice, but in the background she could hear the chatter of Meg and a strapping young lad by the name of Simon, as blond as Meg was dark.

Later that afternoon she played with Joan in the garden, a game of fetch with a soft ball made from rags, and Toby joined in with gleeful delight. When Joan grew tired they sat upon the grass in the shade of an oak tree and drank cool apple juice.

Joan looked at Eleanor and said, 'My father has gone away again.'

'Aye...' Eleanor smiled gently at the child '...but he will soon be home.'

A look of sadness filled Joan's large brown eyes, and Eleanor felt her heart miss a beat at such a look on a young child. 'I had a mother, but I don't 'member her. She went away too.'

Eleanor patted her tiny little shoulder. 'Your father will be home, I promise.'

Joan rose from where she sprawled on the grass and scrambled on to Eleanor's lap. She leaned against her breast, her eyes closing as she settled trustingly into a comfortable position. Eleanor was much bemused, unfamiliar with the weight and warmth of a small child upon her lap. But it felt so natural and so right that she sat up and placed her arms around Joan, hugging her gently, and leaned back against the oak tree's trunk, as she too surrendered to the bliss of an afternoon nap.

From within the manor house, Lady Anne glanced up from her never-ending sewing and looked out the window. She saw Eleanor with Joan asleep upon her lap, and smiled. In the course of the next few days she found that her bones ached most wearily and pleaded with Eleanor for her help on many an errand.

On one such afternoon, as Eleanor strolled through the cobbled streets to the market to buy dried figs and raisins, with Simon as her escort, she resolved to find an apothecary and see if he had any potions that might help relieve Lady Anne from her discomfort. She had been much bound to the house lately and Eleanor was concerned, especially as Lady Anne did not strike her as one that gave in easily to the slightest ache. They crossed Samson Square towards the market, and Eleanor looked up as a party of horsemen clattered by. Simon drew her back, with a protective yet respectful hand upon her elbow.

'My lady,' he murmured by her ear, 'the city is teeming with soldiers and mercenaries. Let us be done with our business and hurry home.'

Eleanor nodded, but smiled at Simon's concern. 'Have no fear, they are English knights, here to protect our realm from the Scots.'

Simon shook his head at her naïveté, 'Aye, but they are not all chivalrous knights, and not all English. 'Tis no place for a lady at such times.'

Looking about, Eleanor noted that though the streets were crowded, teeming with all manner of people as they hurried about their business, indeed there were few ladies of her class abroad, and for good reason.

'They say the King has mobilised an army bigger than when he went to Wales,' Simon told her, 'at least thirty thousand, but many of these will desert. And they will seek wine and women before making their way homewards.' Again Simon urged her to hurry.

They went into the market and Eleanor spent little time perusing the many colourful stalls, heading straight for the seller of dried fruits—raisins and figs from Sicily, apricots from Turkey—making her purchases swiftly. She abandoned the idea of finding an apothecary as the afternoon waned and Simon was eager to head home. They headed for Coppergate; as Eleanor glanced up, across the mass of shifting bodies and faces, there was one that caught her eye. She looked, hardly believing her eyes, and then peered harder as she looked again. Such distinctive shaved blond hair and piercing blue eyes, the stern facial structure and the swaggering arrogance, all were not easily mistaken—Casper von Eckhart! Her instinctive reaction was to clutch at Simon's sleeve.

He turned, looking about at her consternation. 'What is it, my lady?'

'That man—' Eleanor searched through the throng,

but von Eckhart had disappeared. 'No matter.' Smothering a gasp, Eleanor resolved to tell Troye as soon as he returned, and she needed no second bidding from Simon to hasten home.

Once home, Eleanor soon forgot about the Hun, as she settled into the routine of daily chores and amusing Joan, who was still fretful at the absence of her father.

A few days later, Eleanor had cause to go in search of Meg to assist her with the shelling of peas. Jarvis had sent the maid out to the hen-coop to gather eggs. It was late afternoon and the day had been very warm, yet now the cool shadows came as a welcome relief. Eleanor made her way to the hen-coop, but there was no sign of Meg. She retraced her footsteps, and then paused as she thought she heard the sound of Meg's voice in the barn. She went into the dim, hay-filled barn and glanced about, and then she heard a giggle, and the deep sound of Simon's voice. Thinking that the bailiff must be helping Meg with her egg collecting, she took a few more steps, and then stopped. Simon was certainly helping Meg, but in a way that made Eleanor blush. The young man lay sprawled on several bales of hay, with Meg sitting astride him.

'So you promise you'll never make eyes at that Dylan again,' Simon said in a low voice.

Meg laughed and leaned down towards him. 'Aye, it's you I love, Simon.'

Her bodice was open, revealing full breasts tipped with taut pink nipples.

'God, but you're a pretty wench, Meg,' Simon groaned as he reached with one hand to grasp her breast, sighing and moaning as Meg moved on top of him.

Her cheeks flaming, Eleanor backed away, with quick yet stealthy footsteps. She departed from the barn, all but running as she went out into the yard and then into the garden and there she sat down upon the bench. She should be very angry and give Meg a piece of her mind. What if Joan had wandered in? Yet it was not anger that Eleanor felt, but envy. Clearly the two young people had been engaged in an act of mutual pleasure, abandoned and carefree, and judging from the sounds that Simon had made, he enjoyed it very much. How she wished that Troye would moan and groan like that when he made love to her! But was that not the very crux of the matter? Troye had never made love to her. Their couplings had been merely the physical union of male and female. Eleanor resisted the temptation to dissolve into tears, for she had never been a girl to resort to tears at the merest trouble, and lately far too often she had been yielding to the urge. From here on, Troye de Valois would never again make her cry! Standing up resolutely, she made her way back to the manor house, and never said a word about what she had seen in the barn.

On Saturday evening, Troye returned home. He seemed weary, and yet in good spirits. As he walked through the door, Eleanor rose from her chair, and went to greet him. How she had missed him, and she had almost forgotten how very handsome he was! He stooped and kissed her on the cheek, in much the same way as he kissed his mother, and little Joan, who ran with a gleeful squeal to her father. Troye lifted her and embraced his daughter, before setting her down on her feet and accepting a glass of wine from his mother as they discussed his dealings with Antwerp.

They ate supper in good spirits, and Lady Anne mentioned that the High Sheriff had called in his absence. Troye glanced at Eleanor, but she did not notice as she helped Joan pick burrs from Toby's golden fur.

'What did he want?' Troye asked.

'He has news of the King. The Exchequer has established itself in York and a great army has been mobilised to march on Scotland before winter.'

Troye sighed. 'So, it is definite then, we are to war again?'

Lady Anne looked at him askance. 'Surely the King will not ask you to ride with him? Not after your campaign in Wales two summers ago?'

Eleanor looked up then, her heart beat slowing as she waited for Troye's answer.

Yet Troye merely shrugged. 'I am in his service. If he commands me to fight against the Scots, then I must do so. As a serjeant-at-arms we are few in numbers and there will be much need for cavalry against the likes of the Scots, who are just as savage, if not more so, than the Welsh.'

'But—' Eleanor made to protest, closing her mouth at Lady Anne's frown behind Troye's back. With her husband newly returned after his absence, she had no wish to encourage dissent. She rose from where she knelt upon the floor with Joan, and murmured, 'I bid you goodnight, Lady Anne.'

'Goodnight, my child.'

Eleanor, having waited so patiently, and her fears stronger than her modesty, she looked at her husband. 'Troye?'

Realising what she meant, and aware that he had indeed missed Eleanor in the week past, he coloured slightly under his mother's gaze and murmured, 'I will be there anon. Joan, 'tis time you were abed.'

'Carry me, Papa,' Joan demanded, climbing on to her father's lap.

He made much of his complaints, but smiled as he carried her upstairs, while Eleanor followed and went to her own bedchamber. There she hurriedly washed and dressed in her prettiest nightshift, the one with the pink ribbons, and brushed out her hair. Then she climbed into bed and lay upon her side, facing the window, with the covers pulled up close to her shoulder even though it was a warm evening and the light was soft as twilight faded. She waited anxiously, wondering when—if—Troye came to bed she should turn and encourage him, or if she should keep herself to herself and not bother him. She was so torn, between a desire to love him wholeheartedly and with all the warm, vibrant passion in her soul, and to leave him be in peace until he was ready. The day that Lady Anne had spoken of, when he would be ready to turn to her and accept her love, seemed very far off indeed. A great ache of loneliness weighted her chest and as the moments slipped away it seemed that Troye would not come.

Just as her eyelids were starting to droop and her body relax for sleep, she heard the click of the door. She did not turn, but lay still, listening to the sound of his boots dropping on the floor and the rustle of his clothes as he stripped. Then a moment of quiet, followed by the splash of water in the bowl as he washed. The covers lifted, she steeled herself, the mattress dipping as he climbed in. She sensed, rather than saw, that he lay upon his back, and that after a while he turned his head in her direction.

Troye looked at the pale glimmer of Eleanor's bare

shoulder. Her long hair appeared dark in the evening light. It seemed to him, through the dim shadows, that he could almost fool himself that he lay with…but nay, he closed his eyes and his mind on such a thought…it was not right, nor fair, to always compare Eleanor to another. And yet he did…her skin, her body, her hair, her voice, her scent…all were Isabeau, her impression left upon his mind as surely as if she lay beside him now. He stared up at the canopy of the bed for what seemed like an eternity. He could hear the easy breathing of Eleanor. He guessed that she must be asleep, and he leaned forwards to take a closer look. From the soft amber glow of light of the window he could faintly discern the glisten of tears upon her cheek. With a silent and inward groan, Troye realised that once again he had hurt her.

'Eleanor?' he murmured, rolling towards her, pressing his chest close against her back.

Her eyelids fluttered, but she made no sound, and indeed hunched away from him.

'I'm sorry,' he whispered, and he pressed a kiss to the soft, smooth skin of her shoulder.

Eleanor woke then, at the gentle touch of his lips on her skin, the feel of his body pressed against her back. She opened her eyes a little, the lashes lowered, but she did not turn around, or encourage him. Her heart felt too heavy within her, knowing that he had no feeling for her. And yet he was her husband, and she could neither refuse him, nor had any desire to, as his hand slid over the curve of her hip.

His kisses found the vulnerable spot behind her neck, and trailed across her back, between her shoulders, the heat and moistness of his tongue arousing her, the feel of his breath and his lips drawing from within her a response. And yet still she did not turn, nor did he ask her to face him. His fingers slid up under her shift, stroking the slender length of her thigh, brushing his fingertips with lingering gentleness. His hand moved direction and found the soft swell of her buttocks. He squeezed and kneaded her flesh, and she gave a little gasp. As he kissed her spine and fondled her buttocks, his knee nudged her thighs apart, raising her one leg slightly above the other so that he would have access to her womanhood from behind. Eleanor felt her heart drum and desire flare in that secret place, the place that only he had ever known, his to do with as he wished, his fingers moving in a slow sensuous movement, circling the entrance to her body. His manhood was hard and eager, pressing against her back, and her hips moved, undulating to the insistent rhythm of his finger. His other hand slid around her, beneath her ribs, and reached up to cup her breast, teasing her nipple and squeezing the mound of soft flesh in the palm of his hand. Eleanor groaned, and Troye pulled her into the middle of the bed, lifting her shift up above her waist, kissing the small of her back, her buttocks, biting her gently, feeling the contrast of rough hair and silky, moist flesh between her legs. His breath came in heavy pants, pleasure gripping him. He spread her legs and raised her up slightly, thrusting with his manhood. Eleanor smothered a cry, taken by surprise as he entered her from behind. He held her firmly, thrusting gently and slowly, and she was curiously aroused and felt excitement grip her as never before. And yet she wanted to see him, to look on his face, her eyes meet his eyes, so she made a murmur of protest and his rhythm slowed. He withdrew, yet kissed her neck, her cheek, the corner of her mouth, aware that he had never done it like this with Isabeau and somehow, for the first time in months, he felt pleasure that was intense and real, not something he was trying to force himself to feel. He whispered in Eleanor's ear, 'Your bottom feels so nice. I want to take you like this, if you are willing.'

Eleanor felt the heat of a fierce blush sweep over her, startled by his words, he who never spoke during coupling. Yet she could not deny the joy she felt at his words, nor the sensuous pleasure that erupted. He dominated her, possessed her, totally, and she gloried in that. She could not deny him, nor herself, and though it niggled her that it was not quite right she gave in, accepting his fingers as they slid between her thighs and moved up higher, brushing gently yet insistently, arousing, until her hips rocked and strained. Her skin flared with damp moisture, hot and sudden, as his fingers found her swollen bud and tenderly encouraged her arousal, until she did not want gentle or tender, but for him to take her, with all the fierce male ardour that was his.

'Troye—' Eleanor gasped for breath, struggling to say his name, caught up in the heat of the moment, as was he.

'I want to take you,' he murmured in her ear, his broad back covering the slender expanse of her shoulders and waist, her bottom a delicious mound of womanly flesh clenching and quivering beneath his powerful male body. 'Eleanor?'

'Aye,' she gasped, almost faint with desire and her need for him. He groaned as he carefully eased inside her, slowly, savouring the pleasure of her body, then he thrust faster, his hands gripping her hips and holding her tight. Eleanor felt great waves of pleasure building inside her, and she cried out his name, 'Troye!'

He gasped and panted, but made no reply, thrusting hard and fast.

She wanted to lie upon her back and wrap her legs around him, to feel her breasts against his chest, to draw him into her embrace, to feel the intimacy of his heart beating on her heart, and yet she knew that it would soon be over and though she had enjoyed their coupling it was still not lovemaking in the truest sense of the word. The flare of desire ebbed too soon, and a moment later she felt him relax, having spent his seed within her. He sighed, and rolled away, on to his back, catching his breath as though exhausted. In that moment, as disappointment and anger crushed her, she did not know whether she loved Troye, or hated him.

Chapter Eleven

Eleanor pulled down her shift and sought anxiously to think of something to say to Troye, pretending as he did, that nothing had happened. There were moments when they seemed so close to finally reaching some sort of meeting point, common ground, where the past could not reach them. But more often, like now, it seemed they were so far distant that it was entirely hopeless. Her prayers to St Jude seemed to have come to naught. And then she remembered her sighting of Casper von Eckhart, and she turned about, aware that Troye lay motionless, but not asleep. He seemed as much troubled by their relations as she, but she doubted he would be willing to discuss the matter and she feared confronting him, lest he should leave her again.

'Troye?'

'Hmm?'

She inched a little closer, 'A few days ago I saw Casper von Eckhart.'

'What!' He turned his head swiftly in her direction, raising himself up on one elbow as he looked at her in the fast fading light, 'Where? He did not come here to the house?'

'Nay—' Eleanor shook her head '—it was in the city, near the market. It was only for a moment, and I do not think he saw me.'

He subsided, lying down again and clasping his hands behind his head. He stared up at the ceiling, and then said firmly, 'I want you to stay close by the house from now on. In a few weeks we'll be away to Scotland, but until then the city is out of bounds. 'Tis not safe for womenfolk.'

'But—'

'No buts, Eleanor. I will speak to my mother in the morning. She has said you have been of great help to her while I was away, and for that I thank you, but any errands in the city can be done by Simon or that lazy lump of lard Jarvis. Is that clear, Eleanor?'

'Aye.' She nodded her head, and then asked him the question that had often puzzled her. 'Why do you think he is in York?'

Troye shrugged, with a sigh, and turned on to his side to face her. 'The King has hired many mercenaries, he is in great need of cavalry. His wrath is fearsome, but when it suits him he is just as quick to forgive. No doubt he has taken the Hun back into the fold to suit his own purpose.' In the gloom he searched her face. 'You are not afeared?'

'Nay, I doubt he means me any harm.'

Troye nodded in agreement. 'You are now my wife. He would not dare so much as look at you.'

Eleanor smiled at the hint of a growl in his voice. 'And would you fight for my honour if he did?'

'Well, not just for looking—'

She chuckled. 'If he tried to touch me? Kiss me?'

'Then I would kill him!'

They both laughed, softly. Lying so close to Troye, murmuring their conversation, sharing a joke, almost like a normal man and wife, it felt so good and so right. She longed to reach out, stroke her fingers over the hairs on his chest, kiss his biceps that bulged so close, but she did not dare. The only fear she harboured now was that he would shut her out if she came too close. It cost her dear, but she turned away, rolling over on to her other side, and facing the window. 'Goodnight, Troye.'

'Goodnight.'

He lay awake for a long while, and though he was tired sleep seemed to elude him. He had many thoughts on his mind: preparations for the march on Scotland, his mother's mysteriously failing health, the news that von Eckhart lurked in the city, and, most importantly, his failure to satisfy Eleanor. But tomorrow was another day, and it would help nothing to lie awake worrying. He felt relaxed, satisfied, after... He felt heat flush his face as he glanced at Eleanor—he should not have taken a young and inexperienced bride like that, yet they had both enjoyed it, hadn't they? And it had been a long while since he had felt such raw passion... For a moment, for the first time since they had wed, he pondered on Eleanor's response. He was not vastly experienced with women—there had been a few maids willing to initiate a young man—but war and soldiering had much occupied him. Then there had been Isabeau, and no other. He did not wish to compare Eleanor's responses to those of his first wife...and yet...they were not the same, of that much he was aware, and he could blame no one except himself. Eleanor had been a virgin and even now he doubted whether she had experienced, or even had any knowledge of, a woman's climax. Physically he knew that there was no reason why he could not show her how to climax, yet always he held back, he could not give her that, and he could not fathom the reason why. With a sigh, Troye turned on to his other side, his back to the sleeping Eleanor. His eyelids drooped until at last he too fell asleep, his last thought being that he would make amends...a gift mayhap? A new gown or necklet...

* * *

In Troye's absence a fretful Joan had fallen into the habit of visiting Eleanor in the morn, before she rose. The child enjoyed the comfort of a cuddle as Eleanor lifted the covers and welcomed her into the bed. This morn was no different and Joan seemed not at all concerned by the fact that her father lay naked in the bed with Eleanor. They both roused at the click of the door opening, the patter of bare little feet on the wooden floor, Joan's grunts as she pulled herself up onto the high tester bed, and launched herself in between the bodies of her father and stepmother.

'What are you doing?' groaned Troye, abruptly woken from his sleep, and peering at his daughter with heavy eyes, raking back his hair with one hand.

Joan giggled, sitting on her heels and pointing mischievously at her father. 'You look like a hedgehog.'

'Do I?' He grabbed hold of her and began to tickle her. 'And you look like a little girl who should be banished to the chicken-coop.'

Joan shrieked and laughed as her father tickled and wrestled with her, thrashing her little legs and arms about in a half-hearted attempt to evade him. Eleanor had woken at the first familiar sound of Joan's feet pattering on the floor, but now she turned and flinched as small elbows collided with her head.

'Enough,' Troye announced, releasing her. 'You do damage to Lady Eleanor.'

At once Joan's face became most earnest and she

climbed up on to her knees, leaning on the curve of Eleanor's hip as she peered anxiously into her face. 'Lady Eleanor, you are not hurt, are you?'

Eleanor shook her head, with a gentle smile. 'Nay, your papa only teases.'

Joan leaned forward and planted a moist kiss on her cheek. 'Shall we go and walk Toby?'

Eleanor glanced doubtfully at the grey clouds darkening the sky outside. 'I think it will rain.'

'Aye,' said Troye, lifting Joan from the bed and setting her firmly on the floor, 'Run along to your nurse and tell her that I say you are not to go beyond the gardens with Toby from now on.'

Joan looked up at him with her large, innocent brown eyes, promptly asking, 'Why?'

Troye frowned at her. 'Because I say so.'

'Why?'

Eleanor almost laughed at his expression, one of vexation and puzzlement. She sat up and turned towards Joan. 'Your papa wants us to be safe because there are lots of bad men about at the moment. Now run along, dearling, and get dressed. We will be down anon to break our fast together.'

Joan looked from one to other, but then she shrugged and trotted to the door, leaving it open, and she went off in search of her nurse, calling to Toby to follow her.

Troye rose from the bed and crossed the room to close the door. Eleanor felt a blush steal over her cheeks at the sight of his masculine and beautiful male body, at the intimacies she had shared with him. He was so perfectly proportioned, she mused, her glance full of admiration, his shoulders and chest broad, covered with dark hair, now starting to grey, his waist tapering down to slim hips, his legs and arms bulging with muscle hard-earned on the battle-field. As he reached for his breeches his glance collided with hers, and he noticed her blush and the way her eyes warmly admired him.

'Lady Eleanor…' He smiled, walking towards the bed, leaning one knee upon the edge as he leaned down and murmured, 'Shame on you, ogling a man with such lust.'

Eleanor smiled too, though her eyes were modestly downcast, 'But, sir, the man is my husband.'

'Indeed. He had better be.'

This jealous streak in Troye delighted her, yet just when she hoped that he would kiss her, there came a knock on the door and he sighed, rolling his eyes, pulling on his breeches and calling out, 'What?'

'Troye,' Lady Anne called out, 'come quickly, 'tis Dylan!'

'What ails the lad?' Troye retorted impatiently, shrugging on shirt and tunic, 'Don't tell me he has the stomachache again from eating too much plum cake…' he reached for hose and boots '…for he'll get no sympathy from me.'

'Nay, nay, just come quickly, he has been badly beaten!' Lady Anne sounded genuinely panic-stricken, she who always remained so calm and in control. 'Is Eleanor with you?'

'Of course!'

'Then tell her to bring her box of potions. We will have need of them. Come down to the kitchen as soon as may be.'

Eleanor and Troye looked at each, and then quickly she pushed back the covers and hurried from the bed. 'Go,' she urged, 'I will be there as soon as I have dressed.'

He nodded, and left her then, his booted feet clattering down the staircase as he hurried to the kitchen. Eleanor dressed in a clean linen shift and kirtle of duck-egg blue, her fingers shaking as she tried to tighten the laces fastening the sleeves to the bodice. She abandoned her hose and merely slid her feet into kid slippers, reaching for her box of medicines that her Aunt Beatrice had instructed her in, and then following in Troye's footsteps as she too made her hasty way to the kitchen.

There were several people gathered about Dylan as he lay sprawled in a chair by the hearth—Lady Anne, Troye, Simon, Meg and the cook Jarvis. All made various suggestions and exclamations of concern, yet they parted as Eleanor approached, and made way for her. She placed the medicine box on the kitchen table, and turned to Dylan, smothering a gasp as she surveyed his battered face, rapidly swelling to purple about the eyes and nose. She laid a hand on his shoulder, but he seemed little aware.

'What happened?' she asked, of no one in particular, but it was Troye who answered.

'He was set upon by several fellows when he made his way back from the Castle last night. I had sent him there to hear news of the King's arrival. But then he passed out before he could say who the fellows were.' He exchanged a glance with Eleanor, 'But I have my suspicions.' He turned then to his mother. 'No one is to go into the city, except Simon or Jarvis. I will speak to the High Sheriff about providing a guard to protect you while I am away to Scotland—'

'Oh, but surely that is not necessary?' protested Lady Anne. 'We have never had any trouble before. Who would bother us? We are unimportant people and certainly have no great wealth.'

Troye laid a hand on her arm, and drew her away from the kitchen and out into the hall. He lowered his voice, for though their servants had been with them many years, his soldier's instinct insisted that no one could ever be trusted completely. He explained that Eleanor came from a very wealthy and titled family, that there had been some trouble in London with an overzealous suitor in the form of Casper von Eckhart.

'Either that,' he said grimly, 'or Dylan has been unfortunate and 'twas merely a random attempt at robbery. Let us hope so.'

'Indeed.'

'Keep your eye on Joan, Mother. You know how she loves to run about in the garden and play hide and seek with Toby. You must be vigilant at all times. And with rebellion in Scotland there is every chance that the Scots will get beyond Berwick. If that happens, you are to take Eleanor and Joan and seek shelter at the castle at the first rumour of any attack.'

'The Scots will surely not come this far south,' Lady Anne scoffed, 'would they?'

Troye shrugged, 'This time is different. It is not just landed knights who seek to rebel against the authority of King Edward, but the peasants and farmers themselves. I am confident that we will put the rebellion down, but it will do no harm to be cautious.'

They returned to the kitchen and found that Dylan had been cleaned and tended to by Eleanor, and carried away to his bed to sleep off the worst of his injuries. Troye chafed with impatience as he waited for his squire to heal before being able to continue with their training and preparations.

The following day he was vastly cheered when several riders came cantering into the stable yard, astride powerful destriers little seen by common countryfolk, and fully armoured beneath their swirling blue cloaks crested with the insignia of the King's Own bodyguard. The three knights dismounted and tied their horses up, as Troye came striding out of the house to see who they were, his sword latched firmly to his side.

'What ho! And here is the bridegroom himself!'

Troye grinned. 'Austin, you old scoundrel, a sight for sore eyes!'

They clasped hands and there was much back-slapping with Sir Austin Stratford, Sir Percy Warrender and Sir Lindsay Crawford. He urged them inside and in the hall introduced them to his mother, and waved a hand at Eleanor as she rose from her seat. 'And of course you know my lady wife.'

The three knights bowed to her, and Sir Lindsay smiled as he kissed her hand, well aware of Troye's possessiveness and thinking it would do him only good to know that others appreciated the charms of his young wife. 'I hope married life is suiting you well, Lady Eleanor. You look even more beautiful than I remember.'

Eleanor blushed, casting a glance at a frowning Troye. She was only too aware that she was not looking her best from too many sleepless nights spent worrying about such things as married life, but she had the grace to smile at Sir Lindsay and thank him, murmuring a pleasantry in acceptance of his compliment.

'Simon!' Troye called to the kitchen. 'Bring us a keg

of that new ale from the Abbey.' He turned to his friends and urged them to take their seats around the table, 'I take it you are coming with us to Scotland—'

'Indeed.'

'Wouldn't miss it for the world!'

'We'll have Wallace running for the hills before you can say "sheep-stealer".'

The men laughed, and Eleanor returned to her seat, opposite Lady Anne. They exchanged glances and smiled. It felt good to have company, and they both enjoyed the sound of throaty male voices as the knights sat grouped around the refectory table. Meg served roasted pork and fresh bread, the men ate and drank, oblivious to all else as they talked of the forthcoming campaign that would see them cross the River Tweed at Coldstream and lay siege to Berwick, now occupied by the Scots.

'Berwick is a small town, granted,' insisted Sir Austin, 'but the chief royal borough of Scotland and they do much trade with Europe and England in salmon, herrings, hides and imported wines and spirits. We cannot allow the Scots to take control of it, not with the state of the King's finances.'

'Indeed...' Sir Austin nodded glumly '...are we not all taxed up to the gills to pay for Edward's grand designs?'

'Fear not, 'tis the Church that carries the greatest burden, so eager is Rome to keep Philip and Edward from tearing out each other's Christian throats,' Troye pointed out.

Lady Anne and Eleanor sat in their chairs beside the fire hearth, ostensibly attending to their sewing, making for Troye extra shirts from fine wool, to keep him warm in the icy climes of the north. They listened to the conversation of the knights, and Eleanor's exchanged glances with Lady Anne became increasingly anxious, as the talk of weapons and strategy alarmed her greatly. But Lady Anne merely smiled and shook her head, as though to say, 'There is naught to fear. 'Tis merely mantalk.'

Eleanor looked across the room to where Troye sat at the table with his fellow knights, nursing a mug of ale and animatedly discussing the merits of crossbow versus longbow and the tactics of William Wallace. His face was earnest, his voice firm and strong—a man trained from boyhood to fight, and to kill the King's enemies. It crossed her mind that mayhap such a man was not willing or able to love a woman with tenderness, and yet she knew that not to be true, for he had loved Isabeau. With a heavy heart she realised that it was only her he had no tenderness for.

Sir Percy took a deep draught of his ale before adding his thoughts. 'And that's another little spat no doubt we will be trudging off to sort out—Philip of France and Edward have long since been at war since Philip took a fancy to Gascony.'

'Aye,' mused Troye, 'but not this year.'

Sir Percy shook his head, the eldest of the three knights, his full head of hair and thick moustache almost entirely silver. 'I am too old for this charging about. This will be my last campaign, and then I go home to Felicity and put my feet up on the hearth to enjoy my twilight years with her. The poor woman has long since suffered my absences. No matter what say the King, I for one have had enough of war.'

They were all four silent for a moment, and Eleanor looked up to find Troye's eyes upon her, his expression most thoughtful. The hour was growing late, but the knights showed no sign of retiring. Weariness tugged at her eyelids and she set aside her sewing as soon as Lady Anne did. They bade the menfolk goodnight and then climbed the stairs together. Outside her chamber door Lady Anne paused, detaining Eleanor with one hand upon her arm.

'Do not over-concern yourself with what we have listened to this eve—'tis merely men's talk. They thrive on the adventure of war, but eventually they all come home to put their feet up on the hearth, just as Sir Percy says. Be patient, Troye will come to you.'

Eleanor could not believe in such a thing, not when Troye's armour stood ready and waiting in the hall, and their marriage was a source of pain and unhappiness. 'I can only pray that it will be so,' she murmured.

Lady Anne was not one to show great affection with hugs and kisses, her demeanour always rather dignified and aloof, but now, seeing the sorrow on Eleanor's young face, she sighed and reached out, placing a kiss upon her brow, and urging her to have faith. Eleanor replied goodnight and then they parted and each went to their own bedchamber.

Eleanor lay awake, wondering when Troye would seek his rest, but the hours waned and the talk from below in the hall did not abate; indeed, it seemed to only become louder, interspersed with laughter. Eleanor rolled on to her side, listening, pleased that Troye had been lifted from his doldrums and was enjoying the good company of his friends and fellow knights. She fell asleep long before he came to bed as the last of the stars faded at dawn.

They saw little of Troye in the next few days. Eleanor spent much of her time with Joan. At first she had feared it would be difficult, for was she not the spitting image of her mother? But Eleanor was soon to discover that Joan was a little person in her own right, and one that craved company and love as all young and innocent creatures do. When the chores were done and the long summer afternoons stretched into twilit evenings, Eleanor and Joan could often be found playing in the garden, a game of hide and seek, or throwing a ball with Toby, or building ant houses from leaves and twigs.

On one particularly hot afternoon she and Joan strolled down to the river, taking with them Toby, a bottle of lemonade and freshly baked raisin cakes. Together they sat in the shade of a weeping willow tree and dangled their feet in the cool green waters of the river. They made boats from leaves and sticks, and raced them, and Eleanor looked at Joan's smiling little face, and wished that she too could give Troye such a beautiful child. Her smile faded a little, for they had been married now nearly three months and this morn, for the third time, her monthly flow had begun. How she longed to give Troye a son, but no babe had quickened in her womb. And soon, within the next week or so, Troye would be gone. But her heart lifted at the thought that things had been much easier between them of late. She hoped that when Troye returned all matters would somehow, miraculously, be resolved and he would be just as willing to give her a son as she was to conceive one. When Troye returned? *If* he returned... A sense of fear lurked at the back of her mind and now she knew how her Aunt Beatrice and her mother had felt every time that her Uncle Remy and her father had marched off to war.

Joan became bored with sitting by the river, so hand in hand they strolled along the path that wound its way between the tall reeds and grasses fringing the bank, until they came to the village and Joan pointed at the tower of the church.

'My mother is there. Shall we go and see her?'

Eleanor was a little taken aback. She was not certain if Joan fully grasped the concept of the fact that her mother had died, but even though she had little experience with children Eleanor felt sure that a child as young as Joan could not understand the meaning of death. But she merely smiled and nodded, for how could she ever refuse such a request?

They walked through the village, calling to Toby to follow, and then Eleanor held open the gate to the churchyard, following Joan and Toby through the gravestones. As they rounded the corner of the church she heard Joan give a gleeful little shout, and Eleanor looked up to see Troye standing by the grave.

He turned, on hearing Joan's noisy greeting, and leaned down to hug her. Eleanor paused, halting in the shadow of the church, watching father and daughter from a distance. She felt as though she were intruding on something private, something not to be seen by the rest of the world. The ache of pain that swept through her came as a surprise, for she thought that, by now, she had grown well accustomed to the third person in their marriage. And yet it was not so. Troye's love for Isabeau was still a source of anguish for them both.

Quietly she slipped away, and walked back to the manor house alone. But as soon as she entered the front door and stood in the cool dimness of the hall, she felt the presence of Isabeau here too, most especially here, where she had lived, where she had lain in the bed upstairs, with Troye, and given birth to Joan, and where she had died. She was everywhere in this house, in this family. She seemed to permeate and emanate as surely as the smell of beeswax from the dark oak furniture. While Eleanor stood there, in a quandary, in the hall beyond she had a glimpse of Meg and Simon in the kitchen. The maid stood at the table beating the contents of a large bowl with a wooden spoon. Simon came up close behind her, and gently swept a tendril of hair from her eyes. Meg turned and smiled her thanks, and Simon leaned down and kissed her lips. It was such a simple gesture, and yet so tender and so loving that Eleanor felt a burst of envy. When had Troye ever looked at her with such a light of love in his eyes? Or ever given her the gift of tenderness? With a small, defeated cry Eleanor picked up her skirts and whirled about, running out of the door. She ran into the garden and beyond the high hedge to the orchard. She threw herself down in the lush green grass, amidst the fallen rosy apples, and hid her face in the crook of her arm, great sobs bursting from within her and tearing at her throat.

When at last all her tears had been wrung from her, she lay there for a long while, just staring, numb, unable to comprehend anything. Why did the thought of Troye visiting Isabeau's grave upset her so much? Was it the fact that he went to see her first, before returning home? Or was it because she feared the hold that Isabeau still had on him? Or that he preferred the company of a grave to the company of his wife? And yet, in this marriage, who was the wife? It was sacrilege to think it, but it seemed to Eleanor that Troye had two wives, and that was a matter sooner or later they would have to resolve. But how? She had tried everything, she had tried being loving and patient, she had tried being cool and distant, and it seemed that either way Troye was not concerned about the wife who lived.

Lady Anne had invited all her neighbours, friends and acquaintances to a great feast to celebrate the marriage of Troye and Eleanor. The day of the great event was brought forward, and it was as much a farewell as a celebration of marriage, as Troye and some of the guests, including the King, would depart within a day or two for Berwick.

The feast was to be held in the garden, with important guests invited from amongst their neighbours and friends, and the merchants of the city, of whom Lady Anne was one, having inherited the cloth import and export business from her husband. The household was all astir with excitement, for it had been a long while since any celebration had been held.

Beneath the shade of oak trees long trestle tables

were set up for a vast spread of delicious food, and several more to hold kegs of ale and wine and mead. An ox and a hog spit-roasted in a huge pit dug nearby, turned slowly and diligently by Simon as he watched the proceedings with interest, though his eyes never strayed far from Meg, as she threaded her way through the throng of gathering people, offering refreshments.

Through her bedroom window Eleanor could see that the tables and the trees had been decorated with garlands of flowers and colourful sashes. She could hear the musicians tuning their instruments as the first guests arrived. She turned away and surveyed the beautiful silk gown laid out upon the bed. It seemed that lately there had been little to smile about, but she smiled now as excitement and happiness stirred within her at the prospect of this evening. Troye had gifted her the gown, and it was the loveliest she had ever seen, an unusual shade of bright copper, the bodice and the sleeves held together with cream-coloured ribbons. She slipped it on, and set about fastening the ribbons. They were many and she struggled, calling out for Meg to help her, and then remembering that she was outside attending to the guests.

The bedchamber door opened then, and Troye poked his head around.

'Is aught amiss?' he asked.

Eleanor shrugged helplessly, the bodice of her gown sagging as she clutched it to her bosom, 'I merely seek assistance with the lacings of this gown.'

'Ah.' Troye came in and closed the door. He strode across the room, stooped a little as he squinted at the intricate criss-crossings and eyelets of the cream ribbons, and then quickly set about fastening Eleanor into her gown.

Her skin seemed to prickle with a yearning to feel his lips brush the nape of her neck, his fingertips caress her collarbone, and she waited, hoping with tense-held breath, as they stood so close together, for a gesture from him. But none came. Briskly he laced her up; when done, he stepped back and said, 'It looks very nice.'

'Thank you.' Eleanor turned swiftly away, pretending to reach for her hairbrush, so that he would not see the disappointment in her eyes.

But Troye had no inkling of the hurt he had caused, with his brisk manner, and he called out that he would see her downstairs, as he hurried away to greet his friends and offer them refreshments. Eleanor nodded, unable to utter a word, her lip trembling and her throat burning at the sudden breaking of her heart.

Stop! she admonished herself firmly. Stop this nonsense now! Yet as she stood at the window and brushed her hair, and looked upon Meg and Simon, and other couples who seemed to smile and touch and laugh together with that simple, effortless manner of people who loved, the tears rained hot and fast down her cheeks.

She felt so alone! So unwanted and unloved. How would she bear it?

Yet bear it she must, and with a cheerful face. Eleanor set aside the brush, wiped her face dry with her hands, blew her nose on a handkerchief that Lady Anne had embroidered for her with her initials, and then descended the stairs.

It was a memorable evening, a feast that was talked about for weeks to come. Eleanor enjoyed the dancing, for as a married woman she was allowed the liberty of greater freedom to join in. Troye was a competent dancer, though he showed little enthusiasm, and Eleanor watched him as he seemed to prefer to stand on the sidelines, conversing with Sirs Austin and Percy and Lindsay.

The High Sheriff claimed her hand several times, as did several other gentlemen, either neighbours or merchants who were well acquainted with Lady Anne and her family. She did enjoy herself, though it seemed to go on too long; on this long summer's evening, daylight did not fade until very late. It was long past midnight when guests began to drift away, calling out their thanks and laughing as they stumbled home, merry with far too much good wine and ale and rich food.

On the morrow Troye would depart with the King for Berwick, and all his armour and weapons waited for him in the hall. Eleanor paused with one foot upon the stairs, and stared at the gleaming steel breastplate and the shield emblazoned with the heraldic banner of de Valois. Tonight was to be their last night for a long while, and she hoped that Troye was mindful of the fact. When she had made her goodnights, she had glanced at him with meaningful eyes, but he had said nothing beyond his usual, 'I will be there anon.'

With a sigh Eleanor climbed the stairs and went to her bedchamber. She closed the door and made ready for bed, struggling with the intricate side-lacings beneath her arms. Her fingers fumbled with the laces that Troye had fastened too tightly and she was about to call for Meg to assist her when she heard the door below bang, and the thump of booted feet upon the stair. She stood as though frozen, her fingers twisted with laces as she watched wide-eyed while the door opened and Troye came into the room.

He snapped the door shut behind him, smiling at her as he said, 'Well, that's the last of them gone. God, but I could sleep for a week!' He sat down upon the edge of the bed without looking at her, bending to pull off his boots.

For a moment her eyes lingered on the broad width of his shoulders, the sturdy column of his neck, dark hair curling at the nape. To her, he represented all that was strong, all that was good. She went to him then, with no thought other than to bridge the gulf between them, and he half-turned, to look up at her as she stood beside him.

Shyly, with eyes lowered, she lifted her arms, and whispered, 'Please.'

Troye laughed, 'Ah, those pesky laces.' He was in no fit state to deal with the complexities of a woman's clothing, having consumed his fair share of the wine, yet he obliged and took hold of the stubborn laces in the hollow of her armpit. He jerked her slender body about as he wrestled with the knots and then he muttered an oath, impatient and frustrated as they failed to yield. Before she realised what he was about, he had drawn his dagger from its sheath on his belt and deftly cut the knots. Her gown fell away, revealing the creamy, smooth skin of her shoulders and the swell of her bosom as she clutched the bodice to her.

'Troye!'

'I will buy you new laces. 'Tis a small price to pay to get you undressed.'

They looked at each other for an endless moment in time. She searched his familiar face, as his own gaze roamed over hers, and then lowered to her mouth, and to her breasts. They were strangers, yet they were man and wife; they were bonded by an intimacy born of events, and yet they had no real knowledge of each other. There were things that could not be spoken of, the memory of their pasts that existed and yet were forbidden and denied. She felt she would explode with the aching questions and doubts that burned in her heart. Yet she could not ask him for the answers she needed, for her soul was petrified of the truth she would hear if she did.

Instead she yielded when his hands clasped her waist and he drew her body to him. She stood between his spread knees as he sat on the edge of the bed, and her breath was held tightly in her throat as he pressed his face between her breasts. Gently she stroked his hair, brushing the strands from his forehead. He pulled her close, and for a moment she hoped that all her fears and all her pain would soon be banished. His fingers parted the fine fabric of her shift. Her skin flared with goosebumps at the soft touch of his lips on her ribs, tasting her skin, his mouth grasping at the heavy weight of her breasts, his tongue circling and caressing her nipples until they hardened with arousal. She sighed, and her hips moved in a sensuous sway as he held them between his hands. The feel of him so close to her body made her weak and she trembled, eager for his touch, and yet unwilling, this time, to let him take without at least giving something in return. This time she was determined that she would have from him what was rightfully hers.

She leaned down and kissed his forehead as his

mouth sucked on her breast, her voice a soft whisper. 'I love you, Troye. I have loved you these many years.'

He stopped, his mouth abruptly freeing her breast, and his hands released her hips. He pushed her away, and she stumbled, reaching out blindly and clutching at a bedpost for support she pulled up her shift, shielding her nakedness, though her heart lay bare and vulnerable between them.

'Don't. Please don't, Eleanor.' He rose to his feet, towering over her, his eyes very dark and his handsome face set in a hard mask, 'I cannot pretend, nor will I insult you with lies. I am your husband and I try to do the duties of a husband, but more than that I cannot give.'

'But—' Eleanor struggled to find words. 'When we couple…' she blushed, yet hastened on in her desperation '…do you not feel anything for me?'

He snorted then, defensive. 'Most men are like that. They are not emotional creatures and do not require love and all that nonsense to bed a woman.'

She cried out suddenly, hot tears blazing in her eyes, bursting from her throat and her nose as the cruel truth leapt upon them. 'Maybe you do not, but I do!' She thumped her chest then, her heart, with the flat of her palm. 'I want to be loved, I want you to love me, and not use me like you would any whore!'

He turned towards her with hand upraised, greatly

tempted to slap her cheek, but he restrained himself as she flinched and wept.

'Well, I cannot!' he shouted, goaded beyond his endurance. 'I cannot love you! I do not love you!'

'Because of her!' Eleanor retorted, her anger as swift as his. 'Because of Isabeau?'

'Aye. I will love her always.'

'How can you, Troye? She's dead!'

At that, he inhaled a sharp breath, glaring at her in rage, and Eleanor felt the fragile bond between them snap, shocked at the rejection that had reared its ugly head the moment she had mentioned the word 'love'.

'Go then,' she shouted, 'go to the graveyard and lie with your wife!'

Chapter Twelve

Their raised voices had disturbed the household, yet neither of them took any notice of Lady Anne as she stood in the doorway, looking from one to the other.

'Very well.' Troye glared at Eleanor, pulling on his boots and his tunic, snatching up his sword and belt from the floor. He turned to her with a mocking bow, ''Tis best if I go. Goodbye.'

Eleanor watched, tears streaming down her pale face, as he shouldered past Lady Anne and walked out the door. Realising what she had done, what he meant, Eleanor cried out, 'Troye!'

She made to rush after him, but Lady Anne stopped her with both hands restraining her shoulders, using all her strength to hold her back.

'Troye! I'm sorry! I didn't mean it!' Eleanor sobbed, desperately trying to free herself.

'Shh,' Lady Anne hushed her cries as in the distance Joan's wails grew louder. Gently yet firmly she bundled Eleanor back into the bedchamber, reaching with one hand to close the door behind them. 'Let him go, child.'

'Nay! I can't let him go!'

'He'll be back, when his temper has cooled.'

Eleanor shook her head, shuddering with sobs and her face blotching crimson. 'Nay, he will not be back. I have lost him forever!' At the sound of horses' hooves drumming outside, Eleanor rushed to the window, and fumbled with the catch to fling it open, lunging through as it swung forwards, shouting, 'Troye!'

His cloak streamed out behind him as he galloped off down the road; whether or not he had heard her, he did not stop or look back.

'Come now, Eleanor.' Lady Anne drew her away from the window, closing it on the cool, fragrant night air, 'What has happened? Why were you arguing?'

Eleanor subsided on the edge of the bed. She covered her face with both hands as she sobbed. Her voice was muffled as she gulped on a breath and said, 'It is because of her. It's always her. He does not love me. I cannot go on like this!' Eleanor broke down then, sobbing with such loud force that she felt as though her ribs would crack.

Lady Anne stood, stroking her hair and silent— what could she say? She too feared that Eleanor was right.

They were all exhausted after the long day preparing for, and enjoying, the feasting to celebrate a marriage that seemed to have ended before it had even begun. Lady Anne stayed with Eleanor for a while, sending Meg, who hovered on the landing to see what all the fuss was about, to the kitchen to warm some milk spiced with soothing nutmeg and honey. Then she insisted that Eleanor get into bed and lie down, sitting in a chair alongside.

'I shall write to my father,' Eleanor whispered, lying on her side, curled up like a child, with the palm of her hand under one cheek. 'I shall tell him the truth and beg him to seek for me an annulment.'

Lady Anne sighed, but she did not offer advice to the contrary. There were no words of encouragement from her mother-in-law and this brought fresh tears, silent and despairing as they slid from the corner of her eyes and splashed upon the pillow. The dream was over. It did not matter that at last she was Troye's wife, for while his heart was committed elsewhere she could never be a true wife to him, nor he a true husband to her.

Yet in the morning, when she woke, she did not rush for pen and paper as she had vowed to herself during the night. She rose as soon as she wakened, and dressed, eager to leave the bed, to leave this house of sorrow. Outside the morning greeted her, soft and cool, the hem of her gown dampened by the dew, the birds singing their bright, cheerful songs. How can this be? she wondered. How can the world carry on so lovely and whole and peaceful when my own world has been totally shattered? Eleanor walked down to the river, and there sat in a favourite spot she had often shared with Joan, her knees drawn up and staring at the dark green waters of the tranquil river.

Mayhap Lady Anne was right, and Troye would return as soon as his temper had cooled and the heated words they had exchanged had dimmed in his memory. As before. She should not rush to her father with tales of woe too quickly. Had her mother and Aunt Beatrice not warned her that there were bound to be times when husband and wife were not in accord, but that she must remain calm throughout? How she missed them! How she longed to be home, with those who she could be sure truly loved her! She hated herself for the tears that came again, hot and burning behind her eyes, and yet her aching heart had to ease the burden of its pain.

After some while, when the well of her sadness was for the moment dry, she rose and walked back to the house, fearing that Joan would go in search of her and find her missing. She had grown very fond of the child in the weeks past, and she was deeply aware that the sudden and unexpected loss of her mother and the frequent absences of her father had left Joan feeling deeply insecure. She could not abandon the child now, not when she had so readily and easily accepted her as stepmother.

Later that morning, Dylan came with a cart and collected Troye's armour, as well as victuals and monies for the road. Eleanor hastily penned a note, begging Troye to please meet with her before he left.

'You will not forget?' Eleanor urged Dylan, as she pressed the note into the squire's hand. 'Be sure that he reads this before you march.'

'Aye, my lady.' Dylan bowed, and then climbed aboard his cart, waving goodbye with a heavy heart. For the first time, he had no great wish for the campaign they were about to embark upon; somehow the comforts of home had become too dear.

All that day Eleanor stayed close to the house, waiting and listening anxiously for the sound of Merlin trotting up the path from the road. Once she thought she definitely heard a horse and rushed to the window, but there was no one there. Later that afternoon two riders appeared, but they were only wool merchants come to see Lady Anne about a shipment to Antwerp. Disappointment bit hard and it dawned slowly upon her that Troye would not come.

When the merchants had left, unhappy with the undertaking from Lady Anne that the shipment would only leave at the end of the month and not before, for it made no sense or profit to sail with half a cargo, she went to Eleanor and tried to soothe her fears.

'Do not fret. He is surely very busy making ready with all the other knights. No doubt he will come this evening.'

Eleanor nodded, yet hope was soon to die as dusk came and went. They ate their evening meal, she listened to Joan chatter and helped the nurse to put her to bed, and then she sat with her sewing. As the hour grew late Eleanor fidgeted and fretted, until at last out of sheer frustration and disappointment she leapt to her feet, exclaiming, 'Well, if he will not come to me, I will go to him!'

'Nay, Eleanor!' Lady Anne rose to her feet, setting aside her sewing, well aware of Eleanor's impulsive nature. ''Tis too dangerous for you to be abroad at night.'

'I care not!' Eleanor rushed for her cloak hung on the peg beside the door. 'I must see him, I must know what we are to do.'

Lady Anne refrained from pointing out that from Troye's very silence and absence there was nothing to be done. And yet she understood Eleanor's desperation; spurred by a love that was all too obviously deep and true, Eleanor now had suffered the pain of rejection. She could see little hope for this marriage, but she realised that no words from her would have any effect on Eleanor.

'Then I will come with you,' said Lady Anne, for she was anxious to see her son and give him a piece of her mind too. 'We will take Simon with us.'

She went off to rouse him, while Eleanor went to her bedchamber and fetched a gilt dagger from the large coffer standing at the foot of her bed that contained all her worldly goods, her marriage gifts and her dowry. As she closed the lid she glanced to that other coffer, the one beneath the window, and how she wished that someone would remove it! With pursed lips she turned away, tucking the dagger into a loop on her girdle.

Simon was not best pleased to be dragged from his bed at this late hour, but he voiced no complaint as he saddled the horses and brought them round to the front door. He carried a lantern to light their way, and a stout cudgel, praying all the while that they would encounter no ruffians. It was scarce a mile to the castle and, though the city gates stood open, they had to pay a fine to the keeper for passing by so late. Eleanor was not sure what she had expected to find, certainly not the heaving mass of humanity that spread itself all around the grounds surrounding the castle and the bailey itself within. Hundreds of Welsh archers and thousands more foot soldiers from all the shires had been mobilised into service, and had now gathered here *en masse* as they waited for the order to move.

At the gate to the castle the guard refused them entry. A local man of the York yeomanry, he knew Lady Anne well and was reluctant to admit her to the castle, seething with noisy, rough soldiers, peasants mainly who had no good care for the passing of a lady.

'My good fellow,' Lady Anne insisted, pressing a florin into his palm, 'I must see the captain of the King's Own Guard. You know who that is, do you not?'

The yeoman flushed and pressed the coin back into her hand, taking affront at the bribery. ''Tis for your own good now, Lady Anne. You don't want to be going in there, believe you me.'

But we must!' cried Eleanor. 'I beg of you—' she leaned down from the saddle and touched the guard upon his shoulder '—please, I must see my husband before he leaves for Scotland. Please!'

The guard looked up at her, and was moved by the desperation upon her young and lovely face. He called to one of several other guards standing on duty, and told him to show the visitors to the hall, and to fetch Sir Troye from the armoury.

'Thank you,' Eleanor murmured.

Lady Anne once again pressed the florin into his palm. 'For your kindness.'

He turned a darker shade of lobster red and then stepped gruffly aside as he pocketed the coin and let them pass. They rode into the bailey and dismounted, leaving Simon clutching the reins of their horses in one hand and his cudgel in the other, as he looked about with a ferocious glare. Lady Anne and Eleanor mounted the steps of the keep and went inside to the hall. It was bedlam within, with knights and servants rushing all about, seeking food and wine and water, cleaning weapons, preparing chainmail, nursing wounds garnered on the way, poring over maps of the north and taking desperate tallies for soldiers that had arrived and for those that had not. For a moment they stood just over the threshold, staring about. Eleanor wondered how Troye would find them amongst the *mêlée* and at Lady Anne's bidding she went with her to stand to one side. The King's Exchequer and Parliament was here housed too, and there were many clerks and officials going about trying to keep a track of things and to issue writs for this and receipts for that.

After some while, when there was no sign of Troye, Lady Anne stopped a pageboy and asked him to go to the armoury with a message. As they waited on weary legs, the pageboy returned to say he could not find Sir Troye. Alarm was now beginning to ring its bells and together they set about stopping every knight they could to find Troye. At last, they came upon Lord Charteris, an old family friend of Eleanor's father. After exchanging a kiss of greeting, he told them, gravely, and with much regret, that Sir Troye had already left at noon with the advance party, as they went to scout the route ahead for the army.

Eleanor felt crushed by disappointment. She had no way of knowing whether Troye had received her note, if he had ignored it, or whether he had just been unable to respond. She liked to think that he had gone to war harbouring no ill feeling or bitterness towards her, but it seemed unlikely. He had taken his armour that Dylan had collected, and therefore he must have taken her note too, for she was sure that Dylan would not have failed to give it to him.

'Is there aught amiss?' asked Lord Charteris, eyeing her shrewdly. Though he was now well past the age of marching with the army, he would remain in York to oversee the rear party and the provisioning by ship of the main body as it marched with Edward north-wards, through the wild lands of the Scots. 'Can I be of assistance, Lady Eleanor?'

Eleanor shook her head, her lip trembling, fighting hard not to let the ever-close tears reveal themselves. 'I wished to speak with Troye, but now it seems I am too late.'

He stroked his beard thoughtfully, glancing to Lady Anne. 'I fear we are not acquainted? Lord Charteris at your service, ma'am.'

Lady Anne, who thought herself long past her time for blushing, felt her cheeks colour as Lord Charteris bowed to her and she introduced herself, adding, 'I am Troye de Valois's mother.'

'Ah.' The mother-in-law. A widow, mayhap? Lord Charteris wondered, taking a keen interest in the situation, as he himself was widowed and understood the difficulties of dealing with grown-up children and their marriages. 'Mayhap I can send a message to Sir Troye. Would that be of help to you, Lady Eleanor?'

In that moment, of gentle enquiry, Eleanor suddenly realised the futility of her quest, and felt utterly defeated. She shook her head, and turned away, her eyes downcast and her shoulders stooped. Lady Anne murmured her thanks to Lord Charteris and made a move to follow after Eleanor, but he stopped her with one hand about her elbow.

'If I can be of any assistance, Lady Anne, please do feel free to come to me. I will do what I can, but you must appreciate the King is away to war, and his men with him. They are neither much concerned with marital matters at this time.'

'Indeed.'

'But I hate to see a young bride so troubled.' He paused, waiting for an explanation, but none was forthcoming.

''Tis a private matter, my lord. Sadly, there is nothing to be done about it. What will be, will be.'

Lord Charteris bowed with regret in his world-weary eyes. He watched them depart and wondered what it was that so troubled the Ladies de Valois. Should he alert Lord Henry that all was not well in his daughter's paradise?

They made their way home, in silence, and once there Simon was thankful to bed the horses and himself down for the night. Having seen for himself the hundreds of soldiers gathered in York and its surroundings, he went about making sure all the doors and windows were shut and barred, and the animals securely penned.

Eleanor hung up her cloak and bid Lady Anne goodnight as she made her way upstairs to her chamber. There she sat down upon the bed and stared vacantly into space for a long while. As exhaustion finally seeped into her bones and lowered her eyelids she lay down, her cheek resting on the pillow that normally Troye slept upon. She could still smell his scent. Where was he now? she wondered. How she ached within her heart to think of him gone, and with such bad feeling between them. What was she to do? Sit and wait for the return of a husband who could not bear to feel even the slightest emotion for her, and yet seemed to think it his right to use her body whenever he wished? She knew what had to be done, had known for a long while, and yet her heart was shattering into tiny bits and pieces at the mere thought.

Eleanor realised that if she wrote to her father it would take many weeks for him to receive the letter, and she could not bear to disappoint him or anger him with her failure. Now she only wanted to escape, and she could not think beyond that. If she went away, far away, then she would be able to leave the past behind her, and forget that once she had ever loved Troye at all, as surely as he had forgotten her.

But where would she go? She could not go to Castle Ashton—it was too far away and she would never make the journey across a land so dangerous with villains who would find a lone female easy prey. For a moment she thought she could go to her grandmother, Lady Margaret, in Oxford, but that would be no easy journey either. And no guarantee that she would not be turned away, for her grandmother had staunch ideas about marriage: a wife must not abandon her husband, no matter what.

For some strange reason thoughts of Oxford brought to mind the conversation she'd had with her mother before her marriage to Troye. She remembered now the information about her father, her real father, the one who had died in Wales when she was still a babe. Had her mother not said that he came from Canterbury? Surely, if she went to the Blackthorns, and professed to being their kin, they would not turn her away? And it was unlikely that her own family would easily find her in such circumstances. It would be the last thing ever to occur to them. And that was what she wanted, never to be found, to cut away the past and become someone else. But how to get there? Eleanor mulled this over, realising that the best and easiest way to reach Kent would be by ship. There were many ships sailing from York to Europe and the south of England, on their way to Ireland and Spain. Why, she could easily sail for Calais, and then back from there to Dover. She sat up suddenly, remembering the wool merchants, and that Lady Anne had promised a ship would be sailing for Antwerp by the end of the month. Surely from Antwerp she would be able to find a passage to Dover?

Upon the side of a hill far to the north of York, Troye drew rein and paused. He looked back at the magnificent sight of King Edward's army as it marched up the coast towards Edinburgh. Not since the Romans had so large a force invaded Scotland and there could be no doubt in anyone's mind that the English King meant business. The ground trembled to the beat of over two thousand horses of the mounted cavalry knights, led by eight of the noble Earls, including the son of his old friend, Guy of Warwick, as well as Surrey, Gloucester, Arundel and the boy-Earls of Lancaster and Pembroke, eager to be blooded in their first battle and win the glory of their spurs. The bright afternoon sunlight shone on their chainmail, swords and lances, colourful pennons and heraldic banners raised aloft and streaming on the wind.

Behind the knights came the foot soldiers of the infantry, some twelve thousand in number, although the call had been for thirty thousand. Even from this distance, as the great train of the army rolled slowly onwards, he could hear the drums beating and the clink and clank of armour and harness. A great swell of pride stirred within him, his eyes seeking out the King who rode in their midst, surrounded by his bodyguard of the King's Own. Picking up the reins of Merlin, Troye touched his heels to the great destrier's flanks and urged him down the steep hillside, riding to join with his comrades and report on his findings for the route ahead.

They made camp as soon as dusk began to fall, and the commanders set a strict guard, not only to be vigilant for the Scots, but to prevent further desertion. Discipline was strictly enforced. They received word that the ships that were to provide rations for the army had been forced back to port by ill winds. Troye joined the other commanders in a tent, and they sat down to discuss how and where they would obtain enough fodder to keep them going. Providing for this great monster driving its way through the countryside became as important to her handlers as the war itself—victory would not be won on empty stomachs and hungry soldiers were much more likely to desert.

The old Earl of Surrey, a veteran campaigner, stabbed a finger at the map spread out on a trestle table. 'Beyond the River Tweed we will not find much in the way of sustenance, but there is a Benedictine monastery here, and several farms there. We will pick up what we can from them.'

'If Wallace has not laid them to waste first.' The only Scottish Earl present, Angus, spoke gloomily, having given his oath of fealty to Edward, little impressed by the antics of rebels like William Wallace.

The others cast him a sour glance, and while plans were made for the morning to take Dirleton and two other smaller castles in their path to reach Edinburgh, they had the news from Troye that Wallace had fallen back into the forests of Selkirk.

'Just like the Welsh,' said Gloucester, 'disappearing into hills and forests where we cannot find them, nor draw them down.'

King Edward stroked his beard, 'Aye, but this time we will take the towns and castles, their kin and trade; without them they cannot survive for ever upon the land.'

Nor can we, thought Troye, but did not express this sentiment aloud, sharing it with exchanged glances only with the other serjeant-at-arms who stood in the background waiting for their orders. When they came, his were to go to the monastery and secure what provisions he could. At first light he would set out, taking with him several other knights and a score of archers for protection, but for now he was in much need of rest and food. He sought out Dylan, who had made a campfire and placed sheepskins upon Troye's shield for him to lie upon. He ate rabbit roasted to a crisp over the fire, and stale bread, washed down with a skinful of wine. Then he lay down and fell instantly into sleep.

Hours later the cold, damp morning air and the apricot light of dawn roused him from the depths of his dreams, and he sat up, nudging Dylan awake with the toe of his boot.

Troye raked one hand through his shorn hair and shook the night from his head. All around him other men rose, coughing and spitting, yawning, moaning, chainmail clinking as they dragged it on, horses stamping in the lines beyond but ever close to hand should the call to arms come suddenly. He stood up and latched on his sword, mindful of his tasks for the day. Nevertheless, for a moment he paused, his companion of the night still with him, remembering her arms about his back as she had embraced his body against her own slender warmth and softness. Often he had dreamed this desperate dream, to feel her once again, to hold her, love her…and yet, somehow this time it had been different and when he had pushed aside the long swathe of flowing hair to reveal her face, it had not been Isabeau…

Eleanor made her plans to run away in great secrecy. Each day she hid an item in the bundle that she would take with her, clothes and a few coins, but the rest, contained within the great carved coffer at the foot of her bed, she would leave behind, mayhap for Joan. She gave no thought as to why she felt the need to be so furtive, why she could not openly say to Lady Anne that she intended to leave. She bided her time, enduring a heavy heart and loneliness, ignoring any doubts that she might have, until one morning, several weeks after Troye had marched away to war, Meg came tapping on her door and called her urgently to Lady Anne's bedchamber.

Eleanor rose quickly, pushing aside the bedcovers and her feet into slippers. She ran with Meg down the passage, alarmed by the maid's obvious distress.

'Lady Anne?' Eleanor leaned over her mother-in-law as she lay in the bed, and urged Meg to open the shutters so that she might better see. With one hand Eleanor clasped her wrist and felt for a pulse, which was faint and fluttering. 'Lady Anne?'

There came no response, but her mother-in-law stared at her helplessly, her mouth slack and twisted to one side, the hand of her left arm peculiarly bent and stiff. Eleanor had seen the like before, and greatly feared that Lady Anne had suffered a seizure of some kind. Gently she brushed aside the strands of grey hair that clung to her forehead, and tried her best to make her comfortable in the bed, consumed with guilt at having been so absorbed in her own misery that she had not noticed the strain of Lady Anne's burdens. She had seemed tired of late, and preferred to remain in her chair positioned by the window in the hall below, sewing or resting quietly, leaving the running of the household and the care of Joan to Eleanor. And though Lady Anne had been kept busy with the merchants, this had been a matter Eleanor was loathe to involve herself with, having no knowledge of the import and export of the wool business.

Over the next few days there was little improvement in Lady Anne's condition, and Eleanor feared for the worst. She agonised over whether to send a message to Troye, urging him to return home, but wondered whether he would consider this merely a ploy to force him to see her and would simply ignore this summons as he had the other. And yet, as Lady Anne grew weaker and drifted in and out of consciousness, she felt she could not ignore the urgency of the situation, nor deprive Troye of his right to bid his mother farewell before she departed from this world.

Hastily she penned a brief note, stating merely that his mother was ill and he should return home as soon as ever possible. She sent Simon to Lord Charteris at the castle, and he sent the message north with a bearer taking military dispatches to the King; she had every hope that Troye would not fail to receive the news.

Night and day Eleanor sat in a chair beside Lady Anne's bed. She cared for her as best she could, bathing her, feeding her, but there came a time when Lady Anne fell into a deep sleep, and Eleanor feared that from this she would never awaken again.

Late one afternoon Joan pushed open the door to her grandmother's bedchamber and walked slowly into the room, followed by the ever-faithful Toby, who seemed just as aware of the sombre situation as the child, padding behind Joan with tail and head downcast. Reaching Eleanor, she scrambled up and Eleanor let her wriggle and settle upon her lap, while Toby flopped down with a sigh at her feet. For long moments Joan looked at her grandmother, to all intents and purposes asleep in the bed, and then she turned to Eleanor, and stroked her cheek with one tiny hand.

'Are you sad, Lady Eleanor?'

Eleanor smiled wanly. 'Aye.'

'Will Grandmother wake up soon? She likes to walk with me and Toby in the garden.'

'Nay, dearling, I do not think Grandmother will wake up today.'

'Tomorrow?'

Tears burned hot and sudden behind her eyes, and Eleanor shook her head, her voice choked in her throat.

Joan was quick to pick up on Eleanor's emotion and she turned to hug Eleanor with her fragile little arms, burying her face against Eleanor's bosom. After a few moments she whispered, 'Papa said my mother went to sleep. She went away to the church. He said she was very beautiful.'

'Aye…' Eleanor nodded, gently stroking Joan's long braid of dark silky hair that hung down her back '…I believe she was.'

Then Joan looked up at her with wide brown eyes. 'You won't leave me, will you, Lady Eleanor?'

Eleanor sniffed and forced back the tears, smiling as she kissed Joan on her plump cheek and hugged her close. 'Nay, my little sweetpea, I will never leave you.'

On a crisp day in October, Lady Anne died. As usual Eleanor had slept in a chair beside her bed, dozed more than slept, though just before dawn she was so greatly tired that her slumber had been deep. When she had awakened, just as the birds began to sing and the golden light glowed beyond the trees, she went to check on Lady Anne and found her to be cold and still. Eleanor crossed herself, and murmured a prayer for the departing soul. She leaned forwards and closed Lady Anne's eyes, feeling a most peculiar sense of calm and quiet come over her.

Throughout the next few days, nothing seemed at all real. They buried Lady Anne in a grave alongside Isabeau. Many of the town's dignitaries, merchants, and all their neighbours turned out for the funeral mass, but at the end of it all, Eleanor was left alone, with a bewildered Joan, and several servants who seemed sullen in the extreme, harbouring doubts for the future. That night she sat at the table, surrounded by papers and letters pertaining to the wool business, and requests for payment from creditors, feeling quite overwhelmed and bemused as to how she should deal with it all. The servants had gone off to bed, Joan was asleep, and without Lady Anne's company the hall seemed suddenly rather menacing. The dark oak timbers creaked, the wind whistled through the rooftops. Eleanor gazed at the shadows, yet unafraid, for surely if there were spirits about they would be those of Isabeau and Lady Anne? The evenings were now chill as summer faded into autumn, and she shivered, finding the excuse to take herself off to bed.

Inside her chamber she resisted the urge to bar her door, for in the morning no doubt Joan would come pattering in. She undressed and climbed between the covers of the bed, lying down and turning on her side to face the empty space beside her. How she hated this lonely bed! Troye's male scent had long since faded from the pillow, but she stretched out a hand and smoothed it over the space he had once occupied. Where was he now? What was he doing? Did he ever think of her, as she did of him? She closed her eyes and imagined him lying beside her, his warmth, the weight of his body, the feel of dark hair that downed his arms and legs rubbing against her own smooth skin. Her nipples hardened at the remembered sensation of his mouth upon them. She felt an unexpected stab of desire between her legs as the memory of his fingers parting her thighs, his body entering hers, possessing her totally in the only way that a man could possess a woman, flooded her mind. With a small moan she pressed her hand to her sex, surprised at the feelings that leapt to life within her, just at the mere imagining that her fingers were those of Troye. She closed her eyes and rolled over on to her back, her fingers sliding and stroking, pretending that she was telling him what she wanted him to do, pretending that his touch was one of tenderness and love and sweet passion. She gasped, her breath caught in pants between her teeth, and instinctively she continued along a path she had long suspected but never experienced with Troye. The pleasure was sweet, sweeter than anything she had ever experienced, and yet, afterwards, she wept silent tears, realising that Troye had never touched her like that, and how much she longed for him to do so, and how unlikely that he ever would.

In the morning, with Lady Anne scarce buried, there came a procession of people claiming that they were owed money. Eleanor did her best to search through the confusing mass of paperwork, willingly paying those whose claims were proved clearly enough by accounts written in Lady Anne's own hand. But before the end of the week the money had all gone, and she began to delve into her own dowry merely to keep the peace. There were some that she had her suspicions about, and refused to pay, calling for Simon to show one particularly belligerent wool farmer from the door. Sir Malcolm Rix, the High Sheriff, had called twice, with offers of condolence and assistance, his manner both too familiar and rather intrusive, with his hints that mayhap she might be a widow by now and that serfs must be dealt with by a firm master. She had been much pressed to deal with him graciously, reminding him in cool tones that she expected her husband home at any moment, and that the serfs had given her no trouble.

Yet she was to rue her bold words, for one morning scarce a week later she came down to the kitchen to find the hearth fire cold and no food prepared. She called for Jarvis the Cook, but there came no reply. For a moment she feared that she had been abandoned by all the serfs, but Simon came stumbling from his room behind the larder, followed by a sleepy-eyed Meg hastily adjusting her bodice and tying on a linen apron.

'Jarvis has fled,' Eleanor stated.

Simon looked up, halting as he ran one hand through his blond hair. Then a sudden thought occurred to him and he ran out to the stables, only to find that all the horses, except Luz, the three cows and five pigs, had gone. Eleanor and Meg, standing in the doorway, exchanged a wry glance as his rude curses blackened the air.

'Bastard!' Simon returned to the kitchen, having securely bolted Luz in her stable. 'We'll have to keep our wits about us, my lady. They'll be like a pack of vultures now, with Lady Anne gone and the master away.'

Eleanor raised her eyes to both Simon and Meg, asking in her plain and direct way, 'And will I one morning find that you have also gone?'

Simon pulled himself to his full height, and replied firmly, 'We'll stand by you, my lady. We'll not run.'

In support of his statement, Meg dipped a little curtsy, and then blushed as she elbowed Simon and urged him on with a little nod of her head.

'I know 'tis not a good a time, my lady, but I would speak with you.' Simon looked embarrassed, suddenly seizing a broom leaning against the wall and wringing its handle in both hands.

Eleanor smiled, encouraging him. 'What is it, Simon? Please do not be shy to speak, for your loyalty and good service will not go unrewarded, I promise.'

Simon looked from Meg to his boots to Eleanor, and then said in a rush, 'Please, my lady, I would ask permission for me and Meg to be wed.'

The maid's cheeks coloured bright pink and she added, 'I am with child, my lady.'

Eleanor felt a small jolt in her heart, not of shock, but of pure envy. Quickly she nodded. 'Of course.' And then she turned away, briskly urging Simon to fetch wood and get the kitchen fire going again, 'And we will need to purchase another cow. Meg, is there enough milk in the larder for Joan this morn?'

'Aye, my lady.'

'Good. Then let us get on.'

But as the weeks wore on and Simon struggled with his chores—chopping wood, drawing water, walking into town and back bearing a sack of flour for bread, a barrel of wine to drink, keeping a watch at night— Eleanor wondered how much longer she could keep the household going. Meg, having kept her condition secret for these many months, now suddenly became heavy and cumbersome and weary, and Eleanor was anxious for the little maid not to overexert herself. She realised that without Simon and Meg, both of them young and strong, willing and cheerful, her troubles would be much worse. Joan's nursemaid, Agnes, was a dour woman who considered her standing as nurse to be above that of mere serfs, and refused to do any manual labour about the manor. She saw to Joan, and Eleanor had to admit that she could find no fault with Agnes there, but she was of little help with anything else.

As the first snows of December settled on the window sills, the workload increased and the monies dwindled. Small items about the manor began to disappear—a rake here, a barrel there, several chickens—as those unscrupulous in the neighbourhood took advantage of the fact that Eleanor had but one male serf for protection.

Lying awake at night, listening to every sound that now seemed so threatening, she thought of the contents of both hers and Isabeau's coffers. The wedding gifts and the remains of her dowry might prove a great temptation for those who were not content with the stealing of mere implements and livestock. She began to realise that soon she would have to accept the offer of assistance from Lord Charteris, and seek shelter at the castle. She was much reluctant to abandon the manor house, for it was both Troye and Joan's home, yet Joan's life, and those of the serfs, even her own, were more valuable than mere bricks and mortar and the chattels contained within. She prayed that Troye would agree with her.

Chapter Thirteen

In Scotland, Troye fought in battles far more violent and dangerous than any Eleanor would ever encounter, unaware of the events taking place at home. The first messenger that Lord Charteris had sent failed to find Troye, for his horse broke his leg crossing the Tweed and he passed his dispatches on to another, but the hastily penned note from Lady Eleanor to her husband lay crumpled and forgotten at the bottom of his satchel. Yet the second messenger, bearing news of Lady Anne's death, reached Edinburgh early November, where the King and his army were stalled after a disastrous campaign.

Wallace had proved himself a formidable opponent, both a warrior upon the battlefield whose skill could not be doubted, and a tactical leader who inspired devotion with his command. Wallace had devised a fighting order known as *schiltrons,* and these he used to good effect against the much-feared

English army, with its armoured cavalry and vast numbers of experienced infantry. The schiltrons con-sisted of triple tiers of twelve-foot spears facing outwards, which was very difficult for an attacking enemy to penetrate.

Troye, having experienced first hand the devastating effect of these schiltrons upon charging cavalry, nursed two broken ribs and lacerations to his arms and thighs. He felt weary, his focus on soldiering often interrupted by thoughts of home: how fared his mother, his daughter and his wife in his absence? It was difficult for him to think of Eleanor as his wife, for that place had always been held by Isabeau, but during the many miles of marching, and the long lonely nights sleeping in fields, he had recognised the fact that it was Eleanor who had exchanged holy vows with him, and now wore his ring upon her finger. It was Eleanor who shared his bed, and Eleanor who offered him the comfort of her love. He too was much troubled by their parting, the bitter words, the sound of her tears still echoing in his ears. He had never had any wish to hurt her, and though he held her in respect and had hoped their marriage would be based on mere friendship, he could no longer ignore the passion that warred and raged and fought for existence. And she had much endeared herself to him with the way she had taken care of Joan, and his mother, and her good humour with that rascal Toby always brought a smile to his lips. It seemed like a long while since there had been anything to smile about, his world had been so dark and cold and silent since Isabeau had died, but he could not deny that Eleanor had opened a window and let the sunshine in.

He was so brooding, sitting before a fire within the great stone halls of Edinburgh castle, when the King's messenger arrived, and finally he learned of the tragic events at home. He opened the parchment note that Eleanor had written:

To my most dear and respected husband Sir Troye de Valois, greetings from your obedient wife Eleanor. This is to inform you that by divine mercy your Lady Mother Anne de Valois has passed from this world to the next. Her illness was sudden yet swift and her passing peaceful. We await your most urgent return.

He sat staring, his thumb and forefinger almost caressing the paper of Eleanor's note, thinking of her sitting down to write it, considering her words, penning them in this elegant script that he now gazed upon. So it had been all those years ago, when he had been sent a message to say that Isabeau had died. His faith in God had long since faded, for what kind of a God took away those so loved and needed as Isabeau, and now his mother? With a sigh, Troye rose to his feet, carefully folded the note, placed it within his leather tunic, and then went in search of the King.

* * *

Edward stood with his advisors and commanders in a private chamber, poring over maps spread out upon the table, barking at millenars to know the whereabouts and numbers of all the men in his army, and faced with mighty decisions to be made. The provision ships had not reached them and they had only the most meagre of rations, and fighting had broken out amongst the ranks as some of the English men-at-arms and the Welsh archers seemed more interested in past feuds and settling old scores than anything else. The King was well aware, too, that desertion and mutiny were rife as hunger and exhaustion spread its evil.

'We need provisions!' Edward raged. 'God damn it, we need to feed these men and take a firm hold of our gains before winter!'

Troye entered the chamber and stood to one side amongst the throng of courtiers and officials, the military commanders muddy and weary from the field, and at their centre towered King Edward, nicknamed Longshanks because of his great height. He bristled with his usual energy and impatience as he stabbed a finger at the map. 'We must have trustworthy Englishmen hold Dirleton, as well as the two smaller castles at Lennoxmuir and Currie.' He turned to his Chancellor. 'Who do we have? What of Ruthven? He will do well enough for Lennoxmuir, but I'll not be leaving Bishop Bek in Dirleton, he's too soft and too weak!'

'Ruthven was killed at Stirling Bridge, sire,' a secretary informed the King quietly.

'Well, then, what of Stratford? Or Talbot?'

'They are both hereabouts. I will send for them at once, sire.'

'They are neither of them married, as I recall,' mused the King, 'no doubt breeding with the Scots will do little harm to our blood and may well improve theirs.'

Glances were exchanged behind Edward's back, though none dared to voice any objections to the policy of forging alliances with the enemy through marriage that had been in practice since William had first conquered Saxon shores. At that moment Edward looked up and espied Troye, as he manoeuvred himself forwards and hoped to gain the attention of a courtier, and ask for an audience with the King.

'Ah, de Valois,' Edward exclaimed, beckoning him forth, 'what say you to taking Castle Currie? I believe you will do well to hold it for me, and I will sweeten the deal with a Scottish bride and title of laird, as well as a bounty for your good service.'

Troye bowed and murmured, 'I am already married, sire.'

Edward frowned, stroking his white beard, and then his face cleared as he remembered, nodding his head. 'Indeed, the lovely Eleanor.' But his plan was not so easily thwarted. 'Well, send for your wife and install her at Castle Currie. Is she breeding yet?'

Troye answered as calmly as he could, well used to his liege's outspoken and forthright comments, 'Not that I know of, sire.'

'Excellent. You will find Currie to be most accommodating, a fine castle to raise a family in, and I have every faith that you will not let it fall back into the hands of Wallace.'

'Sire—' Troye looked at him askance as the King turned away, having to all intents and purposes settled the matter to his own satisfaction.

'What is it, man? Spit it out, can't you see how busy I am trying to run a war!' He smiled, and there were a few chuckles of obliging laughter for his attempt at humour in the face of a grave situation.

'Sire, my mother has recently died. I would humbly request that I might take a leave of absence to return to York.'

'I am sorry to hear that,' Edward replied, yet for several moments he considered whether he was willing to release one of his most able and trustworthy soldiers. 'Very well. But you will return as soon as possible. Before Christmas I want you at Castle Currie, accompanied by Lady Eleanor, for we will show these Scottish rebels that my word is law and the English are here to stay.'

Troye bowed. 'Thank you, sire. It will be so.'

The day was waning, but before the sun had set Troye and Dylan had fastened on their armour, mounted their horses, and galloped south. Yet with Troye's broken ribs and their horses much exhausted from the campaign, progress was slow. Along the way Troye had time to mull over the future, which now seemed to be in Scotland. What would Eleanor say to the news? Considering their bitter parting, he had a feeling that her plans for the future did not include the defence and holding of a castle in the wilds of Scotland.

Eleanor was indeed worrying about the future. As the cold of winter set in, the workload doubled as Simon struggled to collect enough timber and chop it up to keep the fires, hot water and the cooking for the manor house going. Meg had gone into labour several weeks too early, and though Eleanor was much relieved at her safe delivery, thanks to her experience as midwife to her Aunt Beatrice, they were short of a pair of hands about the house. And funds were very low. There was no income coming in, now that Lady Anne's import-and-export wool business had fallen by the wayside upon her death. She was for ever dipping into her dowry, but with Troye gone, and no word as to his whereabouts or whether he had any intention of ever returning, she was indeed greatly concerned for the future.

One afternoon, as she sat huddled by a meagre fire darning Joan's stockings, a knock sounded at the front door. Eleanor rose and peered cautiously from the window, but she could not see who it might be. She was reluctant to open the door as Simon was out foraging for timber, Meg lay in her room nursing her newborn babe, and Joan was belaboured by a cold and asleep with Agnes upstairs. Alone, she went to the door, now always barred, and called, 'Who is there?'

'It is I, the High Sheriff, Sir Malcolm Rix.'

Eleanor's heart sank, and she bit her thumb in vexation as she considered what to do. If only she had not called out! She could have pretended that no one was home. On his last visit, Sir Malcolm had been keen to remind her of the taxes that Lady Anne had owed, and also to impress upon her how eager he was to be of assistance 'during her time of need'. He had laid his hand on her shoulder, squeezing in a most familiar fashion that had alarmed Eleanor, and she had vowed then to avoid him at all costs.

'Lady Eleanor, 'tis snowing, and I have brought you and your household a gift of plum cake and brandy for the Yuletide.'

Oh, bother! Eleanor sighed, although she saw no help for it but to open up the door and smile as graciously as she could, standing on the doorstep and hoping that Sir Malcolm would soon depart. But she had not reckoned on him shouldering his way past her, and entering the hall without so much as a 'by your leave'. The wintry wind was blowing away any warmth from the fire and quickly she shut the door upon the draught, turning slowly to face Sir Malcolm. He set his basket down upon the table and beamed a jovial smile as he pulled off his cloak and cap and went to warm his hands, and his vast backside, before the fire. Eleanor stood as far distant from him as politely possible.

'Mayhap you would call your maid and have her take this basket to the kitchen.'

Eleanor avoided his glance, as she murmured a polite thanks and prevaricated, 'She is attending to her babe at the moment. I will call her anon.'

With a few more questions, which Eleanor realised too late, he established that she was alone. And then he wasted no more time, indeed, seemed most eager, his hands trembling slightly and his face flushed, as he withdrew from the tunic that covered his protruding belly a sheaf of papers. He went to the table and laid them out, glancing over his shoulder at Eleanor.

'As you will see, my dear, these are the taxes that are still outstanding to the City of York. They are for moorage on the river, the King's tithe on wool, and other payments that are due. I am sure you do not wish me to go into all the dull details. But here...' he pointed one finger '...here is the amount that has been long overdue.'

Eleanor gasped, for the sum was quite considerable. More than she possessed to hand, even with her dowry monies. 'I—I don't understand,' Eleanor stammered. 'This is a matter that you will have to settle with my husband.'

'Ah...' Sir Malcolm mused in a long, sarcastic drawl, 'your husband. How long has he been gone now? Two months? Three?'

'He will be home soon, I am sure. We have sent word.'

'Indeed. But I hear the King fares badly in Scotland. Many have been killed and starvation is their greatest enemy.'

Eleanor was silent, her eyes downcast, but anger slowly mounting at his insinuations. 'I am sorry, Sir Malcolm. There is nothing I can do at the moment.'

'Well, now...' he leaned towards her, one of his huge hands covering hers as it rested on the table, heavy and hot with damp sweat '...I am sure we can come to some...arrangement.'

Eleanor arched away from him, his breath repulsive on her cheek, and her heart suddenly fluttered with alarm. 'I fear there is nothing to be done. I do not have that amount of money to pay the taxes.'

'Mayhap you have something other than money to offer me,' he murmured, looking down at her, his eyes heavy as they lowered to the swell of her bosom.

Eleanor tried to snatch her hand away, outraged at his implication. 'Sir, I—I would never…and—and I—I am a married woman!'

He barked a short laugh. 'Are you, Lady Eleanor? I think it much more likely that you are a widow, like myself. Life is very hard for a woman, left alone and penniless in this world. You would do well to accept offers of friendship where ever and whenever you can.'

'Please go!' Eleanor felt her temper, and her fear, rise and she tried again to free her hand from his grasp.

Yet he would not yield and she gave a small cry as suddenly his arm snaked around her waist and he pulled her towards him, pressing her down upon the table top as he sought to cover her mouth with his. Eleanor shuddered with revulsion as his wet, fleshy lips gobbled on her and she gave a mighty heave with her arms, trying to push the bulk of his corpulent body away, but he was heavy indeed.

From the corner of her eye she saw a shadow pass over the window, and she prayed that it was Simon returned from the woods. As Sir Malcolm placed his hand upon her breast and tried to spread her legs, she struggled desperately, her scream for help muffled by his slobbering face. The front door crashed open, and booted feet pounded on the flagstones as someone charged into the room. She heard the ringing hiss of steel and closed her eyes, knowing that her prayers had been more than just answered—she had been given a miracle.

The silver tip of a sword suddenly pricked Sir Malcolm upon his double chins. With a choked cry of dismay he levered himself away from Eleanor, with hands upraised as he turned to stare at Troye. Free of his crushing weight, Eleanor quickly rose and straightened her gown, she too turning to look upon the man who had so often been the one to rescue her from every predicament, her eyes taking in all aspects of his much-missed appearance.

Without speaking a word, using only the lethal point of his sword, Troye manoeuvred their unwanted visitor to the door, there bowing to him with a sardonic half-smile. 'Be grateful, sir, that I have had my fill of killing in these weeks past. Now be gone, and never seek to lay a hand upon my wife, or to set foot on my land, again.'

Sir Malcolm needed no second bidding and he ran down the road, forgetting his cloak and cap, as fast as his tree-trunk legs would carry him.

Troye closed the door and sheathed his sword, then he turned to Eleanor. They stared at each other for long, silent moments; though his face was dirty and unshaven and he seemed so gaunt, to her eyes he was very dear and handsome. Yet their last parting was up-permost in her mind and she feared his thoughts, rushing to explain all in one breath.

'Troye, I—I did nothing to encourage him, indeed I was trying my best to get rid of him, but he was very heavy, and—and these past few weeks all has been so difficult and I don't know what to do, and Meg has had a babe, she and Simon are wed now, please don't be angry—'

'Shh,' Troye smiled slightly and held up one hand, to halt her flow of words, 'I am sorry that it has taken so long for me to return, and that you have been left alone to cope with it all. Yet before all other matters, first there is something I must do before the day is done.'

Eleanor frowned, her hands clasped pensively to her chest, her voice anxious, 'What is it?'

'Say goodbye to my mother.'

'Of course,' she murmured, although in her heart she feared that once again he would shut her out as he dealt with his grief, and she stood there uncertainly.

Troye could not find words or understand what it was that he felt or wanted, but he held out his hand to her, and said, 'Show me, Eleanor.'

Gladly she went to fetch her cloak and threw up the hood upon the chill wind that swirled about on this winter afternoon. The snow crunched beneath their boots as they walked to the village, heads bowed against the fluttering flakes of snow. Each breath that she took burned with a sharp pain, so cold was the winter air, but Eleanor did not flinch, such was her inner joy to have Troye home.

They reached the churchyard and Eleanor led him to the new grave beside that of Isabeau. She hastily explained that a headstone had been commissioned, but the mason had not yet finished with it, but Troye only stood silent, staring at the mound of dark earth now rapidly turning white as the snow covered it.

'She was no great age.'

'Aye,' Eleanor murmured, watching him from the corner of her eye, wondering what words of comfort she could offer.

'What…how…?' he floundered helplessly.

''Twas a seizure. One morning she awoke paralysed and then she became unconscious…' Eleanor paused, uncertain whether he wanted to hear all the grim details.

'And then she died.' His voice was sharp. 'I never had the chance to say goodbye. Just like Isabeau.'

Troye's face set in a hard grim line as the anger and the pain burst afresh within him. Eleanor reached out and laid her hand upon his forearm, but he shook her off and abruptly turned on his heel as he walked away. He grabbed a stick lying on the ground and flung it at the sky, shouting to the heavens at the top of his voice, 'Why?'

Eleanor stared at him, surprised at this outburst from a man she had grown accustomed to being always so self-disciplined. 'Mayhap—' she offered tentatively, about to voice some words of comfort.

'Don't!' he shouted, pointing one finger at her. 'Don't you dare give me any meaningless platitudes about it being God's will!'

She stepped back, wide-eyed at the force of his anger. He turned away from her, kicking at the drifting snow, until his rage had ebbed to no more than a flicker. He turned then, and looked at her across the distance between them, and asked in a quiet voice, 'What good has it done to take my mother, and my beloved Isabeau? Hmm? Can your God answer that one?' He stared at her for a long, hard moment and replied to his own question in a dull voice, 'No, of course not. I have asked that question a hundred times and never received an answer. Never.' With a heavy sigh he turned away abruptly. 'Come, let us return to the house.'

Eleanor paused as she made to follow. She read the inscription on Isabeau's headstone: *Loved and Cherished For Ever.*

How lucky had Isabeau de Valois been! To have been loved by Troye, and now still cherished by him. How she wished that she was so loved.

Eleanor looked up at him, and saw the unshed tears that glittered like glass shards in his dark eyes that he tried to blink away. Suddenly, when grief for her own aching heart could not be countenanced, she ached with his. She felt his pain, a mirror of her own, and tears slid silent from her eyes. With a small sound that had no words she opened her arms, and after a moment of hesitation he turned and stepped into them. He stooped, pressing his face against the soft, smooth warmth of her neck, the wetness of his tears soon dampening her skin and the tendrils of her hair as she encircled the broad, muscular width of his shaking shoulders with her slender arms. He tried to pull away, to stop himself, but she would not let him. She held him and stroked the back of his neck with one hand, her soft voice soothing, encouraging the festering wound to open, to drain away all its venom. And the sorrow, so long pent up, was like a deep abscess that now burst forth.

'How can it be so?' he sobbed, his voice muffled. 'How could God have let these things happen? To ones so good and so loved. There can be no God, for surely if He loved us He would not have cursed us so.'

She patted his shoulder. Neither she nor any human could have the answer to such questions. There was no reason, no explanation, nor logic. There was only the gift of comfort from one soul to another. They clung to each other while Troye wept, and silent tears streaked down Eleanor's cheeks. Her heart ached for all things that had been loved and lost, that made each day a blackness that could scarce be born, and the despair of it robbed the soul of hope. She had felt so alone…so abandoned…but now, at last, Troye had come to her and that was a miracle in itself and must surely prove that there was a God, one who had love and mercy for the creatures he had created. The tears that washed her cheeks hurt, like splinters of ice that burst from behind her eyes.

Alone they stood, isolated in the graveyard as the winter wind and snow swirled around them, muffling the world beyond, shutting them into their own little domain. At last Troye lifted his face from her neck, sniffed and mopped at his eyes and nose with a corner of his cloak. He flushed and would not meet her stare.

'I am sorry,' he said, stiffly, gazing at the stark treetops. 'Forgive me. I have never cried. Even when we buried her I did not cry.'

'Why?'

He looked at her then, with a puzzled frown, 'Why? I—I…' He did not know how to answer that question, and he floundered for an explanation. 'Because, then, at that time, I could not believe it…and…I am a man, a knight, I must be strong. 'Tis weakness to show one's feelings.'

Eleanor laid her hand upon his chest, over his heart. ''Tis not a weakness.' She felt a faint spark of anger, flickering within her mind. 'How could it be weak to show that you loved someone? How could your grief earn anything but respect?'

His eyes were red and swollen from weeping, as he

looked down at her, with a watery smile, and touched his fingertips gently to her cheek, chilled with frozen tears. 'I live in a man's world, Eleanor, a world very different from yours. Not everyone thinks as you do, with the soft kindness of a woman. Come now,' he said briskly, cupping her cold face, 'you are freezing and this is no weather to linger in. Let us go home.'

'Aye,' she agreed, returning the gesture by cupping Troye's face with the palm of her hand.

For a moment they stood thus, man and woman, clasped hand to cheek, the only contact between their two separate bodies, and yet their eyes, mirrors of the soul, looked deeply one to the other. He knew the worst that had ever happened to her, and she knew the worst that had ever happened to him. And here they both stood, battered and bruised in body and soul, and yet they survived. Eleanor wondered why.

'There must be a God,' she whispered, 'for He has given us each other.'

Troye made no reply, but abruptly turned away from the graves and walked away. She turned with him and fell into step at his side. As they neared the church Eleanor asked him to stop, and for the loan of his dagger. Troye yielded to both requests and watched as Eleanor went to the hedge of glossy dark green holly studded with red berries that crowded around the porch entrance. She cut several boughs and went back to the graves of Lady Anne and

Isabeau. She knelt and laid a bough of holly on each
of them.

As she had many times before Eleanor read the inscription: *Loved and Cherished For Ever.* Silently
she prayed, with heartfelt earnestness, Please, let him
go. I will love and care for him and never hurt him.
Please, Isabeau. Please let him go and come to me.

They walked slowly home, as they had many
times before, but on this late winter's afternoon
they both sensed a difference. There was a peace
that surrounded them, no longer the swirling,
burning, aching tension that had always been
between them before. And yet when they entered
the manor house, the presence between them
returned. Eleanor looked about, sensing that
Isabeau was everywhere in this house and that, as
long as they stayed here, she would always be a
reminder for Troye to cling to.

Dylan had been helping Simon with the chopping
of wood and the house now roared with fires in
every grate. In the kitchen Meg was busy, her babe
asleep in a wooden cradle beneath the kitchen table,
and that evening they sat down to eat a hot and
hearty meal, master and squire, mistress and maid,
altogether as one family at the scrubbed kitchen
table. They exchanged their news, although there
was one item that Troye kept to himself, and though

he had been of a mind to take his entire household with him to Scotland, he now wondered at the wisdom of it.

After the meal had been enjoyed, and the table cleared, Troye went to look in on Joan, and Eleanor retired to the hall, closing the door to the kitchen and taking her sewing into her lap as she sat down before the warm, crackling flames of the hearth. Her gaze strayed to the empty chair opposite, where Lady Anne has so often sat and they had passed the evenings together. Yet before she had time to feel the ache of loneliness Troye came thumping down the stairs. He paused for a moment, glancing at Eleanor, and then he piled logs on the fire, checked the shutters were barred on all the windows, had a few words with Dylan before bidding him seek his bed in the kitchen, and then returned to stand awkwardly before the hearth. He warmed his hands, the silence stretching. Eleanor glanced up at him, and then down at her needle plying its way with uneven stitches through the soft linen of a tiny gown for Joan.

Troye cleared his throat. 'The King…'

Eleanor glanced up, aware of his hesitation, and then smiled gently, encouraging him to continue, 'Aye? And what has the King to say for himself?'

Troye frowned at a spot on a distant wall. 'The King has asked me to take lands in Scotland. Hold them for him. He sweetens the deal with a title and bounty,' Troye stated boldly, and then he looked at her and asked, 'What say you?'

Her sewing fell idle into her lap, as she considered his words. 'Does the King ask, or does he order?'

Troye stared down at his boots for a moment, with a wry smile. 'Well, it is a request that cannot be refused.'

'And…' She hesitated, uncertain what it was that he was trying to say. 'You are eager to obey?'

His glance lifted quickly to meet hers, a slight frown creasing his brows. 'I have no choice but to obey.'

'I see.' Eleanor felt her heart skip a few beats, fear rushing through her veins as she dreaded the words that he seemed reluctant to say. She voiced them in his stead. 'Well, then, you must go. If it pleases, my lord, I would only ask that you provide for your family. There are taxes to be paid, and male serfs are needed to protect Joan and me from—' Her voice broke suddenly, as her mind envisioned a future without Troye. 'If…I—I would ask, then, that—that I might…' she sniffed, angry with her weakness '…if I could please return to my family in Somerset.'

'What?' Troye stared at her.

'I cannot stay here alone!'

It dawned on Troye that she had misunderstood, and he rushed to explain. 'Nay, indeed, you may not return to your family.' He ignored her gasp. 'It is the King's wish that I take my wife with me to Scotland. That we settle there and raise a family.'

Eleanor stared at him, and then flung aside her sewing and rose swiftly to her feet. 'Is that so?' she demanded, the issue that so vexed her and their marriage suddenly rearing its ugly head. 'And which wife would that be, Troye?'

'Eleanor—' he growled a note of warning.

'Nay, Troye, I will not go! I will not live with you, nor lie with you and breed like—like a cow with a bull just to suit the King!'

'It is not like that—' He reached out then, trying to embrace her, but she flung her arms up and struck away his hands.

'Is it not? I think it is, Troye! From the very first day we were wed you have had no feeling for me, and you have bedded me like you would a whore! With no love and no tenderness and no passion!'

He took a step towards her, his voice firm. 'Stop. It grieves me to hear you speak so.'

'Well, it grieves me to be treated so! I will not do it, Troye, I will not go with you to Scotland, nor let you have the use of my body to please the King of England!'

'Eleanor, please—' His ribs ached, but when she went to flounce away from him, he grabbed hold of her and pulled her close, smothering a grunt of pain. 'Listen to me, please.' He grasped her chin between his fingers and forced her to look at him, subduing her struggles as she tried to pull away. 'I am sorry for the way things have been between us, but it is not true that I have no feeling for you. 'Tis not easy to forget…the past…but I have missed you these many weeks away from home, and I would try to make amends. In Scotland, away from here, we could start afresh.'

Eleanor strained in his grasp, arching away from him, reluctant to trust that he would not hurt her as he had before. He pulled her closer and his head lowered, his shoulders stooped as he reached down. She felt the heat and strength of his muscular body, the firm contours of his lips as they captured her own. She surrendered then, sagging against his chest, his mouth moving firmly yet gently on hers, and when her lips parted and accepted him, his tongue slid between and entered her mouth, seeking out her tongue, drawing from her a response with his kiss.

Her body remembered the feel of his, knew each contour as she knew her own, and the heat that flared within her was white hot. His kiss deepened, his hand supporting the back of her head, and she pressed her aching breasts to his chest, her arms sliding around his back, her hips swaying to meet his, all too aware of his male arousal. And yet, as she clasped him, and he groaned, wincing, flinching away, she struggled through the haze of passion and became aware that his groans were those of pain.

'Troye…' She pulled away, and looked up at him, at the grimace on his face, and then down as she felt through his tunic the thick wadding of bandages. 'You are injured! Why did you not say?'

''Tis nothing—' he tried to pull her back '—just a few broken ribs.'

'Broken ribs!' Eleanor exclaimed, shocked. 'Why, you need to be abed!'

He smiled at her, his gaze lingering on her kiss-reddened lips, and moving down to the swell of her bosom, his hands firmly holding the curve of her hips as he drew her to him. 'Aye.' His voice was a warm whisper as he kissed her neck, aware that it had been so long since he had flirted with a woman that he had almost lost the knack, yet he tried, caressing Eleanor's ear with his lips as he murmured, 'Aye, bed is what I need.'

Despite the fever his kisses had woken in her blood, she still feared to yield to his lust when it was his love she wanted. She seized upon the excuse of his injury to delay matters. 'My lord is in need of attention—'

He nibbled her ear, pushing aside the strands of silky hair. 'Indeed.'

'Oh, tush! You stink, my lord, and I only hope that it is dirt and not festering wounds.'

Troye sighed and feigned an expression of great offence. 'My lady adds to my wounds.'

'Nonsense. Get you upstairs to our chamber.' Eleanor pushed him away, and then hurried to the kitchen and roused the serfs, urging them to heat water and bring the bathing tub to the master's bed-chamber.

They were little pleased with this activity, but they obeyed. Once it was all set up, the tub of hot water steaming before the fire hearth of the bedchamber, she thanked Dylan and Simon for their efforts and then dismissed them.

'Shall we return to empty the water, my lady?' Simon asked, glancing with curiosity at Troye as he stripped.

'Nay—' Eleanor too was aware of Troye shedding his clothes '—leave it until morning.'

She bid them both goodnight and closed the door. Then she went to her medicine chest and sought out healing creams to apply to the cuts and blisters on Troye's body. From the corner of her eye, she glanced at him, concerned at how thin he seemed, how battered and bruised. She could only imagine how rough a soldier's life must be, and she longed to hold him in the soft comfort of her arms.

Troye sank down into the hot water of the bathing tub, with an audible moan of pleasure. He washed with the bar of fragrant lavender soap that she handed to him, commenting wryly that he would smell like a woman.

''Tis better than stinking like a pigsty,' Eleanor retorted.

'My lady's tongue is sharp tonight,' Troye replied, eyeing her with wary thoughtfulness as he sat back to enjoy the luxury of a hot bath. Eleanor seemed different…more grown-up…more of a woman…he could not quite put his finger on it, but his suspicions were aroused, and he asked casually, 'I am sorry that you have been left alone these months past, with the likes of Sir Malcolm to deal with.'

She paused as she laid out her jars on the table, glancing across the room at him. 'It has not been easy.'

'I hear from my Lord Charteris that he has been of assistance to you.'

'Indeed. He is a most kind gentleman.'

'And…were there others?'

'Other what?'

'Gentlemen?'

'Oh, indeed,' Eleanor scoffed, 'I was quite inundated with them!'

Water splashed as Troye sat up. 'Name them!'

'Why, there were so many I cannot recall their names!'

Troye rose from the bath, stepping out of it naked and powerful as he strode to her side, heeding not the puddles of water that he dripped, and grasping her wrist as he snatched her close to him. 'Have you lain with other men, Eleanor?'

Too late she remembered his jealous streak, and with a small gasp she strained away and stared up at him. 'Why do you say such a thing to me?'

His glance fell to the pink swell of her lips, and the

curve of her breasts, that seemed fuller than he remembered. Was she with child? By another man? 'It is not unknown that while a knight is far from home others will take advantage. And you seem…different…as though…' he paused, trying to pinpoint what it was '…as though you have learned the secrets of womanhood.' His glance was dark and brooding as he looked her in the eyes. 'Which I know you have not experienced with me.'

Eleanor blushed hotly. It was true, she had experienced her own womanliness, and she might have known that Troye would so easily have sensed this, yet how was she to say that it was by her own hand? That was taboo, and her eyelashes cast down as she glanced away from his penetrating stare.

'I have not lain with any man, except you. That I can promise, Troye.'

He stared at her for long, hard moments, but then he released her wrist and seemed to accept her word. Quickly, to distract him from the subject, she reached for a linen and patted him dry, then applied arnica cream to his wounds, and fastened clean bandages to support his ribs. At the end of her ministrations he thanked her, and climbed between the covers of the bed. He lay back with a sigh, exhausted.

Eleanor moved about the room, tidying away, delaying the moment when she must undress and lie beside him.

'Come to bed, Eleanor,' Troye's voice commanded, his patience utterly worn, and yet he could not fail to note the hesitation on her part, 'Have no fear, I am in no fit state to play the bull. The hour is late and 'tis time to sleep.'

Quietly she blew out the candles and unlaced her gown, shrugging it off, and her shoes, sitting on the edge of the bed as she slid off her hose. Then, still wearing her shift, she lifted the covers and slid into bed beside him. He felt so warm, and the smell of his musky maleness overlaid the scent of soap. She lay back, not at all sure how she should respond if he touched her. She wanted him, but not here, not in this bed, not in this house. She almost jumped when she felt his hand touch her arm.

'Eleanor?'

'Hmm?'

'I—' He did not know how to voice his thoughts, his feelings, so he leaned down and pressed a kiss to the curve of her shoulder, the skin soft and smooth beneath his lips. 'I thought…mayhap…that is—' He cleared his throat, frustrated with his own lack of practice when it came to wooing a woman. He tried another approach. 'You are very beautiful, Eleanor.' He ran his hand from her shoulder down the length of her body, over the high mound of her splendid breasts and down the slender curve of waist and womanly hip. 'Very desirable—'

Eleanor sighed, resigned to her wifely duty, turning her head slightly away as she parted her thighs for him, her voice wooden as she murmured, 'As you wish, my lord.'

He exclaimed softly on a curse, reaching out to grasp her jaw and turn her back to him, wishing that in the dark he could see her eyes, 'I did not mean it like that! Besides, with my ribs broken I am far from capable of mounting you.'

'You wish me to go on top?' She half-turned towards him, lifting the hem of her shift.

'Nay!' His fingers circled her wrist, pulling her shift back down into place, covering her silky limbs, even though the feel of her, so close, was arousing him. 'What I am trying to say, Eleanor—' he raked one hand through his still-damp hair, wondering why he was stumbling like a callow youth rather than a man full grown '—I—I want to…start again…woo you…court you. Let us see if, mayhap, we can love each other, as a husband and wife should.'

Eleanor turned towards him then, her voice soft and gentle as she whispered, 'I do love you, Troye. I have always loved you.'

His hand reached up and gently stroked her cheek with his thumb as he cupped her face, murmuring in reply, 'I know. I cannot understand why, for what have I ever done to make you love me?'

'Love needs no reason. It just is.'

'Aye.' He thought of Isabeau for a moment, and by her silence he sensed that Eleanor knew where his thoughts strayed. 'I cannot ever stop loving her. She will always be a part of me. Can you understand that?'

Eleanor nodded, terrified that now he would speak the words that would for ever separate them, and she trembled, holding back the tears that were so close.

He felt her shiver, and his arms went around her, gathering her close, as he kissed her temple, her cheek, her lips. 'But I can understand and begin to accept that she is my past. And you are the future. I need time, Eleanor, please, time to let go and time to become accustomed to you. It will not be impossible to love you, for I hold you in great respect and admiration and I hope we are the best of friends, but that is something I must to learn feel again.'

It was more than she had ever hoped for, and with a tremulous smile, Eleanor nodded, unable to trust her voice to speak a word. They held each other for a long while, and then fell asleep.

Chapter Fourteen

Troye wasted no time, now that the decision had been made, in packing up his family and his chattels, in preparation for their removal to Scotland. He was urged on by the need to put the past behind him and start afresh, as he had promised Eleanor, and yet constrained by the fact that he could not bear to forget Isabeau. Every time he looked at Joan, he was reminded of her, and the manor house too bore silent witness to their love and marriage. It was a long relationship, stretching back to his childhood, and he felt that he could no more forget Isabeau than he could forget himself.

Yet there was Eleanor to think of now. He had no wish to hurt her with the memories of a woman she had never known, and he did truly want her, them, to be happy together. So it was that he had to reach a compromise, and one that brought much consternation from neighbours and friends. He decided to take

Eleanor and Joan, and the nurse Agnes, with him to Scotland, but to leave behind Simon and Meg, and cut all his ties with York. The manor house was a burden he no longer wished to carry, so he gifted it outright to Simon and Meg, the two servants who had remained faithful and loyal to Eleanor in her time of need, and made them free persons, no longer bound in service to the de Valois family.

'On one condition,' Troye told the stunned young couple, as he handed them the deeds, 'that you hold in safekeeping my late wife's wedding coffer. One day Joan will want to know about her past, and her mother, and she will come to claim it.'

Simon took the parchment papers in his hand, staring at the red ribbon binding them, quite overwhelmed at Troye's generosity, until Meg nudged him and they both offered their profuse thanks, mere words seeming too small for such a great gift. Yet already Troye had turned away, his attention moving on to the next hurdle that stood between him and Scotland.

Eleanor spent every moment of her day sorting through her clothes and possessions and those of Joan, to decide what they would take with them. She constantly asked Troye if they would need this, or that, but he seemed vague and had little idea what provisions would await them at Castle Currie.

'And what of the Scots who live there?' Eleanor asked, a worried frown creasing her brow. 'Will they not be angry to have an English knight take command of their keep? Will we be safe?'

Troye stared at her, realising that she had little understanding of the situation. He sat upon a chair, sorting through a box of letters to do with his mother's estate, but he paused a moment. 'I will not lie to you, Eleanor. It is hostile territory we go to, but I will have a company of knights and at least fifty foot soldiers to hold Currie. Have no fear for the Scots who live there, for they have either been slain in battle or fled. That is why the King settles his own people in these places, so they do not fall back into rebel hands.'

'But—' Eleanor was somewhat perplexed '—it is a Scottish castle, in Scotland. Surely 'tis the right of Scots people to hold it?'

Troye snorted and rolled his eyes. 'For God's sake, Eleanor, that is treason to speak so! Never say such a thing again.'

She pouted, and he almost laughed at her belligerent frown. 'Well, I care not for the King's grand plan. It does not seem fair to me, and no doubt it is the women and children of the land who suffer most.'

He shook his head. 'They are a tough breed. No doubt they will survive.'

Setting aside the candlestick that she wrapped in linen and placed in a wooden chest, to be conveyed to this far-off castle in Scotland, she asked, 'What if we did not go? Would the King be angry?'

'Aye.'

'But surely he cannot force you to go to this—this Castle Currie.'

Troye stared at her. 'My duty is to the King, Eleanor. I would never disobey. Besides, where else would we go?'

Eleanor cast her eyes down, and murmured, 'We could go south, to my family.'

He set aside the box then, and rose from his seat, crossing the room to stand beside her, one hand upon her waist and the other raising her chin, so that he might look her directly in the eye. 'Is it your wish not to go with me to Scotland?'

Eleanor hesitated. 'I—I confess that I have no great desire to live in a land troubled with war, where we are strangers, and one that I hear is wild and cold and wet...' she raised her eyes to his '...but I would go wherever you go.'

He smiled then, and leaned down, gently placing a kiss upon her lips. Eleanor closed her eyes, savouring the feel of his lips moving on hers. Though they had not yet resumed intimate relations, often in the few days past he had been most attentive, with the gift of a kiss here, an embrace there, a smile, the touch of hands often. In all honesty she was somewhat nervous about the time when he would want to claim his rights. She knew that there was pleasure to be had, but would Troye be patient and tender and willing to give it to her? What hope for their marriage if he could not? During the few days before their departure she was glad that he was too busy and too discomforted by his slow healing ribs to make any attempt to couple with her, and he seemed content with a mere kiss good-night.

At last, they rose early one morn as soon as it was light, and Simon assisted Dylan to load the cart with the chests and coffers and leather bags containing food and drink, linen for the beds, furs and covers. They took also the family Bible that Eleanor had often read with Lady Anne, a few precious possessions like candlesticks and pens and ink and books. They took clothes and Joan's few wooden toys, Toby the dog, and Agnes the nursemaid, but much of their old lives and old possessions they left behind. Isabeau's wedding coffer stood locked in the bedchamber, to await the day in a distant future when Joan would come to claim her inheritance.

Eleanor rode Luz, with Dylan driving the cart, his horse tethered to the tailgate. Agnes and Joan sat upon the hard wooden bench beside him, ensconced in thick bear furs, neither looking forward to the long journey ahead, one because she was too old, and the other because she was too young.

Troye was silent as he mounted Merlin and took up the reins of the mighty destrier. He checked that they were all ready to depart, then he glanced up once at the windows of the manor house, nodded a goodbye to Simon and Meg standing in the doorway, and turned towards the road. Eleanor too glanced up at the house, called out her farewell, and then she urged Luz forwards and took her place beside her husband, as together they rode away from York.

It was a long and arduous journey. They spent most nights sheltering at inns and friendly keeps, for the weather was too cold with snow and wind swirling all about to make camp. Eleanor insisted that Joan sleep with them, for she was much disturbed by the rigours and uncertainties of the journey, clinging to Eleanor and easily fractious at any excuse. Troye readily agreed, for entirely different reasons, much aware of the dangers of kidnap and the fragile condition of their marriage. Though he tried to give Eleanor his ardent attention she seemed to shy away from intimacy, a reaction that both perplexed and worried him. It was no surprise, though, given the fact that her experiences so far of the marriage bed had not been all that they should have, and for this he could blame no one except himself. For the moment there was little he could do about it, but once they were safely settled within the solid walls of Castle Currie, he could, and would, deal with the compelling matter of his wife's satisfaction. In the meantime, it made for a most interesting and provocative subject for his thoughts to dwell on, as he rode at the head of their slow-moving party, a slight smile upon his lips.

At Berwick-upon-Tweed they met with an escort that accompanied them to Edinburgh, heavily armoured, with cavalry knights riding to the fore, Welsh and Gascon archers on foot to the rear. Eleanor had to take a firm hand with Luz, skittish with all the warhorses, the clank of armour and lances, the general air of tense anticipation as they rode through dangerous territory. At any moment she expected to see wild Scotsmen in kilts running down from the surrounding hills to attack them, but they reached their destination without much ado. The fortress of Edinburgh Castle, towering on its solid mount of rock, was a forbidding sight and within its dark and draughty halls it was no better.

They stayed for several days, while Troye organised the forces that he would take with them to Castle Currie. Situated a mere ten miles south-west of Edinburgh, the small castle was one of several that surrounded the capital, and of some strategic value. Eleanor was glad they would soon set out, for it had been no pleasure cooped up with a moaning nurse-maid, a fretful child and hundreds of soldiers, who seemed as quick to fall out of sorts and pick a fight as young Joan.

* * *

She felt that it boded well when the day of their departure for Currie dawned bright and clear. It was cold, and the snow lay sparkling diamond-white on the ground, but the sky was a bright blue and the sun shone. Her heart lifted as they travelled with their hearth knights and a large force of some fifty foot soldiers and archers, marching swiftly along the glens until at last she caught a glimpse of her new home. The castle was set beside a loch, close to a hillside that in summer would blaze yellow and purple with gorse and heather, but was now a gleaming background of white. At first glance she thought the sheer granite walls, ungraced by towers or battlements, very stern, but once they were within the courtyard, with the gates firmly closed, she thought there was some charm about the castle. A set of steps led up to the hall, and here she was most happily surprised, with the walls lined with oak panelling and tapestries, fires roaring in all the hearths, and the walls freshly whitewashed in those rooms that were not panelled. Her fears that there would be little of comfort were unfounded; indeed, there were enough chairs and tables, beds and chests, all of a handsome and carved dark oak.

Troye had gone to great pains to send ahead a party to make the castle ready. His orders had been most firm, to clear away the debris and ruin of battle and make it habitable for his lady wife and child. The

Laird and his sons had been killed, his wife and daughter taken as hostage by King Edward, his retainers and serfs fled into the hills to join with Wallace. Though he knew Eleanor to be greatly troubled by the conquest, Troye's sworn loyalty was to his King. He had been entrusted with holding Currie, and hold it he would, his conscience little troubling him.

On their arrival his first priority was to see to their defence. He posted guards night and day and sent out scouts to see what lurked in the countryside. No one was allowed to pass or enter the castle without careful inspection. All the servants taken on to work within it were the English camp-followers of his own English men, and mighty glad were these women and children for the chance to be out of the cruel grip of winter; he had no doubts of their loyalty.

It was a busy time, and most nights he did not find his way to bed until the hour was very late. Eleanor would usually be asleep, with Joan snuggled up close against her back. As Troye undressed, he cast an eye over this tableau, and though at first it pleased him that Eleanor and Joan were so fond of one another, after a few weeks it began to irk him that there was a barrier between him and the soft warmth of Eleanor.

The next day he summoned Agnes, and made it clear to her that Joan was to sleep in her nursery, and not in her stepmother's bed. Agnes dipped a curtsy, blushing red like a lobster as she realised what it was that so vexed the master.

All that day Troye struggled with his duties, his mind frequently wandering to the pleasant thought of lying this night with Eleanor, holding her in his arms and making love to her. He considered ways and means, surprising even himself at his imagination and ardour. He wondered where on her soft body she would most enjoy the feel of his lips, his fingers, his tongue…

'My lord!'

Troye started as one of the serjeant-at-arms called his attention, blushing as profusely as the nurse and striding across the bailey to attend to the summons. Yet at last the day was done and he sat down in the hall to enjoy his evening meal, with Eleanor at his side. He cast her a sideways glance, noting how her hair shone, rippling like a silken banner down her back, how winter-pale and soft her skin, the curve of her mouth shapely and inviting.

Eleanor was anxious that Troye would approve of her housekeeping, for she had never had the responsibility of running such a large household before, though her mother had schooled her well and Castle Ashton had been busy with hearth knights and pages and squires and servants, as was Currie. It was strange how quickly she had felt at home within the walls of this austere Scottish castle, set in a glen miles from anywhere; indeed, much more than she ever had at the manor house in York.

'Try this dish, my lord,' Eleanor urged, ''tis called haggis and is most popular with the Scots.'

Troye eyed it suspiciously. 'Where does it come from? You know well enough we must be careful about all our supplies. The Scots would think nothing of poisoning the lot of us if they could.'

'Have no fear, it comes from Edinburgh and the cooks assure me it is well made.'

Troye sliced himself a chunk and chewed upon it, accepting a mug of heather ale from a servant hovering at his elbow. He nodded, and made approving noises to please Eleanor, though to be honest he thought it foul. His reward was her delighted smile, and his gaze roamed over her face, amazed anew that he had never noticed before just how lovely she was.

He watched as Eleanor ate the ham and pheasant that he sliced for her, and drank the elderberry wine they had brought with them from England. Then his patience began to wear thin and he murmured in her ear, 'Let us retire to our bedchamber.'

Eleanor paused, setting aside her cup, a little bemused by the husky sound of his voice in her ear, and the warmth of his hand upon her thigh, beneath the table. She felt the heat of a blush rise up her neck, and cast her lashes down, wondering if Troye meant what she thought he meant.

'Come, Eleanor,' he urged, 'it has been too long.'

She was in no doubt then as to his meaning, and though her heart thumped in nervous anticipation, there was a glow of excitement too. Demurely she rose, not looking at him, and placed her hand on his arm as he escorted her from the table.

Together they climbed the stairs, though it was a silent trek. When they reached their bedchamber Troye closed and barred the door behind them. Eleanor glanced to the bed, expecting to find Joan asleep, as usual, within its vast expanse. But the bed was empty, and she turned to Troye, who smiled slightly at the question in her eyes.

'Aye, she is safe enough in the nursery. 'Tis my turn now—' he came to stand before her, his hands reaching for her waist '—to sleep with you.'

Aware of the doublemeaning to his words, she smiled, and yet had to force herself to stand still, beside the bed, and not shy away in self-conscious doubt. She loved Troye, she was his, and she had the right to touch him, to hold him, and he had just as much right to touch her, and yet if there was no love to sweeten his touch she had no wish for him to do so. Her glance fell to the broad width of his muscular chest, as he stood head and shoulders above her. The fire flames crackled in the hearth, and cast a golden glow about their chamber. He looked at her, and she at him.

They hesitated, and then it was Eleanor who took the bold step forward and lifted her fingers to his tunic. With trembling hands she unbuttoned the rough fabric, sliding it from his shoulders, and likewise with his shirt. As she drew the material away she felt her lips part at the sight of his beautiful torso. The firm, sculptured bulk of his arms, the scattering of hair across his chest, arrowing down to his belly, the planes of his midriff…how beautiful he was to her eyes!

Leaning forwards, she pressed her lips to his chest, moving down to cover his flat, hard nipple, tease it with her teeth before kissing his ribs and opening her mouth to gently bite his hard-muscled flesh. She felt his indrawn breath, but still he stood there without touching her. Her fingers moved to unbutton his breeches, the palm of her hands brushing the solid length of his arousal. She pulled his breeches down, over his buttocks, and knelt upon the floor as she tugged them down the length of his legs and he stepped out of them. She glanced up, blushing fiercely at the sight of his naked male body, but such was her love and her desire to give him everything that was pleasure and comfort that she did not falter.

As Eleanor kneeled at his feet, at the look of uncertainty and desire warring in her eyes, Troye leaned down and raised her up with both hands beneath her elbows. His fingers began to undo and remove her clothes, until they both stood naked in each other's arms.

Eleanor closed her eyes and surrendered to the sheer bliss of Troye's kiss upon the vulnerable and tender skin of her shoulders. She arched back her neck, her breasts brushing against his chest as he kissed her ears. Her legs felt weak, she felt moist heat burning deep within her. His mouth closed over her nipple and she groaned with the pleasure of it. Her arms slid around his back and she pressed against the warmth and solid bulk of his body, glorying in the feel of his shoulders beneath her hands, then sliding them down the length of his back and cupping the taut half-moons of his buttocks. He moved closer, the length of his manhood straining against her belly. With one hand she stroked him, clasping her fingers around the thickness of him. He groaned, his mouth sucking harder on her nipple, and then he manoeuvred them to the bed and they both fell down upon it.

Side by side they lay, and Troye slid his hand down the length of her body, and up again, his eyes following the path of his hand, the glow of the firelight revealing to him the sight of Eleanor's body. He leaned down and kissed her, his fingers gently moving over the flatness of her belly. Slowly, gently, he explored her breasts, his mouth kissing and touching and tasting.

Eleanor felt weak with dizzy waves of pleasure rippling through her veins, and her own fingers reached out to touch him, smoothing over the hard muscles of his shoulders and arms, and reaching down to stroke the back of his thighs, so muscular and powerful as he kneeled over her. There was no sound, except their sighs, and their gasps, that quickened to pants of pleasure and little cries of longing and delight. She was a little wary as Troye slid his hands beneath her buttocks and nudged her thighs apart, tensing as he knelt between them and reverently kissed her womanhood. Her hand strayed to his shoulder, wanting to push him away, but he whispered his reassurance, promising that he would not hurt her, but only give her pleasure like she had never known before. At his urging she relaxed, and his hands grasped her buttocks more firmly, lifting her slightly as his tongue delved and stroked. Eleanor gasped, her neck and back arching as ecstasy seared through her body like molten honey.

He kissed the inside of her thighs, and then returned to her belly and her breasts, and her mouth, his fingers replacing his tongue as he explored her womanhood, encouraging, well aware that now she was hot and swollen and moist with aching desire. Yet still he held himself in check, wanting this to be as if it were their first time together, erasing all remembrance she might have of all the other times when he had taken her without care. He wanted her to experience fulfilment before he did, and so he waited.

Eleanor strained and writhed beneath him, her fingers and lips touching him, enjoying the feel of his roughly haired chest brushing against her breasts, and the muscular weight of his body, his powerful thighs arched over hers. She sighed and moaned and gasped at the pleasure of his touch, and yet was puzzled that still he had not entered her. Yet now she only felt his finger, moving softly and slowly, and she felt goosebumps flare on her skin at the sound of his voice in her ear, a mere husky whisper asking her if she liked it here…there?

'Aye.' Eleanor sighed, blushing hotly, clinging to the width of his broad shoulders.

He kissed her neck, her ears. 'And now?' he murmured, increasing the rhythm, the pressure, moving down, and then back up, teasing, feeling her body respond, opening, slick with passion's dew and swelling like a raisin plumped in brandy. 'Harder? Faster?'

Eleanor could not speak, so she merely nodded, and then little cries came from between her lips as her body clenched with the most exquisite joy she had ever experienced. At that moment he spread her legs wider and entered her. He covered her mouth with his, muffling her joyous exclamations, penetrating carefully. He rested his weight on his elbows and controlled his response to match hers, his hips thrusting slowly and gently. Just when she thought it was over, her hips rose and fell with a swift and sudden urgency, and he thrust deeper, harder, until the great solid four-poster bed was shaking and creaking with the force of their union. He growled and groaned and then exclaimed, and Eleanor raked her nails into his back as yet another, and final, wave of ecstasy gripped her. At its end they were both sheened with hot sweat, their muscles and skin aching, Eleanor amazed at how her body had reacted to his lovemaking. She was sure that even though he had spoken no words of love, this time they had shared something that had been more than mere male mating with female.

Troye rolled on to his back with a heavy, satisfied sigh, clasping her hand with his fingers linked intimately between hers. Then he became aware of her silence, and turned on his side to look at her, his glance skimming over the riot of her sweat-dampened hair and the rosy flush of her face and neck. Looking at her, the glow in her eyes and the swollen, dark red softness of her mouth, he had no doubts that she too had experienced satisfaction. Gently he stroked her ribs with his fingertips, and she shivered, turning to him with a soft smile.

'Would it please you, Troye,' she whispered, moving on to her side to entwine her legs with his and lie close against his chest, 'if from this night I was to bear you a babe?'

For a moment, he looked startled, for such a thought had not occurred to him, then seeing the look in her eyes, he leaned towards her and kissed her shoulder. 'Aye, it would please me.'

'I hope it is a boy.' Eleanor pressed the palm of one hand to her belly, raising her glance shyly to his dark gaze as she smiled hopefully. 'I would like to give you a son.'

His large hand covered hers, and he smiled too. 'At this very moment my seed may be bonding within you and creating new life.'

Eleanor's smile deepened, his hand moving on hers, stirring her, his lips pressing kisses to her neck, and she whispered mischievously, her body arching at his touch, 'Does my lord wish to make sure with a…um…a second attempt?'

Troye laughed, and gathered her in his arms, pulling her on top of him. 'Aye, my lady, let us start our new life together. Again.'

Epilogue

London—three years later

Eleanor strolled through the garden, the summer sunshine slanting across the flowerbeds filled with pink roses and spiky lavender as the afternoon waned and a cooling breeze rose from the dark waters of the River Thames at the bottom of the lawn. Eleanor paused to gaze back at the façade of the house, hearing the faint cry of a baby through an upstairs open window. She turned and began to make her way back to the house, yet paused again as she heard the sound of voices, and the baby's cries turned to soft, gleeful chortles.

Through the open window she glimpsed Troye, holding their son in his arms. At the same moment he saw her too and lifted his hand in greeting. Eleanor waved and then she quickened her footsteps, looking up as a young girl came running from the door to the downstairs parlour.

'Father is home!' cried Joan, her long dark hair braided and flying back with her skirts as she ran towards Eleanor, fell into step with her and linked arms. 'He went upstairs to pick up Harry—' she pouted a little '—it was my turn to pick him up when he woke.'

Eleanor laughed and hugged her stepdaughter closer. 'There will be plenty more chances, he's only five months old.'

Troye emerged from the door before they reached it, and with unspoken consent the family turned and went to sit upon the cool grass, beneath the spreading arms of a shady oak tree. Eleanor sat with baby Harry—christened Henry after her father—upon her lap, kissing his plump, milky cheek as he nuzzled against her, yet one arm open to give young Joan access to her side.

Troye gazed at them, his lovely wife and daughter, his young son, and counted his blessings. He reached out one hand and stroked Eleanor's cheek. 'Is it warm enough for you today?'

Eleanor looked up, with a smile, gazing into his eyes so tender with concern. She chuckled, for it was an old joke between them that the bitter cold of Scotland had plagued Eleanor. They had endured for as long as possible the hostile land of the Scots, and then when peace treaties had been made Troye had yielded to her pleas and begged the King for release. As quickly as maybe they had purchased this half-timbered house beside the river, not too far distant from the Palace of Westminster and the White Tower, where Troye had been gifted the task of training the young cadets and would never again march away to war.

'I am warm,' murmured Eleanor softly, leaning towards Troye slightly, as he gently stroked back the long skeins of her hair, her eyes inviting. ''Tis your love that makes me glow.'

Troye almost blushed, still the soldier at heart, and Joan giggled, sensing that her parents were about to get all silly and running off to find Toby and bring him out to share the playtime.

Eleanor cuddled baby Harry more securely as she stroked her husband's cheek. 'I love you.'

Troye's eyes were no longer shadowed by the darkness of grief, and looked at her with tenderness as he leaned down and kissed her lips. 'I love you too.'

Author Note

During the years 1296-1305 Edward I mounted his first campaign to subdue Scotland and force their loyalty to the crown of England. It was just the first of several campaigns over several decades. The events of this story are, therefore, only loosely based upon the events of the first campaign.

HISTORICAL ROMANCE™

LARGE PRINT

DISHONOUR AND DESIRE
Juliet Landon

Having run from two previous engagements, Caterina Chester knows that marriage cannot be avoided for much longer. But to be parcelled off as part of a wager to clear her family's massive debts? Caterina is outraged! Yet Sir Chase Boston, for all his impeccable manners and charm, reveals an unexpected and undeniably exhilarating wild streak that taunts and teases her…

AN UNLADYLIKE OFFER
Christine Merrill

Miss Esme Canville's brutal father is resolved to marry her off – but she won't submit tamely to his decree. Instead, she'll offer herself to notorious rake Captain St John Radwell and enjoy all the freedom of a mistress! St John is intent on mending his rakish ways. He won't seduce an innocent virgin. But Esme is determined, beautiful, and very, very tempting…

THE ROMAN'S VIRGIN MISTRESS
Michelle Styles

Silvana Junia knows what the gossips say about her – and doesn't care! Until a mysterious, dangerous stranger rescues her from the sea, and she's instantly drawn to him. Lucius Aurelius Fortis is rich and respected. But his playboy past could come back to haunt him if he cannot resist his attraction to the beautiful Silvana. And in the hot sun of Baiae their every move is being watched…

MILLS & BOON®

HIST1107 LP

HISTORICAL ROMANCE™

LARGE PRINT

NO PLACE FOR A LADY
Louise Allen

Miss Bree Mallory is too taken up with running her successful coaching company to have time for pampered aristocracy! But then an accidental meeting with Max Dysart, Earl of Penrith, changes everything… Bree's independence is hard-won: she has no interest in marriage. But Max's kisses are powerfully – passionately – persuasive…!

BRIDE OF THE SOLWAY
Joanna Maitland

If Cassandra Elliott does not escape from her brother, the Laird of Galloway, she will either be forced into marriage or confined to Bedlam! Desperate, she turns to a handsome stranger and begs for help in the most unladylike manner. Captain Ross Graham *must* help her flee across the Solway to safety. But neither Cassie nor Ross expects a desire as wild as the Scottish hills to flare between them…

MARIANNE AND THE MARQUIS
Anne Herries

Sheltered innocent Miss Marianne Horne had come to Cornwall to care for her ailing great-aunt. Surrounded by smugglers, spies and plots, Marianne hardly knew whom to trust. Instinctively, she turned to the handsome Mr Beck. But Mr Beck turned out to be Andrew, Marquis of Marlbeck, who would *surely* never look twice at the daughter of a country vicar…so why was he paying Marianne such flattering attention?

MILLS & BOON®

HIST1207 LP

HISTORICAL ROMANCE™

LARGE PRINT

A DESIRABLE HUSBAND
Mary Nichols

Lady Esme Vernley's unconventional first meeting with a handsome gentleman in Hyde Park has damned him in the eyes of her family. Felix, Lord Pendlebury, is taken with this debutante's mischievous smile. But his secret mission for the Duke of Wellington in France could jeopardise any relationship between them…

HIS CINDERELLA BRIDE
Annie Burrows

Lord Lensborough was a man well used to getting exactly what he wanted – and he wanted Hester! Convinced that this badly dressed, redheaded waif was a poor relation, the noble lord was about to receive the shock of his life…from a lady who would break all his very proper rules!

TAMED BY THE BARBARIAN
June Francis

Cicely Milburn has no intention of marrying anyone, let alone a Scottish barbarian! But when Lord Rory Mackillin rescues her from a treacherous attack she reluctantly accepts his help – even though his kisses trouble her dreams. The Border Reiver is determined to guard his charge on their journey. Yet he cannot shield his own heart from Cicely's beauty and bravery…

MILLS & BOON®

HIST0108 LP